Wild Grapes

"*Wild Grapes*, set among Jewish immigrants-turned-farmers in early twentieth-century Ohio, is a story of resilience, faith, and grudging re-invention. Miriam Flock's courageous, unsparing matriarch, Bluma Rappaport, is driven to help her daughters escape the circumscribed life that has been her lot; they should root and prosper in the unfamiliar soil of a new country. In our twenty-first-century culture, when populations are still besieged with displacement and bound together with fragile hope, *Wild Grapes* reminds us how families can cultivate belonging even in the most unyielding ground."

—**Michael J. Rosen**, author of *Elijah's Angel*

"*Wild Grapes* does not feel like a debut novel. It is beautifully written, and I was immediately absorbed by this riveting story of an immigrant Jewish family intent on making it in early twentieth-century America. I grew to love the characters. Their hardships and their joys brought me to tears and laughter. An accomplished poet and editor, Miriam Flock was a trusted reader for my writing. No one will be disappointed reading this compelling writing of her own."

—**Sheldon Lewis**, author of *Torah of Reconciliation*

"This historical novel is set in the unusual context of rural Ohio in the early twentieth century, giving readers a new and refreshing take on Jewish immigration from Eastern Europe to the US outside of the teeming cities. Told through the voice of the family matriarch, it gives us an unvarnished view of a woman's experience of displacement and accommodation, marital and family strife, maternal devotion, economic struggle, and determined survival in the New World, including continued holiday, culinary, and birthing traditions from 'the Old Home,' and the use of Yiddish, liberally reproduced in the narrative. Written lucidly, with care to historical accuracy and to the realities of concord grape growing and wine making, home weaving, and immigrant hopes and disappointments, *Wild Grapes* is both an engrossing read and an authentic entree to Jewish historical experience in America."

—**Shulamit S. Magnus**, author of *Pauline Wengeroff, Memoirs of a Grandmother*

Wild Grapes

—— A Novel ——

BY Miriam Flock

RESOURCE *Publications* · Eugene, Oregon

WILD GRAPES
A Novel

Resource Publications
An Imprint of Wipf and Stock Publishers
199 W. 8th Ave., Suite 3
Eugene, OR 97401

www.wipfandstock.com

PAPERBACK ISBN: 979-8-3852-6096-6
HARDCOVER ISBN: 979-8-3852-6097-3
EBOOK ISBN: 979-8-3852-6098-0

VERSION NUMBER 11/24/25

For my grandmothers, Slova and Anna

Let me sing for my beloved
A song of my lover about his vineyard.
My beloved had a vineyard
On a fruitful hill.

He broke the ground, cleared it of stones,
And planted it with choice vines.
He built a watchtower inside it,
He even hewed a wine press in it;
For he hoped it would yield grapes.
Instead, it yielded wild grapes.

—Isaiah 5:1–2

Contents

Acknowledgments

Special thanks to my constant readers, Michael J. Rosen and Jane Jacobson, and to my chavruta partner for *Wild Grapes*, Dalia Sirkin. Thanks also to Amaryah Orenstein; Emil Flock; Kathy Flock; Rabbi Sheldon Lewis; and my husband, Howard Schulman, for their invaluable help on the novel.

Part I

Chapter 1

MY COUSIN MENDEL STOPS the truck in what looks like the middle of nowhere. Surrounding us are only trees and a dirt track leading off the main gravel road. He jumps out of the cab and comes around to the back where the girls and I are perched on our luggage.

"Bluma," he tells me, "I'm afraid I can't take you any farther. The last time I tried to go up that track, I almost broke an axel."

What can I say? It was good of Mendel to schlep my husband, Sender, out here when he bought the place last year. I can't blame my cousin for not wanting to make such a risky trip again. "You mustn't worry yourself," I insist. "Thank God we have legs to walk."

"It's not far—maybe ten minutes," he assures me.

I shoo the girls out of the truck bed, and Mendel helps me unload all of our *pekelakh*—carpet bags and knapsacks and bundles. With a final hug, he leaves us by the side of the road. All three of my daughters stare wide-eyed at their surroundings—so different from Falciu, the little shtetl where we lived in Romania.

As I shepherd the family up the track, my eldest daughter, Sala pipes up. "I still don't understand why you didn't tell Papa we were coming. He could have picked us up in Cleveland." At fifteen, she's full of not-so-helpful suggestions.

"I told you this already, Sala. I want to surprise him." This is a lie. What I wanted was for her father to send for us, like he'd been promising to do for four years, ever since he left us at his parents' house and headed for America. Every year there was another excuse. When he finally scraped together a bit of money, he spent it on this land in Geneva, Ohio. I assumed Geneva was a city, like Geneva, Switzerland. No, the *mishugener* bought a

3

farm. No Jew has bought a farm in Eastern Europe for centuries. We weren't allowed to own land in the countryside.

As if she's reading my mind, Chaia, my middle daughter, looks around at the woods and asks, "Is this what farms look like in America?" She knew every nook and cranny of Falciu and the wide plain beyond, where our neighbors grew small plots of millet and rye. This rutted track with its towering maples is a far cry from Romania.

"It must be a farm," I say airily, "since that's what your father bought."

"But there's nothing growing here," she insists.

"*Chaia, hak mir nisht keyn tshaynik,*" I tell her. It's a strange Yiddish expression—don't bang your teakettle at me—but Chaia knows very well that I mean I don't want to be bothered right now. I always speak to the girls in Yiddish, as I do all the members of my family. It's the home language of Eastern Europe's Jews, the one we scold the children in, the one we think in, the one we make love in (or in the case of Sender and me, the one we bicker in).

So now, I've scolded Chaia, but in my own mind, I'm asking Sender the same question Chaia asked me: "This is a farm?" While I don't know from plowing and planting, even to me, the land doesn't look promising. A break in the trees reveals stony soil, parched in the summer sun. I imagine Sender was so determined to get his little patch of dirt, he didn't look too closely.

I should have realized he was squirreling money away for this half-baked project. He got the farming bug from his Uncle Moish, who was part of the "Back to the Land" movement in Russia. Like Moish, Sender is determined to be "a free farmer on his own soil."

I'm not sure the girls and I were ever part of this pipe dream. At times, I've suspected there was another woman—he wouldn't be the first to forget about his family in the old country. In fact, the Yiddish newspaper in New York runs a column, "The Gallery of Missing Husbands," where women can request help finding their wayward men. Me, I'm not the type to advertise my troubles. Finally, I saved enough money from my sewing and weaving to pay for our crossing myself.

Whatever I've sacrificed to get us to Ohio, it hasn't impressed my five-year-old, Reyzel. "I wish we never came here," she proclaims. "If we stayed in Romania, we wouldn't have to do all this walking."

"And if my grandmother had a beard, she'd be my grandfather," I reply. I'm usually not so short with the children, but I'm on my last nerve.

Reyzel drops the little bag she's been carrying and collapses on top of it, weeping. And who could blame her? The journey has been a *farshlepte krenk*, a long, drawn-out illness: bumping along in the back of a cart from Falciu to Bucharest. Sleeping on top of our luggage on the train to Hamburg. Pitching in the hold of the SS Graf Waldersee and vomiting all the way to New York. Another two days by train to my cousin Mendel's house in Cleveland, and today, two hours in the bed of Mendel's truck all the way to Geneva—and not another Jew in sight, hardly even another person, after we passed Painesville. If I didn't need to keep the girls going, I'd sit down in the middle of the road and cry too.

But I have to put on a brave face, so instead of sympathizing, I say sternly, "Reyzel Rappaport, you've made it this far. Surely you can walk a little farther." Still sniveling, Reyzel picks up her bag. "I'm sure the place is just around that bend," I promise.

The trees have thinned out, but there are no houses to be seen. I wonder how we'll get on in this lonely corner of the world. In the August heat, perspiration escapes the kerchief that covers my hair; it drips down my neck and pools between my breasts. I'm wearing half my wardrobe including a long grey skirt and a fitted brown jacket. By the time we reach a bend in the road, I feel like the sun is singeing my eyelashes.

As we make the turn, Sala, Chaia, Reyzel, and I stop in our tracks like a column of soldiers who've come upon a bombed-out town. The woods have given way to a scraggly meadow. In the center is the most dilapidated house I've ever seen, and I come from a village of thatch-roofed cottages. The porch sags, and what used to be gingerbread trim now looks more like Swiss cheese. The once-white walls are peeling and gray. More than one window is boarded up.

"*Gotenu*," Sala gasps.

"*Vey iz mir*!" I say under my breath.

"Jesus Christ!" Chaia blurts out. Sala and I both look at her in astonishment.

"Where do you get such language?" I ask.

"That's what the sailors on the boat said when the bilge backed up."

"Well, when your bilge backs up, you can say it too. Until then, leave Jesus Christ out of it."

Reyzel's lower lip is trembling. "Don't cry," Sala tells her. "This place isn't so bad. Look at all the land—not like *Bubbe* and *Zeyde's* poky little house in the shtetl." Sala always was an optimist, and given this is where we're going to be living, I guess it's the best attitude to take. I can hear a cow lowing from the no-longer-very-red barn, so at least we'll have milk. A few chickens and geese scratch in the yard. Beside the house, a little orchard is heavy with green apples and ripe peaches and plums, many already fallen to the ground so that the smell of ferment wafts toward us. There are a few rows of grapevines.

"But where are the streets paved with gold?" Reyzel demands.

"Oy, a curse on Columbus," I mutter darkly. "I would settle for streets paved with cobblestones." Then, realizing my daughters are really disheartened, I pull myself together. "I'm sure things are better inside. Come."

We haul our burdens up to the front of the house. As we approach, we're greeted by a familiar sound. A group of men are singing a folk tune:

> Tell me, dear Rabbi, what will happen when the Messiah comes?

> When the Messiah comes, we'll have a banquet.

I sigh. "Romania or Ohio. Wherever your father goes, he's always expecting the Messiah to turn up." I tromp up to the front door, almost tripping on a broken step, and rap loudly.

A man answers. He's tall and wide, with a full beard and mustache and a head of kinky hair covered by a yarmulke. We just stare at each other until he calls out in Yiddish, "Sender, you have company."

At the sound of my mother tongue, I feel a little more at home. The portly man leads us into the front parlor, dominated by (or more accurately, almost entirely furnished with) a wooden table, where a small group of men are sitting in front of large, leather-bound tomes. Sender stands at his place. As much as that man has made me suffer, I can't control a sharp intake of breath when I see him again—the same rush I felt when he first came to court me. It's the architecture of his face: the square jaw, the tilted brows over sleepy black eyes. The only problem comes when he opens his mouth. "Bluma," he yelps, "what are you doing here?"

"Nice to see you too," I say, keeping my face expressionless.

Sala isn't waiting for any preliminaries. She rushes into his arms, burying her face in his old white shirt. "Papa, I've missed you so much!" But instead of the big hug she was longing for, he gives her a quick pat before he releases her. I can see her face fall, but Sender is oblivious. The other two, who don't really remember Sender, peer at him warily, and he seems astonished that such big girls belong to him.

By this time, the rest of the men have approached us. A chorus of greetings rings out: "*Borukhos habayos*—Blessed are the ones who come!"

In front of his cronies, Sender has decided to be expansive. "My dear wife," he says, as though we're in a play, "it's been too long. Come, embrace me." I don't move. After an awkward moment, he sidles over and gives me a small squeeze. "It's true I wasn't expecting you quite yet, but welcome."

I decide it's time to pull out one of my secret weapons. "We are happy to see once again our husband and father," I reply in my best English.

"You speak already the language of our adopted country!" he says, almost impressed.

One compensation for having an absent husband for the past four years has been the freedom to get some education for myself and my daughters. I can read a little Yiddish, which I taught the girls, as well as arithmetic, but that's as far as my own education went. When Sala turned twelve, I hired an English language tutor for the four of us. My in-laws were dubious, but I told them Sender wanted it, which was a total invention he doesn't need to know about. Instead, I just say, "We have many talents we want you should put to use."

The man who opened the door decides it's his moment to hold forth in his own extravagant English: "What a joyous homecoming! I'm your closest Jewish neighbor, Harold Gold," he says. "Praise God, who gathers together the scattered of his people. I was saying to Sender just the other day . . . ."

"Hershel," a Mr. Kaminsky interrupts, returning us to Yiddish (and Harold to his Yiddish name). "Don't you think we should give the Rappaports some time by themselves to celebrate their reunion?"

"*Avade*, of course." Harold beckons to the only young man in the group, a thin boy, a bit stooped as though he's already spent years bending over the holy texts. "Come on, Morris, time to head for home." Morris picks up the Hebrew book he was studying. He looks like the boys in Falciu, outfitted in the standard white shirt and black trousers. I notice he must be in mourning as he has the beginnings of a scruffy beard, which many Jewish men grow when a close relative has died. Behind his wire-rimmed spectacles, his eyes are a pale brown.

"By the way," the older man says, "Morris is my nephew—just come from Poland to live with us."

I nod at him. Morris smiles nervously. "Lovely daughter you have, Mrs. Rappaport," he stammers, looking admiringly at Sala. A blush rushes down from Sala's cheeks to her neck, as if you poured wine into milk.

The other neighbors are also getting up to go. Chaia is fidgeting. Rey-zel is so tired she's swaying on her feet like she did on the boat. I tell Sala to take them upstairs and find some place to lie down.

When all the guests have filed out, Sender turns to me and splutters, "Bluma, what possessed you to pick this moment to come to America? I told you the place wasn't ready."

I look at him, hard. To think I once considered myself lucky to have such a bridegroom.

"Why now? you ask. And I ask, why not four years ago? The minute you left, the Great War started. There was fighting not a day's ride from your parents' house. Then right in the middle of everything, the Russians thought it would be a good idea to have a revolution, so—big surprise—both the Bolsheviks and the Tsar's forces decided to take it out on the Jews. I wrote to you about all that," I say accusingly. "You knew, but you left us in Falciu." If I wasn't worried about waking the girls, I'd be yelling in indignation.

"I just wanted things here to be right for you. I know the farm looks a little run-down. But I've been working with the Jewish Agricultural Society. I'm helping them recruit more families to go back to the land right here in Geneva—so we'll have a community—a minyan."

I snort. "If you're so keen on going back to the land, why do I find you and the other so-called farmers in the parlor singing songs instead of picking the fruit that's rotting on the ground?"

"Singing? We were just finishing our Talmud study. I'll have you know there's a whole section of the Talmud devoted to agriculture. Besides, every man should have some time for contemplating things that are not of this world."

"As my mother, may she rest in peace, used to say, 'If a man is too good for this world, he's bad for his wife.'"

"I don't claim to be too good for this world, only that to be a better man, I must study God's laws."

"What kind of God wants you to spend your time studying while your family is dodging bullets?"

"I know you're angry, Bluma, but that's no reason to take God's name in vain."

"This isn't about God."

"Everything is about God." What answer can I make to that? I'm just searching my mind for a retort when Sender stops me. "You see," he says, "this fighting—this is one of the reasons I didn't send for you sooner."

It's true: Sender and I can't be in the same room more than five minutes before the arguing starts. Back in Romania, we quarreled about money, we quarreled about how much time Sender spent at the house of worship, we were quarreling about him going to America without us until he actually walked out the door with his belongings tied up in a sheet. I can't say I've missed the squabbling, as tired as I was of living like a widow in Falciu. Yet I don't believe arguing is the real—or at least the main—reason Sender never sent for us.

I decide it's time to be honest. "Look, *mayn man*," I say. "Do you think I don't realize how you feel about me? I'm not the 'woman of valor' from the Proverbs with the law of kindness always on her tongue. I'm not much to look at. You may not have realized it, but my father made my sister Malke smear ash on her face when you came to meet me, so you wouldn't want to marry her instead."

Sender can't help chuckling. "He thought I didn't know what he was up to."

"It's a good thing Hodel was so young or he would have cut off her hair and dressed her in knickers."

Somehow the image of my little sister as a boy tickles me, and I also start to laugh. Suddenly we're both cackling. When we finally stop, Sender says, "You know, Bluma, I never complained about our match."

This is technically true. Sender never made any of these complaints in so many words, but if he ever gazed at me lovingly, I must have been look-ing in the other direction. "Let's not quibble," I answer him. "You got stuck with me. But you have to admit, I've always been a loyal wife. I brought in money from my needlework so you could spend your time studying. I did all the chores your mother didn't want to do: plucking the chickens, hauling the water, scrubbing the laundry on the washboard. Most important, I gave you three beautiful daughters, who need you."

"That's true," Sender admits.

"And, from the looks of this place, you need us."

"There is some fruit that needs picking."

"And the barn needs painting, and the stairs are broken, and the—" I see his defenses go up, and I stop in the middle of the sentence. "But there's time enough for all that. Tonight we need sleep."

"I think the girls took the only bed in the house."

"That's okay. I'll climb in with them. It won't be the first time."

9

Chapter 2

DID I EVER END up in bed with Sender? As Orthodox Jews, we've always had separate mattresses, but you can see from the fact we have three daughters, we sometimes pushed the beds together. It was always a dutiful affair. According to Sender, the Talmud specifies how often a man should be intimate with his wife, and, good Jew that he is, Sender complied. I tried to imagine there was some desire when he reached for me. But to be touched out of duty—it's as if you're being kneaded like dough. The day after we arrived in Geneva, we did set up a bed for me in Sender's room, but there's been no passionate reunion. I guess the Talmud can only take a man so far.

We also stuffed some ticking with hay for the girls, giving Sala one room, and putting Chaia and Reyzel together in the other. Today, I decide it's finally time to get the kitchen up and running. As far as I can tell, Sender never cooked anything, depending for his meals on Shabbas dinner at the homes of other Jewish farmers and for the rest on raw fruits and vegetables or potatoes he baked in the fireplace. I'm ready to change all of that. Thinking to make some bagels for breakfast, I open the door of the cast iron stove to light it. I'm greeted by the sound of frantic squeaking as a brown field mouse tries to protect her nest, where a clutch of tiny babies squirm.

"Gevalt!" I cry out, slamming the door shut.

"What is it, Mama?" Chaia has appeared from nowhere, taking my still shaking hand in hers.

"Nothing serious, little duckling. I was just surprised by a mouse nest in the oven. I'll have to dispose of them."

"You mean kill them?"

"I should invite them for Shabbas dinner?"

"No, but you don't have to murder them." Gingerly, Chaia cracks open the oven door. "They're babies!" she says accusingly.

"What do you suggest?"

"We could take them out to the orchard. I'll put the nest by a tree, and then they'll have food to eat."

I figure it would take the mother mouse about ten minutes to find her way back into my kitchen. "How about way out in the woods?" I counter. "You've been wanting to go exploring."

We agree on this course of action. I outfit Chaia with some of Sender's gloves, the leather fingers protruding beyond her small hands like flippers. I've already made myself a straw broom, which we use to scoot the nest and the squealing mama into a deep wooden box Chaia finds in the barn. Then off she trots.

I'm not usually a squeamish woman, but shivers run down my spine when I think about that jiggling mound of eyeless pink creatures in the space where I'm supposed to cook my family's food. The abandoned oven reeks of mouse droppings and damp straw. Crumpling onto one of the rickety kitchen chairs, I begin to cry.

That's the way Reyzel and Sala find me. "Mama, what's happened?" Sala wants to know.

Hastily, I dry my tears and try to compose myself. "Nothing, darling. I'm just tired."

"What's that smell?" Reyzel gags dramatically.

"I'm afraid we had some uninvited guests living in the oven—a whole family of field mice. Chaia's out finding them a new home in the woods."

"Ew!" Reyzel squawks.

"Let me help you clean that out," Sala says. "I'll heat some water in the fireplace, and I'm pretty sure I saw some lye soap in the cupboard."

For the girls' sakes, I know I have to get a grip on myself. They're already unhappy with America. To hear Reyzel tell it, Romania was paradise: "Bubbe would make us kvass, and we would drink it in the shade of the beech tree and sing songs." Reyzel actually hates kvass, its sweet-sour tang a taste she never acquired. Plus, she isn't that fond of Sender's mother, who has a habit of rapping naughty little girls on the head with her thimble.

May God forgive me, but I have to say, my mother-in-law is a bitter woman. Of course, she's had some cause. Before they came to Romania, the family lived in a Russian shtetl, where there was a terrible pogrom. Houses were burned; people were killed. She once told me how the community had gathered to bury their dead when the Cossacks (may they crawl on their bellies) invaded the cemetery. They seized a young girl, murdered her parents right in front of her, and then raped her, one after another, while everyone else was forced to watch.

The old country was no paradise for Jews—that's for certain—but Reyzel is not alone in pining for it. Chaia isn't happy about her new chores on the farm. Her hands are numb from milking and the geese peck at her when she tries to feed them. Sala misses her gaggle of teenage girlfriends, all crowded into the little houses of our shtetl. And everyone seems to think I'm a fitting target for their complaints. I'm starting to feel like Moses, with the children of Israel kvetching about the cucumbers and figs they had back in dear Egypt—where they'd been slaves for four hundred years!

Not that Ohio doesn't have its share of modern-day Egyptians. The first day we were here, I went up the road to see if I could buy some flour from Tillie Johnson, a nervous woman with an old-fashioned sun bonnet and faded gingham dress. She was just about to get me some from her kitchen when we heard her husband, Corbin, bellowing, "Who's that strange woman? Is that the Jew from down the road?" She left me standing in the yard.

Fortunately, not all our neighbors are so inhospitable. Elsie and Harold Gold had us over for dinner last night (which was mostly an occasion for Sender and Harold to debate the meaning of the weekly Torah portion and for Morris to make eyes at Sala). There's also a nice Italian family down the road, the Giordanos. And I've already learned something useful from Ethel Blankenship, who owns the next farm over with her husband, Walter.

I noticed Ethel had set up a farm stand, and I strolled over to see what I could get to supplement Sender's meager output. Ethel was selling a pile of red stalks I recognized from clumps of the stuff sprouting in our weed-infested garden. I'd taken a bite, thinking it was celery. Oy was it sour! Assuming it was a weed, I was planning to dig it up.

"Excuse me, Mrs.," I said to Ethel, switching to my somewhat shaky English, "can you tell me please how you are calling this—thing?"

Ethel looked at me carefully. I figured she knew I was a foreigner, so I fully expected to be snubbed. Instead, she answered me, "That's rhubarb."

"And excuse me, but you are using this rhubarb how? It seems too sour for chicken soup."

When Ethel finally stopped laughing, she explained that although rhubarb is a vegetable, most people add sugar and use it in desserts. She even wrote out her recipe for rhubarb custard pie, which I will make as soon as I can get Sala to translate it. I learned to speak some English from the tutor, but I never did master reading it. Sala and Chaia both took to it like fish to water.

Sala's reading skills prove to be a lifesaver today, as the girls help me get the house in order. Chaia is supposed to sweep and dust though Sender catches her daydreaming and gives her an exasperated swat. On the other hand, he seems to have endless patience for Reyzel, who's been sprinkling the garden with an old milk can he converted into a watering pot. Sala's job is to straighten out the parlor/dining room, which is home, in addition to the table, to a sideboard with a collection of odd lengths of string, scraps of paper, and broken bits of farm equipment. In one of the drawers, she discovers a letter with a note written on the outside in red ink. I don't have to be able to read English to guess it isn't bringing good news.

"Mama, look at this," Sala says, waving the mail beneath my nose. "This envelope from the Unionville Savings and Loan is marked 'Past Due.' It's addressed to Papa, but do you think we should open it?"

Sender is out in the orchard, shamed, I guess, into bringing in the peaches. Sure I won't get a straight answer out of him, I tell her yes, let's take a look. It's pretty much what I feared. Sender is behind on the mortgage. The bank is giving him one more month before they repossess the farm. My English isn't very good, but I know what that means.

"Will we be kicked out?" Sala asks in a hushed tone. "I mean, I don't like it here, but where will we go? What will happen to us?"

"Don't worry, *Mamele*. We'll figure it out."

I wish I hadn't needed Sala to read the letter to me. This news is more than a teenager should have on her shoulders. Of course, I was almost a wife by the time I was her age, but for Sala, I had hoped for better.

Oh, well. At least I was prepared for something like this. All I had to do was remember what happened to Sender's Uncle Moish. The Russians let the "Back to the Landers" buy some forestland that anyone with experience would never have tried to cultivate. After that failed, they set off for Louisiana where some con man sold them an island in the Mississippi River. A year later, the entire community was swept away—houses, cattle, machinery, and crops. Not one to give up, Moish joined a new settlement in South Dakota. The first year, hessian flies decimated the wheat fields. Then, there was a drought. In the third year, hail mowed down all the standing crops. It was like the ten plagues. A normal man would have said "enough already," but Moish was a true believer. Finally he settled on a chicken farm in New Jersey that, last I heard, was limping along with help from the Jewish Agricultural Society.

Did this tale of woe discourage my husband? On the contrary. Because he was a horse trader back in Falciu, Sender figured he knew more about farm animals than Moish and his bunch. The rest of farming couldn't be that difficult, he told me (which shows you how much he knows about agriculture). Somehow he persuaded the JAS to help him secure a loan for this land. Apparently, he hasn't figured out a way to pay it back. He isn't able to eke out much of an income from his produce. Only the grapes bring more than a few pennies a pound.

More than once over the last two days, I've thought about taking the girls and leaving Sender to his fantasies. I suppose some people would think I should be grateful—at least there wasn't another woman. But in his own way, Sender has been faithless to me. All the love in his heart belongs to this worn-out piece of land.

I like to think I could manage without him. Cousin Mendel would take us in, and I could earn my way weaving. I don't even need a loom. When I first went to live with Sender's parents, I didn't have one, so I invented a new way of making afghans. I used only a forked stick strung with twenty strands of yarn to make long streamers. Then I crocheted the strips together to form blankets. The money I made from those afghans helped buy our passage to America. Plus, I have a little put by—my emergency fund.

Financially, I could make a go of it without my husband. But if I leave Sender, how will life be better than it was in Falciu? There's not much space for a single woman in our world. At Sender's parents' house, I had no say in any decision beyond what affected my own children, and even then, my mother-in-law was always interfering. Mendel's wife would be kinder, but it wouldn't be my home.

Besides, I was always telling the girls how wonderful things would be in America: They would be reunited with their father. They would get an education. We could live as equals with everyone else. I'm already disillusioned, but can I dash their hopes so easily?

That night, after the girls are in bed, I draw the past-due bill from my apron pocket and put it in front of Sender on the parlor table, where he's studying a chapter of *Gemara*.

"Would you like to tell me about this?"

Sender stares at the gaping envelope and hisses at me, "You opened my mail?"

"Somebody had to. Do you realize the bank is threatening to take back the farm?"

"That's my business."

"How is it only your business? You have a wife and three daughters!"

"Who weren't supposed to come here until I sent for them."

"Sender, what does it matter if we're here or in Romania? You're about to lose our life savings."

"My parents were taking care of you until I could get on my feet. But you couldn't wait."

"I waited four years. And besides, I was taking care of your parents as much as they were taking care of us."

"Do you think this nagging is helping?"

I have an answer for this question. I might say, "*Shmendrik*, you don't know what a nagging wife is, but if you keep ignoring the bills, I'll be happy to show you. Or better yet, you can see how things go without any wife at all. I'm leaving!" All of this is waiting behind my clenched teeth. But then I look at his face—the shame behind all that bluster. Four years in America, and he's about to lose everything he's been working for. I sigh. "I want to help, Sender," I say earnestly. "I really do. Wait here a minute."

When I return to the parlor, I'm carrying the jacket I wore the first day we came to the farm. It was too hot for a jacket then—it was too hot every day of our journey from Europe, but I never took that jacket off. I sit down at the table with it and my sewing scissors. Sender is still fuming, but now he's also curious. I turn the jacket inside out and begin taking out the bottom hem. Two gold coins clatter onto the table.

Sender gasps. "Where did you get those?"

"I earned them. Two years ago, the local landowner's daughter was getting married. He heard of my skill at the loom and ordered a whole trousseau. This is what he paid me."

Sender reaches toward the coins, but I scoop them into my hand. "I'll give you the coins for the mortgage," I say, "on one condition. Right now the farm isn't paying for itself, and if you keep going the way you are, it never will. I'll come up with a plan for us to make some money, but you have to promise to work on it. You can't spend all your time studying Torah and helping the Jewish Agricultural Society get some other poor schmoes to move to Geneva."

I know Sender is itching to argue, but I'm holding the coins, and as the saying goes, when you have money, you're wise and beautiful, and you sing well, too.

Chapter 3

HAVING HANDED OVER MY "emergency fund" to Sender, I guess I've de-cided to make a go of things in Geneva. My first priority is constructing a full-size loom, which I piece together laboriously from a few boards and some cotton cord. Somehow, I squeeze it into the parlor, and Sala and I begin weaving linens for sale. I also finish cleaning the stove. On the oven door, under the grime, I uncover an enamel panel stenciled with the words "Home Comfort." When the scent of my first challah fills my nostrils, I say to myself, "Ah, now it's home."

Today, I had to figure out what I could make to feed the "scholars," who are back for their Thursday-night Talmud study. What's in the garden? Potatoes and onions. Add eggs and that's the recipe for latkes, which Sala and I are busy frying. I pick one up fresh from the iron skillet and am just about to pop it in my mouth when Chaia gives me her imitation of puppy-dog eyes. She's supposed to be helping, but I guess her real job is taste-tester; this is her third pancake. With her mouth full, she says, "I met somebody today when I went down to the river. His name is Pasquelino Giordano."

"Oh, yes?" I say. "I've met his mother. Very friendly."

"He taught me how to swear in Italian."

I'm sure she expects me to be scandalized, but I say, "Mazel tov."

Chaia brings her fingers together and shakes her hand dramatically. "*Pasta Fazool!*"

"Chaia, I'm afraid pasta fazool means noodles with beans," Sala says. "I met Mrs. Giordano on the road today, and that's what she called the dish she's making for dinner."

I have to laugh, but Chaia doesn't see the humor. "That sneaky Pasquelino Giordano," she says. "I ought to punch him right in the kisser."

"I have a better idea," I offer. "Tell him you're going to teach him how to swear in Yiddish." I make the same gesture Chaia did and shout, "*Gehakte leyber*! You know it means chopped liver, but he won't."

Chaia is just about to try it out, but I interrupt. "Enough, now, with the foolishness. You need to get some sleep. School starts soon and you have to get on schedule. Make sure you don't wake Reyzel when you get in bed."

Reluctantly, Chaia climbs the stairs. I wipe my hands on my apron and, with a tired sigh, slump into a chair at the kitchen table. I pick up something Sender has been reading. "What's this?" I have to ask Sala.

"That's the newsletter from the Jewish Agricultural Society Papa's always talking about."

"So, read me something. I'd like to know what the great JAS is doing."

"'The Jewish Farmer, August 1918,'" she begins. Then, she flips through the pages, reading out the headlines: "'Chicken farmers in Petaluma, California, form an egg co-op; Jewish settlers in Greeley, Colorado, build a synagogue.' Oh, here's something interesting: 'Midwestern Jewish Farmers Make Progress: Not only does the Jewish farmer in the Middle West keep pace with his neighbors but in some instances, he is also keeping ahead of them. For quite some time the largest vineyard in Ohio—sixty-three acres—has been owned by Harold Gold, who has been crowned the 'Grape King' of the state.'"

"Grape King! No wonder that man lives like God in Odessa. How many acres do we have?"

"I don't know about acres, but we have maybe eight rows."

"And all that land on the north side of the hill sitting idle. I wonder how many rows the Golds have."

"More than I could count."

I arch an eyebrow. "And how would you know how many rows the Golds have?"

"You remember: Elsie Gold asked me to tea in her grape arbor. Really, I think, she just wanted me to talk to Morris. He was out in the vineyard."

"A nice boy, Morris," I say distractedly.

"Nice but awkward. I mean, I do feel bad for him. His parents both died in the Lvov pogrom, which is why he's living with Harold and Elsie. I'm sure he's very smart, but—" She's saying more, but the plan I've been struggling to come up with for our farm suddenly takes shape in my mind. I pick up an old paper bag and begin doing calculations on the back of it.

While she's still expanding on Morris's shortcomings, I blurt out, "I figured it out! We're going to plant that hill in Concord grapes. You'll see. Someday, I'll be the Grape Queen of Ohio and you'll be the Grape Princess."

"Mama, I was trying to tell you something."

From the parlor, the sounds of Talmudic chanting are beginning to wane. "Sorry, darling. You can tell me all about it later, but I hear the scholars winding down. Go and take them this tray of latkes. And say hello to Morris Gold," I tease.

She harrumphs, but she picks up the tray. I follow her into the parlor. The minute she appears, Sender begins *kvelling*. "Such a wonderful cook is my Sala. My mother told me that back in Romania, people came from across the river in Moldova just to taste her rye bread."

Well, really, it was my cousin Anshel visiting from Kishenev, and anyway, it's my rye bread. But Sala does help me bake, so I let it pass. The men are reaching over each other to grab latkes. There are cries of "*Azoy geshmak*" and "Manna from heaven."

Sender maneuvers Sala over to the table, where Morris Gold is still consulting a Hebrew text. "Sala," he says, "you met Mr. Gold's nephew, yes? What a mind this young man has! He just brought us a teaching from Rabbi Isaac ben Moses of Vienna on the law of tithes."

All this puffery is making Sala sassy. "So, in your scholarly opinion, Mr. Gold, how much of this year's crop should we be setting aside for the high priests?"

"Well, Miss Rappaport," Morris sputters, "we may not tithe for the priests anymore, but we still set aside ten percent of our income for the poor."

"And what if we are the poor?"

Harold Gold has been listening to the conversation and decides this is the moment to butt in. To Sender, he says, "Your daughter has some chutzpah, arguing Jewish law with Morris."

Sender nods gravely. "This is why women don't study Talmud." Still, I can tell he has his eye on Morris as a match for Sala, so he adds, "You have to admit, though, Sala knows how to make latkes."

"Thank you, Papa. I'll have that engraved on my headstone." She nods at Morris and pushes back through to the kitchen. Morris looks after her wistfully. As soon as the men take their leave, I join her.

Heating up water to wash the dishes, Sala smiles wryly when I join her at the sink. "Did you hear Papa singing my praises to Morris? Like the only thing I'm good for is making latkes."

"It's not a bad skill to have."

"But it doesn't compare to understanding the law of tithes," she says with mock reverence.

"Not in your father's mind, I'm afraid."

"I don't see what's so great about it. Morris may know a lot about the Talmud, but he can't carry on a normal conversation. In all the time we spent together in the Golds' arbor, Morris can't have said more than. . ."

At that moment, Sender walks into the kitchen to scrounge a leftover potato pancake. "You don't like Morris?" he demands.

"He seems perfectly nice, but I'm not thinking about boys right now."

"At your age, your mother was already engaged."

"And we see how well that worked out," I say under my breath.

But neither of them is listening to me. Sala is on her high horse. "Yes, Mama married you when she was just sixteen," she says, "but that was in Romania. Things are different in the United States of America."

Sender is not having it. "You may live in 'the United States of America,' but you also live under my roof, little girl, so watch how you speak to me."

"Papa, I'm sorry, but I just don't want to get married until I finish high school."

"Who told you you were going to high school?"

There is a moment of total silence. Sala looks at me incredulously. "Mama told me. She said that was one of the reasons we were coming to America, because Jewish girls can go to school here."

That *was* one of the reasons. In Romania, a new law kicked all of the Jewish students out of the public schools. Apparently, we were foreigners, even though our family has lived in Romania since the seventeenth century. To compensate, the Jewish community managed to set up a system of yeshivas for boys, but unless the girls lived in big cities, they were out of luck. I really did intend to send all of my daughters to school in America, but I hadn't realized what state the farm would be in when we arrived. We're going to need Sala's full-time help to make a go of it. I kept putting off talking to her about it, and now Sender has beat me to it. I guess the old saying is true: You can't hide an awl in a sack; eventually the point will poke through. I look at my daughter guiltily.

"I'm sorry, Mamele."

"But Chaia's going to school," she protests. "You just said so."

Sender breaks in. "Chaia is nine—too young to help much around here—and Reyzel is practically a baby. But you, we can use on the farm. Besides, what book learning does a girl really need? Your husband will only care about the things you already know: to bake, to weave, to keep a kosher kitchen."

"I thought I might be a teacher," Sala says brokenly.

"Who puts these ideas in your head? You will teach your children. As the Proverb says, 'Train a lad in the way he ought to go; he will not swerve from it even in old age.' Now, no more silliness about school." Sender grabs another latke and heads blithely upstairs to bed.

I try to put an arm around Sala, but she shakes it off. "Sala," I say, "I didn't want you to find out about school this way. I was going—"

She interrupts me. "What does it matter how I found out? The result is the same. I'm going to end up like you."

Nothing she could have said would cut me more deeply. It's a glimpse into how she sees me: a brainless drudge. In the two weeks we've been in Ohio, her childhood image of her father—strong and capable—has been replaced with this truer, more disappointing picture of Sender. And her mother is powerless to protect her from the damage he leaves in his wake. Well, I'm hurt, but I suppose I deserve her scorn. I shouldn't have made a promise I couldn't keep. Besides, I don't want her to end up like me, and I think we can still prevent that. At least I can keep her from the kind of unhappy marriage I've had.

In the meantime, I'd like her to understand. I begin, "I know I said you would go to school. That honestly was my plan. But I had no idea how bad things were here."

"And how am I supposed to change that?"

"You're already doing it—canning, weaving, taking care of Reyzel. We're going to set up a farm stand and sell fruit and linens, which will at least get us through the winter."

"That's not very far."

"No. In the long run, there's no way to earn anything from this land unless we put a lot more of it into a crop that people will pay good money for—grapes. With every penny extra we make, we're going to buy grape cuttings and plant that hill in the back. If you and I and Papa all work hard, we should see a profit in a few years."

"A few years?" I hear the defeat—and the resentment—in her voice. "I see. I guess next you'll marry me off to Morris Gold so you can have yet another set of hands."

"You're not going to marry anyone you don't love." Sala looks at me levelly. I'm sure she doesn't believe my promises anymore. I try one more time to explain. "Look, Sala, I'm sorry your father bought this wretched farm, but he did, and now we're going to have to make it feed us. Tell me you understand."

"I understand," she says, but there's no feeling behind it.

"Tell me you forgive me."

"Please, I'd like to be alone now."

"You'll see, Sala. It'll work out. You *will* be the Grape Princess of Ohio."

"Mama, please."

I realize it's selfish of me to want her absolution. There's nothing I can do right now but let her come to grips with the situation on her own. She's resilient, I try to reassure myself.

"Go to bed, now," I tell her. She turns and climbs the stairs without a word. I go back to the sink full of dishes, thinking, '*Der mentsh trakht und Got lakht.*' A person plans and God laughs.

Chapter 4

SEPTEMBER 1918

SENDER WASN'T ENTHUSIASTIC ABOUT my plan to earn money for some new grapevines. "You'll make bupkes," he warned me. But I reminded him about our bargain, and he helped Sala and me scrounge up some lumber for the farm stand. I chose our location: right in the path of people heading east to the county seat in Ashtabula or north to the resort town of Geneva-on-the-Lake, where many city folk spend their summer weekends. They say even John D. Rockefeller and Henry Ford vacation there. Although neither of them has visited our stand, we've had a reasonable stream of customers.

On this mild September morning, a lull in traffic finds me biting into one of our late Granny Smiths. It doesn't resist my teeth the way a perfect apple should. Of course, Sender hadn't done anything to protect the orchard from pests, so our fruit has some dings and holes. Still, it'll make decent pie. We sold a bunch this morning to a family from Trumbull, on their way to the county courthouse, and to several picnickers headed for the beach. I shake our jar of coins. "You see," I tell Sala. "It's not even one o'clock and already we have almost a dollar. If that lady comes back for a tablecloth like she promised, that will be another two dollars. I'm sure we'll have enough money to plant some cuttings by January."

"Yes, Mama," Sala says without enthusiasm.

That's how it's been with Sala since she learned she wasn't going to school. She's polite and obedient, in fact, too much so. The energy—and the sass—are gone from her voice. I honestly don't believe she means to punish me; I think she's despondent. I just don't know what to do about it. We sit in silence for a few minutes until I spot Morris Gold hurrying up the road. He has the Orthodox man's habit of walking with his hands joined behind his back and his head slightly bent, lest he seem arrogant.

"Ho! Look who's coming," I say, maybe a little too heartily. "Morris, my boy! What brings you out our way on this fine afternoon?

"I've come to buy some"—he looks at our little display of produce—"apples. For Shabbas."

Sala is not fooled. "I thought I heard your uncle bragging about how abundant your apple crop was this year."

"Abundant—yes—but everyone says the produce from the Rappaport farm is the best," he improvises.

Sala surveys our somewhat sorry-looking crop. A bit of a spark flashes in her eyes. "Do they also say, 'Everything that comes out of a cow isn't butter'?" she asks.

Undeterred, Morris plunges on. "The girl is beautiful *and* witty."

"And she makes excellent latkes," Sala says acidly.

I'm glad to see Sala return to her old bantering self—if only for a moment—but I have to intervene before she eats the poor boy for dessert. "Sala, stop *dreying* the kind gentleman and weigh him out his apples. How many would you like, Morris?"

"I'll take all of them."

Sala looks at him askance, but she rustles up a basket and fills it. It weighs more than fifteen pounds. "Are you going to carry these all the way back to your farm?" she asks him doubtfully.

"Of course. My aunt needs them for her, um, noodle kugel."

"The whole bushel?"

"Sala," I scold her, "leave Morris in peace. Maybe they're having company." I take his money—two dollars and fifty-five cents for the kitty—and thank him.

"Well, good Shabbas to you both," Morris says, clearly wishing he had another excuse to stay a few minutes and talk with Sala. Sala summons her reserve of basic courtesy and wishes him a good Sabbath. Heaving the bushel onto his shoulder, he staggers off. About a hundred paces down the road, he stops to wipe his brow and looks back toward us hopefully. I wave. Sala sits expressionless.

I see what Sala means about Morris's lack of skill in the small-talk department, but I feel sorry for the boy. I remember how it feels to be lovestruck. "A long way to come for apples," I observe. "I wonder what else Morris was looking for."

"Well, I hope it wasn't me."

"You could do worse."

"I'm not saying Morris is a bad person. He's a mensch. But whenever I do get married, it's not going to be to someone like him."

"What's wrong with Morris?"

"First, he wants to be a farmer. He told me Papa introduced him to the Jewish Agricultural Society, and now he sees how important it is for Jews to go back to the land. He'll be a farmer like Papa is: full of theories but not so good at actually running a farm."

I'm impressed that a teenager has seen through Sender's shtick so quickly. But then, she probably doesn't have a high opinion of me right now, either.

"Not only that," she goes on, "Morris thinks that after he's mastered farming, he'll go to Palestine. He feels we should all be helping build a Jewish state there. I understand why our people want our own homeland, but I'm not interested in crossing the ocean again and trying to carve out a new place in the middle of the desert."

This is more words than I've heard from Sala in days. Clearly, it's something she's been thinking about. Grateful to have her talking again, I decide not to push my luck and kibbitz her. I let the conversation lapse. I'm just about to close up shop for the day—Shabbas is coming, and I still need to make my own kugel—when I see Chaia dawdling up the road, dragging her school bag. It's too early for her to be home.

"Chaia Sora Rappaport, what are you doing here?" I greet her. "Did Miss Dupont let you out early?"

Sala looks at Chaia expectantly. Digging the toe of her lace-up shoe into the dust, Chaia practically whispers, "The teacher sent me home."

"Sent you home? Why?"

"She was mad at me. She hit me with her pointer." Chaia lifts her hand to show me a big, red welt.

If that's supposed to make me feel sorry for her, it doesn't work. How could my daughter have misbehaved so badly that the teacher needed to hit her with a pointer? Unlike Sender, I'm not usually a spanker, but one thing I won't tolerate is Chaia getting into trouble at school. Not when we've come halfway across the world so that the girls can be educated. Not when Sala wants so desperately to go to school but has to work on the farm instead. I grab Chaia by the arm and give her a good smack on the *tuchus*. "What foolishness did you get into that the teacher hit you with her pointer?"

Chaia's lip begins to quiver, and soft-hearted Sala jumps in. "Mama, at least let her explain before you punish her all over again."

"All right," I allow, "tell us what happened."

According to Chaia, it all started the very first day of school. Chaia's voice gets stronger as she recalls the injustice of it all. "When Miss Dupont called the roll, she kept saying the name Chay-ya. Chay-ya. Honestly, Mama, I didn't know who she was talking about. Finally she said 'Chay-ya Rappaport,' and I figured she meant me, so I raised my hand. All the kids were laughing at my name, and she was getting angrier and angrier. I figured I would make it easier for everybody, so I told Miss Dupont she should call me by the first English name that popped into my head. I thought we met someone named Charlie at Cousin Mendel's house, so I told her to call me that."

"But Chaia," Sala says, "Charlie was a boy."

"Well, I remember that now. Everybody just started laughing harder and yelling, 'That's a boy's name. That's a boy's name.' Miss Dupont rapped her pointer on the desk so hard it almost broke. Finally, the class got quiet. She said to me, 'I will call you by your Christian name,' which I don't have one."

I'm stumped by that too until Sala explains, "That's what Christians call first names. They get them when they're baptized."

"Now you tell me," Chaia says.

"So what did you do?" I ask.

"I've been hunching down in my chair, hoping Miss Dupont won't notice me. Today, I ran out of luck. She wanted me to come to the board to do an arithmetic problem. Again, she's with the 'Chay-ya.' I thought, I just won't answer till she calls me Charlie. That was a big mistake. She marched over to my desk and made me put my hand on top. Then she whacked me real hard and told me to go home until I learned better manners."

By now, I'm good and mad. "I see. All right, Charlie," I say, emphasis on the Christian name, "come with me. We're going back to school. Sala, mind the stand."

Sala tries to intercede. "Aren't you being a little hard on her?"

I don't answer—just hold out my hand.

"No, Mama, don't make me go back there. Sala wants to go to school. Send her instead, and let me stay home to help you."

"You do as you're told, Chaia Rappaport. Now give me your hand."

She flinches as I grab her sore knuckles, but she comes along with no further protest. We walk back to the schoolhouse in silence. Long before we get there, I can see the bell tower rising above the corn fields. It's a simple red building with only one room. There's a flagpole outside, and Miss Dupont is taking down the flag when we arrive. She's younger than I expected—maybe twenty-two—and so thin that, as my mother would have said, she only has one side. Her hair is pulled back in a severe bun, part of an effort, I'm guessing, to look a bit more mature.

"Teacher," I call out to her as we approach. She continues lowering the flag and folds it carefully as we stand waiting for her.

Finally, she says, "Ah, you must be Mrs. Rappaport, Chay-ya's mother."

I wince at the way she says it but quickly smooth my face into a smile. "I'm pleased to make your acquaintance," I reply. This is a line we practiced with the English tutor, so I'm quite proud to pull it out now, even if I can tell from Chaia's expression that my pronunciation might be off. Undeterred, I continue, "We have in our house only respect for teachers. If my daughter, God forbid, misbehaves, you have from us our blessing to do anything what you think is needed." Chaia's shoulders sag.

"I'm relieved to hear that, Mrs. Rappaport," the woman replies. "I feel the schools are the key to all children's future, but especially those who—" I can see she's looking for a tactful way to say this—"who may lack certain advantages. You'll forgive me for saying so, but some of our immigrant families don't understand the way we expect young people to comport themselves in the classroom. It's all we can do to keep order. I feel it's an important part of my job to teach newcomers how we do things in the United States."

"I understand," I say. And I do. It's hard to imagine this slip of a girl controlling a bunch of rambunctious children in all the grades from one to eight. So far, I haven't noticed much difference in the way American and immigrant children "comport themselves," whatever that may mean, but I let it pass. Instead I add, "But, Teacher, I have to tell you that my daughter meant no—how do you say?—" (I search a few seconds for the right word) "disrespect about her name." Chaia looks up at me hopefully. Fortunately, her face is turned away from Miss Dupont because here's where I start concocting a story. "You see," I continue, "we did just change her name to Charlie."

"Oh?"

"Yes, you see, came over to us from Romania last week a letter that my Aunt Charlie, may she rest in peace, died." Now Chaia is staring at me incredulously, as she doesn't have an Aunt Charlie. I plow ahead. "God did not bless Charlie with children of her own, so we gave her name to"—can

I make myself say it?—"to Chay-ya—to keep alive her memory." This is a total fabrication. By this time, Chaia's eyebrows are up to her hairline.

"I see," says Miss Dupont. "You people have such, um, interesting customs. You do realize that Charlie is a boy's name."

"Not in Romania."

"All right, then, in future I will call your daughter Charlie if that is your wish."

"It is." I turn to Chaia. "Now Charlie, tell Miss Dupont you're sorry for causing trouble in school."

Chaia takes her cue. "I'm *so* sorry, Miss Dupont. I'm going to be such a good student. You'll see." Miss Dupont nods curtly.

"All right, Charlie," I say severely, "you go home and do homework. And I don't ever want to hear again that your teacher had to hit you." Knowing better than to wait around, Chaia scoots off down the road.

I turn back to her teacher. "I'll say goodbye now, Miss Dupont. You shouldn't have anymore a problem with Charlie." I make as if to leave, but then, I add, like it just occurred to me, "I hope you should forgive me, but there is one more thing."

"Yes?"

"If you ever hit my child again, I'll come back with my husband's horsewhip. Then you'll see what a smack really feels like." Before Miss Dupont can respond, I stalk off, leaving her holding her carefully folded flag.

Chapter 5

AFTER A STRING OF hot days, the weather has turned damp, with sudden squalls leaving the roads studded with puddles. Even so, on the off chance someone will come by, Sala and I are sitting at the farm stand. Sala is still often silent. I wouldn't say she's sullen. It's more like the dreams that used to animate her are gone, and she hasn't found any to replace them. Grape Princess is just not the honor she's looking for. In our conversations, I'm reduced to comments like the one I make now. "Looks like this might be the end of the farm-stand season." I can't believe I'm actually talking to my daughter about the weather.

"Yes," she says dutifully. "It doesn't look like we'll have too many customers."

When someone does trudge toward us, it turns out to be our neighbor, Corbin Johnson. I've never exchanged more than a nod with Johnson, who has a forbidding scowl permanently plastered on his face.

"Ugh, I don't like that man," Sala says with more spirit than she's shown in a while. "Once when you weren't at the stand, he came up and leered at me. I could smell whiskey on his breath."

"I'm not surprised," I tell Sala. "He makes his own moonshine. Chaia and Pasquelino were exploring, and they happened on his still way up in the woods."

"So that's why he has a steady supply."

"Not only that. Marta Giordano tells me he sells liquor to all the bigwigs in Ashtabula County—without a license."

By this time, Mr. Johnson is abreast of us. Big and beer-bellied, he's swaying slightly, and his eyes are slits. Tobacco stains his beard and overalls.

The smell of sour mash is like a cloud around him. "Good afternoon, Mr. Johnson," I say. "You would like, maybe, a pound of apples?"

His bleary eyes stray to Sala, or more accurately, Sala's chest. "I wouldn't mind having some of those apples," he slurs.

I'm so outraged, I'd like to pelt him with apples. But I'm a lone woman sitting on an empty road with her teenage daughter. I decide to bite my tongue. Keeping my face as stony as possible, I say, "The apples what we have for sale are on the table."

I watch the man react to my still-thick Yiddish accent with contempt. "Aw, I don't want your Jew apples anyway."

He's really trying my patience now. "As far as I know, Mr. Johnson," I spit out, "apples have no religion."

"Don't get cute with me. I don't truck with Jews, and I'm not the only one around here who feels that way."

I know I should keep holding my tongue, but I didn't come all the way to America to be harassed by a *shiker* like this. "Well," I say icily, "maybe you should go to hell, Mr. Johnson. You won't find down there too many Jews."

With difficulty, he brings his eyes to focus on me, staring ferociously. "Think you're funny, woman? Just you wait. Someday you won't be laughing. You'll find out how folks around here deal with Jews." He bangs on the table, scattering apples on the ground. Then he wheels around and lurches up the road.

Sala cringes. Unwilling to let her think Johnson has intimidated me, I call after him, "Do you think you worry me? Go frighten the bedbugs."

"Pu, Pu, Pu," Sala says to ward off the evil eye. "What a horrible man!"

"May leeches bleed him dry," I say fervently. We begin restacking the apples.

"Do you think you should have goaded him like that, Mama?" Sala asks, drawing her shawl around her more closely but still giving an involuntary shudder. "What do you think he meant about how folks around here deal with Jews?"

"Nothing, *Zisele*. There are Corbin Johnsons wherever there are Jews. We had a couple of bullyboys like that back in Falciu—always making a loud noise about what they were going to do to us."

"I thought that's why we left Falciu. America was supposed to be different. Remember all the things you said: no anti-Semitism, easy money, free public school?" She says the last with special bitterness.

"America *is* different. In America, the bullyboys run from the police. Back in Falciu the bullyboys were the police."

"I don't know, Mama. Corbin Johnson frightens me."

As we've been talking, Sender comes up the road, returning from pulling someone's car out of a ditch with our horse, Barney. In the rainy weather, we sometimes make more money rescuing stuck vehicles than we do selling produce. Sender has Morris in tow. Both are spattered with mud.

"Look who happened along to help me drag that Model T out of the ditch. He was on his way here to buy some apples." I have to smile. Morris has been our best customer all season. I don't know what Elsie is doing with all the fruit he buys.

"Was that Corbin Johnson I saw leaving the stand?" Morris asks. "You should stay as far away from that man as you can," he instructs Sala.

She bristles. "A drunk, for sure, but Mama knows how to handle him," she retorts.

"I'm sure we've dealt with worse," Sender says. "As the Torah tells us, 'Fear not to go down to Egypt, for I will make you there into a great nation.' God is saying he will protect us wherever we go, even from *paskudniaks* like that man."

"Of course, of course," Morris says respectfully, "but Corbin Johnson isn't just a drunk. I heard he's a member of the Ku Klux Klan."

"The Ku Klutz Klan?" Sender asks skeptically.

"No, the Ku *Klux* Klan, may their names be blotted out. It was started by a bunch of former Confederate soldiers and sympathizers after the American Civil War. Since the war put an end to slavery, the Klan made it their goal to terrorize Black people. They go around in white robes and hoods, burning crosses, raping women, lynching."

"It sounds like the pogroms," Sender says.

"It's just like the pogroms," Morris answers. "In the South, Black people are treated like the Jews are in Europe. They can't buy land. They can't send their children to the regular public schools. In fact, it's worse for them. They can't sit next to white people on the trains. They can't even drink at the same water fountains. And these bands of thugs are always threatening them."

"That's horrible," I exclaim.

"But I've never seen any Black people in Geneva," Sala protests. "What would a group like the Klan be doing here?"

Ever the scholar, Morris gives her the details. "The Klan had practically died out years ago, but they've started to get new recruits up North by complaining about immigrants, especially Jews and Catholics—anyone who doesn't fit their idea of what it means to be one hundred percent American."

"There are many people in this group?" I ask.

"Unfortunately, it's a popular message—and they're not just appealing to uneducated farmers like Corbin Johnson. There are judges, business-men, school board members, all kinds of people in the Klan."

Sender is all bluster. "Just let them try their nonsense around here." He looks at me and Sala. "My horsewhip is by the front door. If that man comes back, you call me." Then he strides off toward the barn, dragging Barney behind him.

Sala turns to me accusingly. "This is the Golden Land you've brought us to? With neighbors like Corbin Johnson?"

"Don't you worry, Sala. I know Corbin Johnson's type. He's just a *knaker*, a big talker. Morris, help us close up the stand, and take the rest of the apples for your aunt—a gift from the Rappaports."

Chapter 6

DESPITE WHAT I TOLD Sala, I was uneasy about Corbin Johnson. But when trouble visited us next, it came from a different direction: the Spanish Flu. All around us, people were getting sick. One entire Jewish family perished: father, mother, and two teenagers. Chaia's friend Pasquelino came down with it a week ago. Of course, she wasn't far behind. Yesterday, she was sent home from school with a cough, and Reyzel with her since she had been exposed. They brought a sign with them we had to hang on our door: Influenza! Keep Out of This House.

I put Chaia to bed, hoping she might have a light case, but by evening, her fever was so high, two quilts couldn't stop her chills. This morning, she's sweat through her sheets and nightgown. Her curls hang in wet clumps, exposing the white skin of her scalp. So sore is her throat, she can't swallow. Beyond complaining that her eyeballs ache, she just moans.

When I don't show up for breakfast, Sala knocks hesitantly at her sisters' door. "Don't come in," I warn her firmly. "Maybe we can keep you from coming down with this thing."

"But I want to help."

"You will. You're going to have to milk the cow and feed the animals. And kill a chicken," I add, "for soup." That really worries Sala. Chickens are so valuable for their eggs that we rarely butcher them. There's an old saying, "When a Jew kills a chicken, one of them is sick." True, but I tell Sala we'll be fine. "Just move your blankets to the parlor and don't come up to the second floor except to leave supplies. We'll need buckets of water, clean rags, pots of tea, and toast."

Hoping to protect Reyzel, I moved her from the room she shares with Chaia to my bed last night. She seemed okay this morning, but by afternoon, she has a fever high enough to set the bedclothes on fire. Sender has also started coughing. He's nauseated, but he manages to eat some challah.

For a while I run from room to room with cold compresses and glasses of tea. Finally I realize it will be easier to have everyone in one place. I lift Chaia—so weak she can't keep her head up—and I carry her to our room, putting her in bed with Sender. He's now so ill, he doesn't even register that she's there. Reyzel I put in my bed.

Chaia has sweat through the sheets again, but I don't have any more. I change her into one of Sender's shirts and put some clean rags under her. Reyzel keeps vomiting, no matter that there's nothing left in her stomach. Otherwise, she lies on the mattress, glassy-eyed, until the chills come and rattle her teeth like dice in a cup. The day feels like a week. I make up a mat for myself on the floor next to Reyzel. Finally, I get a little sleep around midnight.

Toward morning, Chaia calls out to me. There's terror in her voice. "Mama," she rasps, "why is Bubbe Klein here?" My mother has been dead for years. Rushing to Chaia's side, I put the back of my hand against her forehead. I have never felt a human being so hot. In a panic, I gather her to me and race out to the yard. There's a hint of frost in the air, but I put her right underneath the pump and begin frantically raising and lowering the handle. Water gushes from the spigot, making Chaia cry out in misery.

"I'm so sorry, little duckling," I say, "but I have to get your fever down." She tries to evade the cold water, but she's too spent to move away. I pump until she closes her eyes, whether sleeping or unconscious, I can't tell. When I pick her up, she's covered in mud but cooler. In the dark kitchen, I clean her up as best I can and put her back in bed. Exhausted, I get about an hour of sleep before Sender wakes me, retching into the pot I left by the side of his bed.

I rouse myself, give him some water, and check on Chaia, who's still sleeping beside him. When I brush her hair away from her face, I feel dry, cool skin. Her fever has broken! Relief floods my chest, but before I celebrate, I turn to kiss Reyzel's forehead. No change: fever high, skin clammy. My movement arouses a groan, but she doesn't seem to see me.

Retrieving the supplies Sala has left by the door, I put a cool compress on Reyzel's head. Then I help Sender slurp a little soup. He keeps it down, but it triggers a spasm of coughing, which wakes Chaia. She's surprised to find herself in bed with her father, an unheard-of occurrence.

"How did I get here?" she whispers. "I don't remember anything after you put me in my bed."

"How *did* she get here?" Sender croaks.

"She was sick during the night," I say—a calculated understatement. "How are you feeling, Chaia?"

"My throat still hurts, but it's not too bad."

"Then put her back in her own room," Sender growls, the nausea making him even more irascible than usual. "Isn't it enough that she brought this curse on us?"

"Sender!" I bark angrily. I can see Chaia is shattered. "Come, my heart," I tell her. "We'll get you settled in your own rom."

Chaia goes to climb down from Sender's bed and sees Reyzel, her limp body covered in compresses. "Is she dead?" she breathes.

"No, darling. She's going to be fine. I'm just bringing her fever down." My words are much more optimistic than I feel.

Chaia sits next to Reyzel and takes her hand. She would stay there longer except Sender suddenly calls out, "I'm going to be sick! Get her out of here."

I scoot Chaia down the hall, the sound of heaving following us. As I tuck Chaia in, I see tears gathering at the corners of her deep brown eyes. "This is all my fault," she says.

"Chaia, darling, that's your father's fever talking. Sometimes when people feel very sick, they say things they don't mean."

"But he's right, isn't he? I brought the flu home."

"If you think that way, maybe we should blame Pasquelino, who gave it to you."

"No!" she interrupts, "Pasquelino couldn't help getting sick."

"Well, there you are. It's nobody's fault. Now listen, *Chaiale*, I'm going to need to look after Papa and Reyzel right now. There's some chicken soup and toast in the hallway. You really should eat. Is there anything else you need?"

"Will you bring me *Little Women*?"

Miss Dupont lent her this book, and she's fascinated by it. I know there's a character who dies of scarlet fever—Chaia came to me weeping the first time she read it. I worry this is not the best time for such a scene. But then I think, maybe it's exactly what Chaia needs: a story about sisters who care for each other. I get it down off her shelf and hand it to her. "Come and get me if you need anything," I tell her.

35

Back in the sickroom, Sender is clutching his head. "Oy, yoy, yoy," he groans. I call down to Sala to fix some milk and cinnamon. When Ethel's husband Walter had the flu, she said it helped reduce his fever. I'm ready to try anything. Meanwhile, I refresh Reyzel's compresses though they don't seem to have done much good. I try to get her to speak to me. She shakes her head back and forth, but no words come. When Sala leaves the milk outside the door, I dose Reyzel and Sender. They both throw it up.

And so we spend that day and the day after. Sala communicates to me through the door, letting me know she mended a break in the fence near the Johnson property and took in the rest of the field corn. The farm goes on no matter what shape its owners are in. She also tells me that Chaia is asking for mamaliga, the corn porridge that was a staple back in Romania. I take it as a good sign.

Sender is still miserable, but at least he's not delirious. Reyzel may be hallucinating, but she doesn't speak, so I can't tell. She's feverish, and she's started coughing like her insides are going to come out. I'm terrified it's pneumonia, so I don't try the pump cure on her. I just pray.

Though I'm a religious woman, I'm not usually a praying woman. I follow the laws and customs of the Jewish people. I keep a kosher home. I make sure we have all the necessities for the holidays: the challah for the Sabbath, the apples and honey for the new year, and the matzo for Passover. But talking to God—that's Sender's domain (and he's often busy at it when I wish he were plowing). Me and God, mostly we leave each other alone. But now, since he's visited this plague upon us, I come knocking at his door. "Master of the Universe," I plead, "if you want to take one of us, take me. Let my Reyzel live."

The next day, I think I'm going to get at least part of my wish. When I wake up, my throat feels like someone has taken a grater to it. It hurts to move. I'd like nothing more than to lie there, but I hear Reyzel breathing heavily. Now I'm sure the pneumonia has come.

When my hot feet hit the cold floor, I can't help crying out. Sender keeps snoring, but a second later, the door opens a crack, and I see Chaia's worried face peering at me. "Mama," she whispers, "what's wrong?"

"Reyzel isn't doing so well," I admit. I hate to put Chaia to work, but since she's just recovered from the flu, I know that she can't catch it again from the rest of us. Besides, I'm desperate. "Can you help me prop her up so she can breathe a little easier?" I ask. "We'll need whatever you can find to put under her back."

"I'll bring my feather pillow." Chaia pads back to her room and returns with one of her prized possessions. She collected the down for it herself, braving the pecking geese. Together we lift Reyzel and slide the pillow behind her. As we work, Chaia touches my arm and gasps. "Mama, you're so hot. You're sick too!"

"I'll be fine, Mamele."

By this time, Sender is up. He adds his advice, coughing between each sentence: "Tell Sala to get some mint from the yard and boil it in a big pot. Reyzel should breathe in the steam. That's what my mother used to do." Chaia calls down to Sala with the instructions, and soon a soup pot full of hot mint water is outside the door. Chaia sets it on the bed. I sit behind Reyzel and hold the sheet like a tent over the pot, urging her to inhale deeply. She must at least understand what I'm saying as she tries to breathe in. As she does, I can feel the congestion in her lungs. It sounds like she's breathing through glue. Hoping it will help, I begin thumping on her back.

Suddenly, the smell of the mint is too much for me. I lean over the bedside and throw up into the pot. Chaia takes the pot out to the yard and washes it under the pump. When she returns, I'm covered in sweat.

"Mama, you need to rest," Chaia tells me, climbing into the bed and gently relieving me of Reyzel's little body. I go back to my mat. I don't remember much from the next two days except Chaia's stoic round of sickroom ministrations: applying cold compresses, removing foul-smelling pails of vomit. I feel her small, cool hand on my forehead, and I hear her usually boisterous voice gently urging her sister to drink soup and breathe deep.

Finally, Sender feels well enough to get up and help. Of course, his idea of helping is to open his prayerbook and recite the *Misheberakh* for the sick. I don't expect much from the ritual, but then again, my fever breaks in the night.

Reyzel, however, seems impervious to compresses and prayers. She's been running a fever for seven days. She hardly sleeps from coughing, and I notice brown spots have started to appear on her cheeks, a sign the pneumonia is worsening. We're all in quarantine, so I can't send Sala for the doctor. Even if I could, I know they don't have much to offer: a few aspirin tablets. I try to talk to Reyzel, to encourage her, but she doesn't seem to hear.

Finally, Chaia has an idea: "Reyzel likes music so much. Maybe we should sing to her."

"It couldn't hurt," I say. "Let's try that song about raisins and almonds, 'Rozhinkes mit Mandlen.' She always fell asleep to that lullaby when she was a baby." So the three of us, our voices hoarse, begin to sing:

> In the old house of study in a lonely, dark corner,
>
> a young widow sits with her baby and sings.
>
> Her little one fusses and frets in his cradle,
>
> but her haunting lullaby quickly takes wing.
>
> Ah, lyu, lyu, lyu.

As we begin the verse, I think I see the ghost of a smile on Reyzel's lips. Before we finish, she's drifted off.

I can't swear it was the music, but that afternoon, Reyzel's fever breaks. By the end of the day, the brown spots have disappeared from her cheeks, and she begins to breathe easier. She can even keep down Sala's soup. A miracle!

#

We aren't in what the Americans would call "fine fettle." Already slender, Sender looks hollowed out from the days when he couldn't keep anything down. Still, he returns to the barn and his autumn tasks: mending the horse's harness, sharpening the plow, and of course, praying to the Almighty for "the wind to blow and the rain to fall." Chaia is ready to take back her chores and to provide some company for the jubilant Sala, who's been alone with her worries and all the farm work for the past week. I'm up to making challah for Friday night. Reyzel is still bed-ridden (in her own bed by now). Her cheeks have lost their fullness, and dark smudges remain under her eyes. Still, she's back to her old chatty self. Sala shows her how to make paper dolls, and Reyzel invents whole sagas about their adventures. If it weren't for her extreme pallor and some unsteadiness on her feet, I could pretend I don't remember how close to death she was.

When our two weeks of quarantine are finished, Sender disappears for the morning and comes back with his pocket bulging. He won't reveal what's inside until we're all gathered together in Reyzel and Chaia's room. He can barely contain his excitement as he announces, "I have a little something for my Reyzel, who was so brave when she had the flu." With that, he reaches into his pocket, and with a flourish, pulls out a tiny puppy, white with brown spots.

"Oh, Papa, he's so cute. I'm going to name him *Rozhinkes*," she says decisively.

Of course she's delighted, and we're delighted for her, but I can't help noticing a hurt look pass over Chaia's face. She too had the flu. Not only that, but she also nursed the three of us, a burden that was really too much for a child. And though Sala is too old to be jealous of a puppy, she might have appreciated a few words of praise from her father for looking after the farm.

That evening, I take fifty cents from my grapevine fund. I give twenty-five cents—along with my profuse thanks—to Sala to spend on whatever she wants. Then, with Sala's help, I write a letter to the bookshop in Geneva, asking that they send *Jo's Boys*. This is the sequel to *Little Women*, which Charlie once told me she's been yearning to read. We ask that the bookshop include a card: "To my own little woman, with love and thanks, from Mama."

Chapter 7

IN COMPARISON WITH THAT bout of flu, the rest of the winter seemed easy. Chaia and Reyzel were back at school. Sender, God be praised, replaced the boarded-up windows and fixed the porch. Sala and I were busy weaving. In March, we put our earnings toward fifteen rows of grapes.

Now Purim is upon us, a time when all seven Jewish families in Geneva will get together to hear the megillah of Esther and how she saved our people from annihilation in ancient Persia. Sala and I started about a week before the holiday making *shalakh mones*, gifts of food that we'll exchange with the others, especially those who are struggling. I sometimes wonder how this custom might look to someone who's not Jewish. Basically, you make hamantaschen—triangular cookie pockets filled with prune or poppyseed—and give them to your friends, who make the exact same cookies, which they then give to you.

It's not entirely clear what hamantaschen (or Haman's pockets) have to do with the story of Purim. They're named for the villain, a vizier who schemes to slaughter all the Jews in the realm. I've seen a lot of pictures of Haman over the years. Sometimes his hat is tri-cornered, but I've never seen him with pockets of any kind, let alone triangles. Whatever his trousers looked like, the megillah tells us he hated the Jews. Why? Some people just do.

Besides exchanging hamantaschen, another custom of the holiday is the Purim spiel, a slapstick play that makes fun of everyone in the story and sometimes the people in the audience as well. While Jewish holidays can be on the sober side (as are most Jews), Purim is our version of Carnival. We're supposed to drink so much that we can't tell the difference between the evil Haman and Esther's Uncle Mordechai, the hero of the story. The farmers have stocked up on schnapps for the event as we soon will have a harder time getting liquor from our usual source in Cleveland. Ohio has been at the forefront of the campaign for Prohibition and will be the first state to go dry in May. Supposedly, there will be exemptions for alcohol used in religious ceremonies, but I'm not sure the state is going to understand our tradition to get thoroughly drunk on Purim.

In fact, getting drunk is where this evening's trouble started.

Well, to be honest, that's where the trouble got out of hand. It started weeks before when they cast the spiel. First there was a *tararam* about who could be in the play. In Europe, Purim spiels are performed only by men (and what isn't?). One faction, led by old Mr. Kaminsky, wanted to follow this tradition, but the other pointed out there were only eight men in the community, including Mr. Kaminsky, who said he was too old to participate, and Harold Gold, who, though he didn't say so outright, implied that such shenanigans were beneath him.

Finally they decided that Queen Esther could be played by an honest-to-goodness female, but that was not the end of the controversy. Elsie, who didn't share her husband's scorn for the project, wanted to be the beautiful Jewish maiden. I suppose that might have been in keeping with the silliness of the spiel, since Elsie hasn't seen the younger side of forty for several years now. But Dov Fishkin, the community's unofficial master of ceremonies, decided that Esther should be none other than my lovely daughter, Sala. I have to say, if you need a princess, Sala's your girl. Her skin is fair, tinged pink across the apples of her cheeks. From her father, she inherited a pair of black eyes so deep you could fall into them. I can see why Dov chose her, but I'm afraid he set us all up for tonight's less than happy result.

Things started out calmly enough as we assembled at the Golds for the megillah reading. But as the men made their way through the scroll, they also made their way through several bottles of schnapps (with a little help from their wives). By the time we got to the last chapter, there were loud complaints about such crucial matters as how one reader pronounced the *komatz* vowel and whether a final letter *hey* with a dot should or should not be sounded.

Several more rounds of schnapps follow the successful completion of the reading. So it is that we find ourselves reassembling for the Purim spiel with most of the men and a few of the women *farshnikert*. The play opens with Dov, stuffed with batten to twice his normal size, appearing as Akhashverosh, the ruler of more than 127 provinces from India to Nubia.

Fastened to the front of his costume is a sign: "Grape King." I sneak a peek at Harold Gold, who does not seem to be sharing the general hilarity. He's even less amused as Achashverosh begins talking. "Tell me, my courtiers, how I shall choose a wife worthy of my greatness," Dov intones, gesturing toward his huge belly.

Dov has enlisted Sender as Haman, who replies, "Oh, your immense-ness—I mean your eminence . . . ." There's more in the same spirit. By the end of Sender's monologue, Harold is red in the face, and a vein at the side of his forehead pulses.

At the suggestion of his counselors, Achashverosh/Dov is presented with a parade of potential queens. These are all played by the men and introduced with the names of the women in the community. It's no great surprise to me when the shortest of them comes out as "Princess Bluma of Falciu," his skin darkened and his tuchus padded with towels. I learned a long time ago to pretend to laugh at such teasing.

Elsie, it seems, never learned that lesson. When "Princess Elsie of Lvov" appears, the wrinkles on "her" face drawn in black pencil, Elsie rises from her seat and shouts, "This is how you treat your friends, Fish-kin? Whose house do you think you're at? Should we sit quietly as you mock us?"

The answer to that question is actually yes. Mockery is at the heart of the Purim spiel. But Elsie's outburst inspires all of the other tipsy guests to voice their own unhappiness.

"Rappaport," Gold yells, "who are you to make fun of me? Why, my vineyard is the biggest in Ohio."

"Your belly is bigger than your vineyard," Sender shoots back.

"Well, your vineyard is a *shtikl drek.*"

"Oh, sit down, Gold," rasps old Mr. Kaminsky. "We're all tired of hearing about how important you are."

"You ingrate," Elsie shoots back. "Who brought you meals for a whole week when you were sick last year? This is how you repay us?"

"Who asked for your help?" cries Mrs. Kaminsky. "Your chicken soup tastes like dishwater."

By this point, all the revelers are on their feet, hurling insults. I must confess, I'm enjoying some of these exchanges, but I see things are getting out of hand. Chaia regards all such adult tomfoolery with the interest of a naturalist, but poor Sala, positioned at the end of the line of princesses, is covering her face in embarrassment. I have to hold my hands over Reyzel's ears as the group lets loose with a few choice curses. "You should grow like an onion with your head in the sand!" "May all your teeth fall out but one— and in that one, you should have a toothache!" Fisticuffs may be next.

Finally, since no one else is doing it, I decide to take matters in hand. I march up to the front of the room and stand beside the players. "*Genug iz Genug*," I say in my steeliest voice. "Enough is enough." When the grown-ups begin to quiet down, I quote them all a little Talmud, cour- tesy of my husband. "Sender, didn't you once tell me that the Temple in Jerusalem was destroyed because of baseless hatred among the people? Just imagine how we might suffer because of our squabbling. We're seven Jewish families in a sea of strangers. If we fight, who will be there when we need each other?" Several people sit down sheepishly. Although Sender mutters, he takes his seat.

But not Harold. "I should forget this insult?" he says indignantly.

"We're all sorry you were insulted," I allow, not entirely honestly, but peace is at stake. "Besides, of course you would be the model for Achash- verosh. What other king do we have in Geneva, Ohio, but the Grape King?"

Harold seems ready to be appeased, but Elsie gives him a dirty look. "And what about my wife? How about the insult to her?" he asks dutifully.

"Harold and Elsie, I think you both laughed at Princess Bluma of Fal- ciu," I remind them.

They have to agree, if grudgingly. I press my advantage. "Look, Purim is supposed to make us laugh—even at ourselves. So let's do that. Let's sit down and see how this story comes out."

And so we do. Achashverosh chooses his queen, she speaks up for her people and rescues them from Haman's evil decree, and Haman is sentenced to death. Curiously, a Purim spiel often makes Haman a sympa- thetic character at the end. While we drown out his name with noisemakers during the megillah reading, he gets his moment at the end of Dov's play.

Hands bound behind his back, Sender delivers Haman's big speech on the way to the gallows: "Is the beggar who goes from door to door seeking scraps of food to assuage his hunger condemned to a worse fate than mine? If only I might live under the bright sky! To what can a once-proud vizier compare himself? To a mosquito on a whitewashed wall, squashed by a child with the palm of his hand."

Old Man Kaminsky wipes a tear from his eye. "*Gut gezogt*," Morris pronounces. "Well-said." Even Harold nods judiciously. I guess that even in Haman, we all recognize a little of ourselves.

Chapter 8

AFTER ALMOST TWO YEARS on the farm, I have some repeat customers for my weaving. Beside me is a stack of linen napkins ordered by one of my farm-stand regulars. I need to hem them with mitered corners, a fussy bit of hand sewing I've been putting off. I'm just about to force myself to begin when I hear a car struggling up our dirt road, a rare occurrence. Rozhinkes is barking furiously. Going out to the porch, I recognize my cousin Mendel's truck. Right away, I imagine there's been a calamity back home in Falciu. Why else would Mendel drive all the way from Cleveland in the middle of the week? Before the truck even comes to a stop, I'm running toward it. When the passenger door flies open, a slight figure practically hurls herself into my arms. It's my younger sister, Hodel! She embraces me, and I think she might collapse if I don't hold her up.

"Hodel, *shvesterke*, what's happened? What are you doing in America?"

My sister begins to weep although no tears fall on my neck. I wonder if she's already used up every drop.

Mendel looks flustered. "She arrived on our doorstep last night. The only thing she's been able to tell us is that she wants to see you. Other than that, she just cries."

I guess Mendel took pity on Hodel, whom he knew as a girl in Falciu, and despite his reservations about our road, he decided to drop her at our door. She certainly doesn't look like she could have walked it by herself. She's so skinny, her shoulders poke out inside her light jacket. Her cheeks are practically without flesh, and her wrists are flimsy as reeds. Though she inherited the hazel eyes that were my mother's, every trace of sparkle has drained from them; they're like flat seltzer.

"All right, Hodel," I soothe her. "I'm here now. Come in the house, and I'll get you some tea. Mendel, will you have something?"

"I'd love to, Bluma, but I still have a long drive back to Cleveland."

"Well, a blessing on your head for bringing Hodel to us."

"Of course, and I'll come back soon to visit." He glances at my sister but looks away before she sees the concern in his eyes.

When we get to the kitchen, Sala is just coming in from the barn. "Aunt Hodel?" she says incredulously. "Oh, how we've missed you. How are you? How is Grandfather?"

This occasions a whole new bout of weeping. It's all we can do to get Hodel settled in a chair by the Franklin stove. Finally, with a little tea in her, Hodel stops crying. We don't press her, but after a few minutes, she says, "Didn't you get Papa's letters?"

"No, Zisele, we haven't heard a thing from Romania in months. I'm afraid the post isn't very reliable. Do you feel up to telling us what happened?" Sala puts her arm around Hodel. It seems to steady her.

Apparently, it all started last September when a troop of infantrymen returning from the war with Hungary marched into Falciu. There were a few Jewish soldiers, and one of them, Zavel Bercovici, was billeted with my father and Hodel. Papa wasn't pleased, as they hadn't had a lot to go around even though there were only two of them since Malke and her husband, Berel, moved to Iassi.

"That must have been hard," I sympathize.

"It wasn't hard for me! Not after I laid eyes on Zavel. He was so dashing in his blue uniform jacket and plumed hat." No sooner has Hodel drawn this picture of the handsome young soldier than she breaks down again. When I put my hand over hers on the table, her skin is dry, flaky, and cold. I wait for her to collect herself.

"We had so many wonderful conversations over the dinner table, with Zavel telling us about his adventures in the war and his plans for the future," Hodel finally says in a rush. "He was such a fine person. I thought we were made for each other, and it seemed like Zavel did too. By the time his regiment was demobilized, he'd asked me to marry him. He was going to come back to Falciu after he'd had a chance to see his family in Iassi."

"Papa approved?"

"Papa thought Zavel was the answer to all our prayers—" She trails off, unable to keep from crying.

"But he never returned?" Sala prompts her.

"Only three weeks after Zavel left for Iassi, Papa got a letter from Berel. Our brother-in-law knew about my engagement, and he felt duty-bound to tell us a rumor he heard: Zavel had married someone else."

"Oh, no, Hodel!" Sala cries.

"How is this possible?" I want to know.

"I've asked myself that question so many times. How could I have been so deceived?"

"In the whole month he spent with you, there was never any sign that Zavel would do such a thing?"

For a moment, she becomes animated. "Bluma, he was the kindest, most considerate man I ever met. He helped Papa chop wood. He carried water from the well and butchered the chickens that his commanding officer kept demanding of us. He bought us oranges and pomegranates. And when he asked for my hand, he promised we would live in Falciu since otherwise Papa would be alone. Then this. I just don't understand it."

"Of course not," Sala says indignantly. "I can imagine how you felt."

"For two weeks, I didn't get out of bed. I couldn't show my face in Falciu, with everyone knowing I'd been abandoned. And I couldn't go to Malke and Berel in Iassi because Zavel was there. Finally Papa decided to send me to America to stay with you."

"And right he was," I agree although my mind is already trying to calculate where I'll put her and how I'll feed her. Well, as my mother, may she rest in peace, used to say, "Where there's room in the heart, there's room in the house."

I have Sala keep Hodel company while I do some surreptitious reorganizing upstairs. I take everything out of the big linen cupboard, remove the shelves, and squeeze a little featherbed in there. That will be Reyzel's room. I'll put Sala and Chaia together and give Sala's room to Hodel.

Not long after, Sender comes in from trimming the grapes. He's shocked to see Hodel, of course, and knowing him, I imagine he's not keen on hosting her. Before he can say anything inhospitable, I head him off. "Look who's come to help us out on the farm," I declare though it's hard to imagine, looking at my sister, what work she can do in her current state. Still, Sender gets the message and makes lukewarm welcoming noises.

I wish my youngest daughter was even that friendly. When she comes home from school and discovers she's been moved to the linen closet, I have to use my harshest warning look to keep her from complaining about it in front of Hodel. Of course, she has very little memory of my sister from the old country. Chaia, on the other hand, always liked her aunt, and her good opinion is bolstered by the Toblerone chocolate bars Hodel brought for the girls. After dinner, they each get a precious square.

As soon as it's seemly, I send everyone off to bed, but I stay with Hodel at the table. We're quiet for a long time. Hodel is so much younger than I am that we never really had a chance to get to know each other as adults. I was married and out of the house when she was quite little. Until then, I was often tasked with caring for her, and she didn't make it easy. She fidgeted and screamed every morning as I braided her hair, with my mother scolding me from the kitchen to be gentler. I had to cut the crusts off her bread and blow on her soup to cool it. She whined to be played with constantly, no matter how many other chores I had to do.

I confess, I was jealous of her—the *mezinke*, the littlest one in the family and everyone's pet. She was a late-life baby, a delightful surprise for my mother, who'd had several miscarriages after Malke was born. My father, who had no use for me, thought Hodel was sent to him specially by God.

I considered her a spoiled brat, but now that I've had my own children, I see she was just a normal little girl. In the end, she had to grow up too fast. When she was only twelve, my mother died. I tried to help out as much as I could, but I already had Sala and Chaia, and we were living in Sender's parents' home, where I had my own responsibilities. Malke was also married with little ones. When she and Berel moved to Iassi, the burden of keeping house for my father fell on Hodel's young shoulders, which accounts for the fact that she was still unmarried at nineteen. That sacrifice made Papa treasure her all the more. How happy he must have been to think she and her husband would live with him! When the match fell though, I can easily imagine him scraping together the money to send her off to America in the hope it might make her happy, even if it broke his heart.

After sitting with Hodel for several minutes of uncomfortable silence, I blurt out. "Well, I have only one thing to say about Zavel Bercovici. May he have thunder in his belly and lightning in his pants."

"Oh, no, Bluma. Don't curse him. He must have had his reasons."

"Had he, maybe, left the other woman waiting for him in Iassi when he went off to the army?"

"If he was in love with someone else, she must be a special person."

"It's a mitzvah to be so forgiving."

"But I still love him. You don't know what it's like to lose your true love. You have Sender coming in from the fields to sit with you at dinner, give your forehead a kiss before bed, sing 'A Woman of Valor' to you every Friday night."

I debate how much to tell my sister about the state of my marriage. It's true that Sender does recite that Proverb to me weekly, but he does so because it's tradition, not because he loves me. I suppose I could hide the fact that Sender hasn't kissed me on the forehead (or anywhere else) for many years, but soon enough she'll notice that we're more like business partners than lovers. I decide Hodel has enough of her own troubles right now; she doesn't need to worry about mine. "Marriage is a little different than falling in love," I say blandly.

"I guess I'll never get to see the difference. I can't imagine ever finding someone else I'd want to marry."

Just the kind of declaration a nineteen-year-old would make, I think to myself. Aloud, I say, "Despair is not a good thing, Hodel. It's healthier to be angry, to put some fire back in your heart."

"My heart is dead. But I promise, the rest of my body is strong. I can work; in fact, I think that will be the best thing for me."

#

The truth is, I could use another pair of hands around the farm, but those thin wrists worry me. Still, I decide to take Hodel at her word, starting the very next day. Planting season for the garden is in full swing. While I work on that with Sala, I give the kitchen over to my sister, who, it must be said, is a terrific cook. We're at our sparsest season in the larder. Besides our staples, there are just some potatoes and onions in the root cellar; the last dregs of some barley, cornmeal, and beans; the remainder of our canned vegetables and fruits; milk and cheese from our cow, Bubale; and a few skinny chickens and geese. From this Hodel manages to eke out soup with kreplach, cholent for Shabbas, and pots of mamaliga, which is good for anything that ails you. I think Hodel must be dipping into those pots, as she begins to fill out. A little pink grazes her cheeks, and her bones no longer look so sharp you could cut yourself on them.

Also, Hodel is a fine weaver, who, like me, learned the trade at our mother's knee. Soon, our pile of linens begins to grow, with Hodel doing the hemstitching that the fancier ladies prize in their tablecloths and pillow shams.

What pleases me most is that she makes a special effort to get along with my daughters. The first full day she spent with us, she decreed that she would no longer take a bedroom to herself. Out of Reyzel, she pries the information about the old sleeping arrangements. (Come to think of it, there probably wasn't much prying required.) She returns Reyzel to her old room with Chaia, making an ally out of Reyzel. Then she sets up the feather bed so that she and Sala can share the other bedroom. This turns out to be a match made in heaven, which is no great surprise when you think of it. Sala isn't much younger than Hodel, who insists Sala stop calling her "aunt" immediately. With no school friends and only me and her sisters for company, Sala has been lonely. Now she has a live-in confidante. Sometimes I hear them giggling together in the night. Hodel is certainly helping to bring back the old Sala, and maybe my daughter is making the memory of Zavel Bercovici fade. Still, I like the idea of setting fire to his pants.

Chapter 9

I'M IN THE FRONT yard, shucking the first peas from the garden, when my littlest one comes home from school. Reyzel is not as enthusiastic a student as Chaia, who has, true to her word, become Miss Dupont's star pupil. But Reyzel likes the songs Miss Dupont teaches them, and today I'm treated to "Where Have You Been, Charming Billy?" in her chirpy soprano. Rozhinkes greets her with enough barking to wake the dead. "There's mandelbroit on the table, and milk," I say. "Where's Chaia?"

"Miss Dupont made her stay after school," she calls over her shoulder.

"What?" But Reyzel has already waltzed into the house for her snack.

About ten minutes later, Chaia comes up the road. I flash back to the same scene two years ago, but that frightened little girl is gone, replaced by a self-confident eleven-year-old. Her Yiddish accent has disappeared, and her gangly awkwardness has been replaced by the physical confidence of a girl who spends her days milking cows and roaming the woods. Still there's something in her manner that makes me suspicious.

"So what happened?" I greet her, unsmiling. "I hear you had to stay after school."

"Reyzel is such a tattletale."

"Never mind about Reyzel. We're talking about you. Did you get in trouble again?"

"No, no!" she rushes to reassure me. I guess she's imagining the swat that would await her. "But what happened is worse."

"The other children were making fun of you?" Chaia's been having some trouble with her classmates, who resent that she's become the teacher's pet. I'm relieved Miss Dupont has gone from smacking her to kvelling over her, but sometimes I worry these attentions are making Chaia even more of an outsider. Just last week, Miss Dupont gave all the children her age a deadline for memorizing their multiplication tables. Chaia was the only one who succeeded. As a punishment for missing the deadline, everyone else had to stay inside for recess, while Chaia had the dubious honor of playing outside, all by herself. Afterwards there were some snide comments, reported to me by an almost gleeful Reyzel. "Did they call you a goody-goody again?" I press her although I'm still not clear why being good is such a disgrace among American eleven-year-olds.

Chaia shakes her head.

"You were, God forbid, hurt?" I leave my peas in the bowl and come closer to inspect her.

She shrugs off my hand. "No, no. I'm fine."

"Then what?"

"Miss Dupont told me I had to stay after school, so I figured I was going to get rapped on the knuckles again, even though I couldn't think of anything I did to deserve it. Then, instead of whacking me, Miss Dupont tells me Gertrude Higginbottom got the measles and she can't be in the district elocutionary contest."

"*Electionary* contest?" I repeat the word carefully. "This has something to do with elections?"

"It's *elocutionary*, and it has to do with poems and speeches and that kind of stuff. Kids from all over the county go to Ashtabula and recite their pieces, and the person who does the best job wins. 'Charlie,' Miss Dupont says to me, 'you have the loudest voice in the class and you're a good reader, so I'm going to enter you in the contest instead of Gertrude.' She's making me learn the poem Gertrude was going to do."

Relief spreads through me. "That doesn't sound so bad. I like poetry."

"You may like poetry, but you aren't going to like this poem."

"Why, what poem is it?"

"'The Wreck of the Hesperus.' It's about this sea captain who takes his daughter with him on a voyage, but they get caught in a storm."

"That sounds exciting. What's the problem?"

She takes a little book out of her school bag, opens it to the right page, and declaims:

Then the maiden clasped her hands and prayed
That savèd she might be;
And she thought of Christ, who stilled the wave
On the Lake of Galilee.

"And there's more like that. Imagine if Papa heard me."

"Well, we can't let that happen."

"Please tell me you're not going to march me back to school and tell Miss Dupont that no child of yours is going to recite a poem about Jesus Christ. She already thinks we're screwy."

"I thought you were on Miss Dupont's good side these days."

"I am. But that's not going to last if you insult Jesus."

"Couldn't you just tell her that you don't want to be in the *electionary* contest?"

"No one says no to Miss Dupont."

I'm silent for a moment, thinking. The poem really isn't about religion. It's just about a girl who cries out to her God in her troubles, like we do to ours. Surely Chaia understands this. But will Sender? Not a chance.

"I suppose," I start tentatively, "your father doesn't need to know about this contest."

Chaia looks at me in amazement. "You mean you'd let me go?"

I consider it. It's not like saying "Jesus Christ" a few times is going to convert Chaia into a Christian. She's not even that involved in her own religion. Besides, I don't want to dampen Miss Dupont's interest in my daughter. I wish there'd been someone to encourage me when I was a girl. "When is the contest?" I ask.

"That's the other problem. It's the Saturday after next. She's going to pick me up in her car."

There are many things Jews don't do on the Sabbath because they're considered work. Driving or riding in cars is one of those things. I'm sure, if the rabbis had been able to imagine it, reciting a poem with Jesus Christ in it would be another. But I think of the old saying, "If you're going to eat pork, eat till the juice runs down your chin." I guess the English equivalent would be "In for a penny, in for a pound."

"Tell her you'll be ready. Just have her meet you at the bottom of the road," I tell Chaia.

"But what will Papa say?"

"He won't know. I'll tell him we're going to walk over to visit that new family, the Cohens. I'll do that. You just won't be with me."

Chaia grins at me, and I can't help grinning back. "Okay!" she says. "Now I've just got to learn this poem."

She starts up the steps, but I stop her. "Maybe it would be better if you didn't recite it in front of Reyzel or Sala."

"Right. Is it okay if I practice out here? I'll pretend I'm helping you with the laundry."

Without waiting for a reply, she picks up one of Reyzel's wet night dresses, the orangey smell of Fels-Naptha blooming into the air. With her book in the other hand, she begins emoting:

> It was the schooner Hesperus,
> That sailed the wintry sea;
> And the skipper had taken his little daughtèr,
> To bear him company.

Putting down the book, she hangs the nightie while she practices. She's looking up and to the left as she consults her mind's eye. The night dress is askew, but she doesn't notice.

> It was the schooner Hesperus,
> That sailed the wintry sea;
> And the captain—

She stops and consults her book. Then she begins again.

> It was the schooner Hesperus,
> That sailed the wintry sea;
> And the *skipper* had taken his little daughtèr,
> To keep him company.

By this time, she's forgotten about the clothes. She refers to her book again. "No," she says, "'to *bear* him company. The skipper had taken his little daughter to bear him—'"

"Chaia," I interrupt, "it's one thing to help you enter the contest, but I don't think I can live through your practicing. Why don't you go out to the barn and 'pretend' you're feeding the cows?"

Chaia complies absently. As she heads for the barn, she continues reciting.

#

The next day, I'm outside the schoolhouse when the final bell rings. Children explode through the door. Chaia looks a little worried when she sees me, and Miss Dupont looks terrified. I clasp my hands in front of me to assure her I'm not dangerous. "Miss Dupont," I say, "It's to thank you I've come—for giving Charlie the chance to be in the *electionary* contest."

"Oh, you mean the elocutionary contest." She says the word slowly, emphasizing every syllable.

"Yes, that," I reply, not ready to give her another opening to correct me. "We're happy Charlie will recite the poem."

Looking relieved that I haven't come to thrash her, Miss Dupont turns to Chaia. "How are you doing with 'The Wreck of the Hesperus'? I don't imagine you've already memorized it."

"Yes, I have," Chaia replies proudly, "and so have a horse and a cow."

Miss Dupont smiles in spite of herself. "Well, let's hear it. Give me the last stanza."

In a firm voice, Chaia recites:

> Such was the wreck of the Hesperus,
>
> In the midnight and the snow!
>
> Christ save us all from a death like this,
>
> On the reef of Norman's Woe!

Chaia's voice drops to a whisper on the word *Christ*.

"What was that last line?" Miss Dupont demands.

Chaia recites the line again, again mumbling the word. Miss Dupont looks at her appraisingly. I see a light dawn in her eyes.

"That's very good work, Charlie Rappaport. I think you're ready for Saturday. But if you're going to win, you must make sure to say all of the words clearly," she coaches.

"Yes, ma'am."

Miss Dupont looks at me. "For the next contest," she says, "we'll find something more, um, appropriate."

"We are grateful. What time will you be back?" I ask.

"Around three o'clock."

"I'll be waiting."

#

That Saturday afternoon, I walk back from the Cohens, where I've spent a lovely day dandling their baby while Edith Cohen tells me all the trials of having a hungry infant, a subject I know something about. I'm back at the intersection of the main road with the track up to our farm a little before three o'clock. There's no sign of Chaia or Miss Dupont. At a quarter after, I begin pacing back and forth. As the minutes drag by, I learn the color of every piece of gravel, of every beech and maple tree lining the road. When I estimate an hour has passed, I get frantic. I'm worried something happened to them, and, God help me, I'm panicked at the idea Sender will find out his daughter was in a car accident—on Shabbas! When I finally see the car speeding toward me, I'm so relieved that I'm almost not angry. Almost.

Miss Dupont brings her roadster to a screeching halt by my side and jumps out before Chaia even has her door open. I greet her stony-faced.

"I'm so sorry, Mrs. Rappaport," she says, panting like she's just run a race. "I'm sure you've been worried, but I promise you, it was for a good cause. I really did think we'd be back by three o'clock. But Charlie made it to the finals of the contest. That's unheard of for a new contestant."

By this time, Chaia has come to my side, sporting an enormous red ribbon embossed with the words *second place*. I feel my wrath begin to melt.

"Second place," I say. "Not bad for a first try."

"Charlie really should have been first," Miss Dupont assures me. "She lost out to a girl wearing pink hair bows and reciting the poem 'Just Before Christmas.' It's drivel, but there were two ministers on the judging panel."

For the first time, I think I may come to like Miss Dupont.

"That's all right," Chaia says gamely. "Give me a shipwreck any day."

I look at my frizzy-haired child, who hasn't worn a bow since she cut her own hair last year in frustration over the time it took me to get the tangles out. The starched collar I put her in this morning is askew, and her boots are dusty. While she may never be able to win out over a girl with blonde braids and pink ribbons, well, give *me* a shipwreck any day. I hug her and thank Miss Dupont for taking her to the contest. I think the teacher is just glad I didn't bring the horsewhip. "My pleasure," she says, hopping back in the car and speeding away.

"Well," I tell Chaia, "you'd better hide that red ribbon before Papa sees you. And we'll need to keep our story straight: we were helping Mrs. Cohen with the little one, and time got away from us. It's a good thing Hodel has a cholent in the oven. Your father never asks too many questions when his mind is on dinner."

Chapter 10

"SO, MY WIFE, NOT a bad year we've had." Sender and I are sitting on the porch one mild evening. Surveying the vines on the hillside, I can just make out the new ones we put in last year, small but purpling. And we've been able to add another nine rows.

"May God protect us from the evil eye, but I'd even go so far as to say it was a good year," I venture.

"I have to admit, you were right about the grapes. And you squeezed money from the orchard too. As the Proverb says, 'The good wife sets her mind on an estate and acquires it; she plants a vineyard by her own labors.'"

I'm pleased in spite of myself. Getting a compliment out of Sender is like getting a nickel out of a miser. I decide to return the favor. Even though I still don't like the amount of time he spends helping the Jewish Agricultural Society, I say, "You've made progress too. Now we have fourteen Jewish families in Geneva. More than enough for a minyan."

It's such a fine night we stay on the porch schmoozing. He does his usual bragging about the littlest one's musical abilities—she's forever singing his favorite schmaltzy Yiddish folk songs—and his usual complaining about his middle daughter. Chaia, he grouses, has no interest in her chores. Though I try to point out Chaia's achievements in school, academic excellence in a girl doesn't impress Sender. "What good will all those A's be when I have to find her a husband? Speaking of which, we still haven't made a match for Sala." Somehow I manage to convince him that things are different in America. After all, she's only seventeen. Still, I know there's a matchmaker in her not-too-distant future.

Sender doesn't even suggest trying to find a match for Hodel, which is just as well. She's settled nicely into our family, but every now and then,

56

I catch her staring off into space with silent tears coursing down her face. I assume she still hasn't gotten over Mr. Bercovici. I know Hodel doesn't want me to speak ill of him, but I don't have her forbearance—even about my own husband, who didn't desert me.

The sun has already set when we finally get up to go in. As I turn toward the house, I spot something on a hilltop not too far away. "Wait, Sender, what's that?"

Peering into the darkness, he says, "It looks like a fire. Wait, I think it's at the Cohen's place." He starts down the steps.

Suddenly the light flares into a huge cross. "*Got in himl!*" I gasp. What can this mean? A flaming cross on a Jewish farm? Have we come to America only to find a new kind of anti-Semitism?

In the spectral glow, we can make out dozens of white-clad figures wearing pointed hoods. At this distance they look like strange insects. "Who are they?" Sender demands.

Rozhinkes, who had been sleeping under a bush, begins to bark furiously. In a moment, Hodel rushes out. "What's this?" she cries. "A pogrom?"

Sala is right behind her. "Oh no! It must be the Ku Klux Klan Morris was telling us about. He said it's a secret organization that hates Jews and Black people and Catholics."

"Not so secret, it seems," I say.

"But not brave enough to show their faces," Sender growls.

Sala is remembering our run-in at the farm stand with our surly neighbor. "This must be what Corbin Johnson meant when he told us that someday, we'd see how folks around here deal with Jews. I bet he's one of those men in the hoods."

I can't help shuddering at the thought of a whole parade of Corbin Johnsons, liquored up and brutal. "It's like they're telling us we don't belong here because we're not Christians."

"We'll see about that," Sender announces and marches into the house—to get his horsewhip, I imagine.

I'd like to think of something more effective to do. There's one horse-drawn firetruck in downtown Geneva, but we're an hour away on our workhorse, Barney, and an hour back in the truck. By that time, the Cohen's farm could be in ruins.

I try to quiet the dog, but I understand his terror. The Klansmen form up into a line and begin marching down the hill singing "Onward Christian Soldiers." The anthem fades in and out as the wind shifts. We catch the acrid smell of burning wood and gasoline. I can't imagine how Edith Cohen must be feeling, with her little one and a new baby in the house.

Striding outside, whip in hand, Sender announces, "I've got to get over to the Cohens. You three go back into the house—and lock the door." He heads off to find Barney. "Get in the house!" he repeats as he mounts the horse bareback and rides off.

Sala, Hodel, and I hang on to each other and stare at the cross. Usually, I would be able to recover my self-control for my family's sake, but this cross burning is too discouraging. I shiver right along with the girls. Of course we should do as Sender said, but we're mesmerized. As we're standing on the porch, we see headlights come up the drive. We're about to flee in a panic when I recognize the Golds' Packard.

Harold leans his head out the window. "We're driving up to the Cohens', but Morris insisted we stop here first to make sure you're all right. Is Sender still here?"

"No," I say, "he's taken the horse."

Morris comes bounding out of the car. I'm sure if he thought he could get away with it, he would fold Sala into his arms. Instead his words come out in a tumble. "Sala, thank goodness you're safe. And you, too, of course, Mrs. Rappaport, Miss Rappaport. And the young ones?"

"Sleeping through it, God be praised," I answer.

Sala is silent. She's frightened, but I don't think she was waiting for a knight in a roadster, at least not this knight. Finally, with a shade too much dignity, she says, "Morris, it was good of you to check on us, but I think right now, the Cohens need you more than we do."

"You heard the lady," Harold says. "*Gib zikh a shukl*! Let's get a move on. They're running a fire line from the Grand River, and they need as many men as they can get." Morris looks crestfallen, but he jumps back in the car. With a wave, the Golds are off.

We remain on the porch watching. In a little while, we see the silhouettes of the men on the fire line, and gradually, the flames at the bottom of the cross are doused. Then the top collapses, the tiny, shadowlike figures scooting back to avoid the still-burning wood. Finally, the fire is extinguished, leaving the hill in darkness.

We stay a few more minutes in the now-black night. With no moon, the stars glimmer feverishly. It's like we're standing in the world as God made it, without the garbage men have strewn across it. Finally, we go back inside, and I send Sala and Hodel off to bed. I'm still awake when

Sender clip-clops up to the house. It's hard to tell if the horse or the rider is more exhausted.

"So, *nu?*" I say.

"So, thank God we managed to put the fire out before the embers leaped to the Cohen's barn. No one was hurt, just frightened out of their wits."

"That's what these people count on—that we'll be scared and run away."

"Well, they don't know who they're dealing with. Most of the Jewish farmers were on the fire line tonight. We've already decided we're going tomorrow to see the county sheriff in Ashtabula. Gold is getting the word out to the others, so we should have a good-sized group. We'll see who's scared."

"I'd like to come to this meeting," I say.

Sender just looks at me. "This is not a job for a woman."

"And why not? Isn't Mrs. Cohen a woman? Who will speak for her and for me and for your daughters?"

"Bluma, please, now is not the time for your silly *narishkayt*. I'm going to bed."

I can't say I expected anything different from Sender—or from any of the other men, to be fair. I just hope they get some action from the sheriff. America is not Romania, it's true, but I'm learning it's not the Promised Land either.

#

The next day, Harold Gold motors up our road carefully, trying to avoid the worst potholes and preserve the undercarriage of his precious roadster. He has on his three-piece suit with a heavy watch chain draped across the vest. Sender is dressed in his Shabbas best: black slacks, white shirt, black coat. I can see Josef Cohen in the back seat in a similar, worn Sabbath uniform. Plus they've got Old Man Kaminsky. Great, I think: Cohen and Kaminsky barely speak English, Gold loves to hear himself talk, and Sender's usual mode of argument is to threaten someone with his horsewhip. This should turn out well.

As Hodel prepares dinner, my sister looks like she hasn't slept. I'm sure her mind is throwing up the images of pogroms we used to see in the Yiddish newspaper: Jewish towns razed to the ground; elderly men with their beards yanked out; women and girls assaulted; bodies stacked like cordwood.

We work together silently until she blurts out, "Bluma, what have we done that God should punish us like this?"

"I don't think these Klansmen have anything to do with God. That's the problem."

"But God could protect us."

"Maybe he has," I venture. "We're still here." I know it's not really an answer.

We didn't tell Chaia and Reyzel about the cross burning, which was a mistake because no one at school was talking about anything else. "Why don't people like us?" Reyzel wants to know, the tears running down her chin. It's something I plan to ask God when I finally meet him. For the moment, I just stroke her hair.

Chaia is more detached. "People just do stupid stuff. I had to beat up Pasquelino twice because he called me a dirty Christ-killer when he got mad about something." This is sobering, but if Chaia has come to an understanding with Pasquelino, I'm not going to be the one to criticize.

Sala, still anxiety-stricken, says nothing. It's one thing to learn about the incident secondhand; it's another to stand on your porch and watch a nine-foot flaming cross on your neighbor's hillside. Corbin Johnson haunts her.

Sender returns from Ashtabula just before supper. I can tell from the way he slams Harold's car door that he's angry. He pounds up the porch steps and on up to the bedroom without a word. At the dinner table, he's mute beyond the occasional demand to pass the kugel. It isn't until the girls have gone to bed that Hodel and I get the story out of him.

"That sheriff (may he go on a voyage and not live long enough to come back!) he kept us waiting outside his office for almost an hour. There were twelve of us, and they wouldn't even find chairs for us to sit down. When we finally got to see the sheriff, he starts out by saying how busy he is (as if we're not). He can only give us fifteen minutes. Of course, Gold, the big *macher*, decides he's going to be the spokesman for the group. It takes him at least five minutes to tell the sheriff how very honored we are that he'll meet with us at all."

"Sounds like the Grape King," I grumble.

But Sender is not to be interrupted. "When Gold finally gets around to telling him about the cross burning, you know what the sheriff says?"

Sender puts on an oily voice. "'Oh, yes. I heard about that. I understand no one was hurt and no property was destroyed.' Then he tells us Cohen could press charges for trespassing—if we could identify any of the men involved. They were wearing hoods, for God's sake!" By now, Sender's shouting, not that I blame him.

"He isn't going to do anything about it?" I ask though I can guess the answer is no.

"He had the chutzpah to tell us that the members of the Klan are really upstanding citizens, just trying to preserve the American way of life. 'Sometimes,' the sheriff said," the oily voice comes back, "'they 'get a little carried away.' Well, I'll tell you one thing, Bluma. If they 'get carried away' on my land, they'll be the ones who are carried away."

It's big talk, and maybe it makes Sender feel better. But really, we are fourteen Jewish families out of a population of sixty-five thousand in the county. Sender's horsewhip is just not up to the job.

Chapter 11

THE GOLDS HAVE INVITED us all over for lunch. Harold wants to talk to Sender about the cross burning and some idea he has for a Jewish self-protection association. Sala begs off. I find her sitting at the loom. When I give her one last chance to come with us, she tells me, "I heard enough about the Klan to last me a lifetime. Besides, I don't want to spend another awkward hour with Morris going on about some fine point of Talmud. Last time, he actually explained why scorpions are impure but touching them does not make you impure. When's the last time you saw a scorpion?"

I laugh, but I recognize his rambling as the outpouring of a bookish young man in the presence of loveliness. Frankly I'm pleased that Sala has no awareness of her beauty; it makes her unassuming. On the other side of the coin, she's not very sympathetic to the palpitations she provokes in a shy person like Morris. "Morris is just nervous around you because he wants so much for you to like him."

"He shouldn't try so hard."

"Well, *Ketsele*, if you have any interest at all in Morris, you might try being a little nicer to him. He's been mooning over you for a long time, but Harold and Elsie are getting fidgety about him being twenty and still single. They're insisting he see a matchmaker in Cleveland."

"Mama, I don't know how many times I can say this. I'm not going to marry Morris Gold. He's very nice, but—I don't know—kind of *pareve*, not meat or milk."

Morris is not the only suitor Sala has found wanting. Cousin Mendel's partner's son made a special trip to Geneva to meet her, and I think he would have proposed on the spot if she'd given him any encouragement. "He smells like onions," she complained. Sender thinks Sala is being persnickety and that I'm indulging her, which may be true. Pretty soon, he'll engage a matchmaker with or without my agreement.

"You know, you could go to the Golds and just settle yourself in the kitchen with me and Elsie," I suggest.

"No, I'm going to stay home and finish this tablecloth for Mrs. Blankenship. You and Papa enjoy your visit."

"As much as a person can enjoy having her ear talked off by Elsie Gold. But you know what they say, 'An empty barrel makes the most noise.'"

At that moment, everyone comes careening through the parlor on their way to the buggy. "Come on, Mama," Reyzel says, grabbing me by the arm. "Maybe Mrs. Gold made donuts."

I consent to being dragged along, but at the door, I turn back for a look at Sala. She's humming the song "*Margeritkelekh*," about a girl who lets herself be seduced by a handsome young man with "eyes as black as coal." Gracefully, Sala throws the shuttlecock back and forth across the warp of the fabric in time to the music. Today, her black braids are pinned up to form a coronet. A far-away smile flits across her lips. It will be a long time before I see her this untroubled again.

#

It's getting toward five o'clock when we turn back onto the drive to our house. Reyzel has fallen asleep in my lap—too many donuts. Chaia is deep in a book she borrowed from Miss Dupont, even though focusing on reading while the buggy is moving always makes her sick to her stomach. I'm consulting with Hodel about what we can put on the table before everyone starts *nudzhing* us about dinner. Unsurprisingly, Sender is complaining about Harold.

"Some plan that guy comes up with," he scoffs. "We'll alert each other immediately if someone's home is in danger! He's the only one of the farmers who has a phone. We'll all buy rifles! Can you see old Mr. Kaminsky with a gun. Mrs. Kaminsky will get shot before any Klansmen do."

"You're the one who wanted to consult with that *trombenik*," I reply.

"If he blows his own horn any harder, his eyes will pop out," Sender agrees.

"I think you're just trying to butter him up so he'll give his blessing to a match between Morris and Sala, which is pointless because she isn't interested in him."

"Interested, shminterested. The question should be, do my parents think he'd be good for me? I blame you for giving our daughters other ideas."

Before the buggy has even pulled up to the barn, Chaia jumps out. I give Reyzel's shoulder a gentle shake, and she opens her eyes. "We're home, Mamele. Go on in the house and change out of your good clothes." I lift her down from the box seat, and she totters sleepily toward the front door. Hodel makes a beeline for the kitchen while Sender and I take the rig into the barn. When the horse in his stall, we head for the house, with Sender still kibitzing me about Harold Gold.

"Where's Sala?" Chaia greets us the minute we enter.

Sender glances into the parlor. "I thought she stayed home to work on that tablecloth, but it doesn't look any bigger than when we left," he says. "Sala? Sala?"

"She's not in the house," Hodel informs us. "I already checked. "

A spark of worry travels up my spine, but I don't want to make the others anxious. "I bet she's in the cowshed," I say. "Bubale looked ready to calve this morning. Maybe she's in labor. I'll go find out."

Once I'm clear of the house, I start calling. Sala isn't in the cowshed or at the chicken coop. We didn't see her in the barn when we brought in the buggy. "Sala!" I call, my disquiet growing. It's a cool night, and I can't imagine what she'd be doing outside.

Suddenly I hear the sound of an automobile coming toward the house. Recognizing the Golds' car, I go down the track to meet it and am surprised to see Morris driving. Sala is in the passenger seat. I'm reassured until I notice the state she's in. Her blouse is half open with several buttons ripped clean off. Her crown of braids falls loosely around her face. Eyes red and swollen, she can't stop shaking. I help her out of the car and throw my shawl around her shoulders.

"Morris," I practically shout, "what have you done to my daughter?"

Sala rushes to his defense. "No, Mama. It wasn't Morris. He just drove me home."

"From where did he drive you home?"

"From his house. I . . . I ran there." Her lip is quivering.

"What happened, Mamele?" I take her hand. It's like grabbing a fish straight from the Grand River—cold and floppy.

"The knaker was here," she says. "I guess he wasn't just a big talker."

"Oh, my God. Corbin Johnson! What did he do?" My voice has gone up so high, I don't recognize it.

"He tried to do to me what the animals in the barnyard do." Her words come out broken by sobs.

Morris gasps.

"You see?" Sala moans. "What man will ever want me now?"

Morris believes his moment has come, and he seizes it. "This man," he says pointing gallantly to his own chest. "This man will want you no matter what. I would marry you tomorrow."

"Morris," I say quickly, "I don't think this is the time to talk about marriage. Sala's very upset. Why don't you go on home, and we'll discuss this later?"

I take my daughter in my arms. Morris raises himself up on his toes and tries to catch her eye. "I love you, Sala," he insists. She's really crying now.

"Morris, go home," I insist. Reluctantly, he gets back in the car and drives off.

As gently as I can, I lead Sala into the cowshed, settle her on a hay bale, and find an old blanket to cover her. Bubale moos at us in greeting, but there's no sign of her going into labor. Just as well. We have more pressing matters.

"Dearest," I tell Sala, "I'm so sorry I wasn't here when that monster came. Are you hurt?" She can't stop crying long enough to answer. In the weak light of a kerosene lantern, I manage to determine there are no marks on her body—only on her soul.

Feeling useless, I whisper the kind of meaningless things mothers say in these situations. "Everything will be all right, Sala. You'll see. Soon, all this will only be a memory." Maybe if I say it with enough conviction, it will be true. I stroke her cheek, untangle her braids, hold her icy hands. Her only response is to weep and shiver.

By this time, I'm shaking right along with her, but in my case, it isn't shock and it isn't the fall chill. I'm so angry, my body can't contain it. This— this helplessness in the face of men who act like pigs—this was another of the reasons I brought the girls to America. For too long, we European Jews were at the mercy of thugs who tormented us at their pleasure.

In America, I imagined, the law would shield us. At least, I thought so until the cross burning, when the sheriff let us know American laws don't really apply to us. Now I realize that goes double for us women. I gave myself the luxury of standing up to Corbin Johnson, and for a moment there at the farm stand, I felt powerful. Hah! Then, when I wasn't home, he simply walked into my house and attacked my child. Would he have done this if he thought he would be punished for it? Will that sheriff care what crime he's committed?

Finally, Sala's sobs taper off. "Come," I say, "let's go into the house and get you warm."

"No, no!" she says in horror. "I can't face anyone. They'll look at me and see what Corbin Johnson has done."

Of course, none of the family would make such a leap, but they would certainly realize something was wrong. I understand Sala is in no state to tell them about the attack. "It's all right, Sala, I can explain it to them."

Now she's even more horrified. "I don't want them to know. I don't want any of them ever to know."

"All right, all right, Salushke," I soothe her. "Don't worry. You stay here, and I'll tell everyone you're with Bubale, helping with her labor. I'll bring your coat and maybe a bite to eat."

Fortunately, everyone has been so busy with dinner, they didn't hear the car. I tell them Sala's in the cowshed, though what I'll say tomorrow when there's no calf, I don't know. In the meantime, I take the coat and a plate of soup out to my daughter, whom I find as I left her. "Do you feel up to telling me what happened?" I ask.

She's stopped crying, but now her voice is so flat, it worries me even more. "I guess," she stammers. "Right after you left, he rapped on the door. I couldn't see who was standing there, but I opened it up anyway. I was so stupid. It never occurred to me it would be that man."

"Of course it didn't! Who could have imagined such a thing?"

Not listening to me, she rushes on with her tale. "He pushed his way inside. He called me . . . " Her voice trails off. I just wait. In a second she resumes. "He called me a 'Jew whore.'"

"The devil!"

"Then he knocked me to the ground and ripped open my blouse. He climbed on top of me." There's a long pause.

"And then?" I ask, not sure I can bear to hear the answer.

"He was so drunk, he fell asleep on top of me."

It's not much better than what I was picturing, but I'm thankful nonetheless. Sala continues, "I just lay there until I was sure he was out cold. Then I crawled out from under him and hid behind the corn rows till I saw him leave. After that I didn't know what to do. I thought you might still be at the Golds', so I started running over there. Somehow I ended up in their vineyard. That's where Morris found me."

"Well, thank goodness you had the presence of mind to get away. And at least Johnson didn't"—I choose my words carefully—"violate you."

"How can you say that? He rucked up my skirt. He lay on top of me with his stinking whiskey breath in my face. He thrust himself between my legs. I told you he was leering at me. You saw it yourself at the farm stand, but you just *had* to tell him to go to hell."

That's the rebuke I've been expecting, the one I suppose I deserve, but it hollows me out like a gouge. "*Hartsele*," I say, "for whatever part I played in bringing that man to our door, I will never forgive myself. But nothing he did changes who you are."

"Oh no? What did Bubbe Rappaport always tell us? 'A girl is like a silk scarf. Once she gets a stain, even seven washings won't rub it out.'"

"That woman always talked too much."

"She was right, though, wasn't she? I'm damaged goods."

"Sala, you're a beautiful girl, a prize for any man. And you're still a virgin, so no one ever has to know what happened."

"But I'll know. I won't be able to look any man in the face."

"You feel like that now, but that feeling will pass. You still have your whole life in front of you. You just need some time to see things more clearly."

"I see things clearly enough," she says resignedly. "Tell Papa to draw up a marriage contract between me and Morris Gold."

"What?"

"Tell him. Tell him to arrange my marriage with Morris."

"But Sala, you told me just this morning you weren't interested in Morris."

"That was this morning. Tonight I'm grateful he still wants me."

I would argue with her, but I can tell that nothing I say is going to move her at the moment. "Okay, Sala," I say to pacify her. "I'll talk to your father about it. But right now, what you need is some food and a good, hot bath." At my urging, she swallows some soup. Finally, she's willing to go inside.

By this time, the rest of the family is upstairs in bed. I draw water from the pump in the yard and put it on the stove to heat. When it's ready, I pour it into our big tin tub. Sala gets into the water gingerly. She lets me soap her back, as I used to do when she was a young child. Clearly, she's not that anymore. When she's finally in her night dress, I embrace her. "Go to sleep now, my sweetest one." After she leaves, I straighten up the kitchen. As I work, I raise my eyes to heaven. "God," I say out loud, "you're lucky you rule from the heavens because if you lived on Earth, someone would break all your windows."

Chapter 12

THE NEXT DAY, I have to dream up some creative fibs. One mustn't lie, but the truth, sometimes, one must also not tell.

"Bubale's labor was a false alarm," I inform Sender, "like when your cousin had contractions and the baby didn't come for another month." I also tell him I need the buggy to go to Ashtabula for a craft fair I made up on the spur of the moment. "It's a good chance to sell some linens," I say. If there's money to be made, Sender won't inquire too deeply.

As soon as the girls are off to school, I tell Sala I'm going to make sure Corbin Johnson never bothers us again. I don't know if she believes me, but she seems determined to put every thought of last night out of her mind. Her whole focus is on getting married, and the sooner the better.

"Have you talked to Papa about Morris?"

"Not yet, Darling. I wanted to give you some time to be sure it's what you want."

"I think I know my own mind," she snaps.

Is Sala ready to hear a different idea? I have to try. "You know, you don't have to get married now or ever if you don't want to," I begin. "There are worse fates than being single. Look at Hodel."

Sala scoffs. "Do you think she's happy?"

I almost say, "Do you think I'm happy?" But I stop myself. The truth is, I might not like being married to her father, but without him, there would be no Sala. I wouldn't want her to think for a moment that I regret having her and her sisters. Choosing my words carefully, I answer, "I'm just saying, you shouldn't feel any pressure to get married. You have the skill to make your own way as a weaver, like I did before we came to America."

She stares at me as if I'm the village idiot. "If I had an education, maybe. I would have liked to be a teacher." A stab to the heart, and Sala is not yet finished. "But an old maid weaver? Some fate—making linens for other women who have husbands and homes and their own dinner tables to put cloths on. Thank you very much, but I'd rather marry Morris."

"Sala, you're a young woman. You'll have many other chances to get married."

"I don't feel young anymore."

Hoping to placate her, I agree to talk to Sender when I get home. Maybe she'll rethink things while I'm gone. Hitching up the buggy, I throw some of my weaving in the back, just for show. It takes over an hour for me to reach Ashtabula and to find the office of Sheriff James McComber. I realize the men had no luck with him when they went to complain about the Klan, but I have an idea I think may work. Instead of righteous indignation, like they tried, I'm going to go for fresh-off-the-boat ignorance.

The sheriff's office and county jail are housed in a red brick building that commands the public square. When I enter, a high counter separates me from the offices behind. In the background, I can hear someone banging on what I imagine are the bars of a cell and a deputy shouting at him to quiet down. Another deputy sitting at the counter peers down at me. "Can I help you?"

"Excuse me, Mister. Bluma Rappaport is my name." My English is getting better, but I'm a little flustered and I pretend to be even more so. "It is possible I should see Sheriff McComber?"

"Is he expecting you?" the deputy asks skeptically.

"No, but, you see, there's been a crime."

"I can take that information."

"Oh, so kind of you. But it's—how do you say in English?—um, delicate. I really must talk to Sheriff McComber."

"Sheriff's a busy man, Ma'am."

"Of course, of course," I concede. "I can wait."

And wait they make me do. I sit for over two hours while various mischief-makers and officers traipse through the station. I don't see any of them go through the door that says "Sheriff," so I'm not sure what he's so busy with, but I sit patiently. Finally, just before lunch, the deputy tells me the sheriff can give me five minutes. I follow him submissively as he ushers me into the office. McComber is sitting behind a massive oak desk, flanked by the Ohio state and American flags. He looks like someone who was very strong in his youth but has gone to seed. His biceps stretch the fabric of his jacket. His belly bulges. A fedora hangs on the hat rack behind him. Waving at a chair, he says with a voice Sender captured perfectly, "Mrs. Rappaport, is it? Have a seat. My deputy tells me you want to report a crime?"

"Well, Sheriff, not exactly."

He looks me up and down. I can imagine how he sees me: my hair is covered in a flowered kerchief, and my clothes—a full skirt and button-up jacket—are nothing like the sleek column dresses of the women in Ashtabula. I'm a rube to him, which is just the reaction I was hoping for. "Well," he says condescendingly, "that's what we do in the Sheriff's Office, Mrs. Rappaport. We investigate crimes."

"I know who did the crime," I say, "so I'm not asking you should in-westigate." (I purposely trip over the word.) "I just want you should make sure the crime never happens again. An important man like you—I just know you could help me."

He takes out a cigar and goes through the elaborate ritual of cutting and lighting it while I wait. I can tell he's decided it will be amusing to hear me out—when he's good and ready. Sending up a great plume of cherry-scented smoke, he says, "I'm all for crime prevention, Mrs. Rappaport. Tell me how I can be of service."

"Do you happen to know, maybe, a Mr. Corbin Johnson?"

"Indeed I do. We attend the same church."

Of course, I think to myself. No wonder this man told the Jewish farmers that the Klansmen are upstanding citizens. Still, I don't let the realization show on my face. Instead, I rush to say, "A very Christian man, I'm sure. But do you know also that he's—I hope you can forgive me for saying this—a drunk?"

McComber laughs heartily. "Is that the problem you came to talk to me about? Well, Mrs. Rappaport, many people think that Prohibition made it illegal to drink, but actually, the Eighteenth Amendment bans only the manufacture, sale, and transportation of alcohol. A man can drink, and the law won't bother him unless he makes a nuisance of himself."

"I see. Thank you for explaining this to me," I say meekly. I wait a beat. "You would say that attacking my daughter in her own home was—how you said?—making a nuisance of himself?"

McComber sobers quickly. "That's a very serious accusation. Do you have any proof of this alleged attack? Did you witness it?"

"Would I not have stopped him if I'd been home when he broke in?"

"Then why didn't your daughter come with you to file a complaint?"

"Sheriff," I explain with as much patience as I can muster, "my daughter is sixteen years old. Rather she would die than talk to a man about what happened."

McComber seems relieved. Using the smarmiest tone, he says, "In the absence of a complaint from her, Mrs. Rappaport, I don't see what I can do. I would need to take a full statement. Then there would be a trial, an unpleasant experience for a young woman. And at the end of the day, unless someone saw Mr. Johnson at your place, we'd have a 'he said; she said' situation. Very difficult to prove beyond a reasonable doubt. I understand you feel very upset about this situation, but I'm afraid that's the way the law works."

I nod, as though I see the wisdom of his words. "Again, I thank you, Sheriff, for being so understanding. But you see, I'm worried because I have two other daughters at home. What if Mr. Johnson comes back?"

"You'll just have to keep a better eye on your girls," McComber chides me.

If life were fair, I would give this man such a slap right now, I'd send him into next week. But if I've learned one lesson about sticking up for myself and my daughters, it's this: I can't do it head on. Fortunately, I've already planned another way.

"Sheriff, you must believe me, I try. But children—you know they sometimes go off on their own, no matter what you do. Like my younger daughter. Why just the other day, she was in the woods above our farm, and guess what she found!"

He's clearly starting to lose interest in what he imagines is the prattling of a bumpkin. "Mrs. Rappaport," he breaks in, "I am glad we could have this chat, but I really need to get back to—"

"She found a still, Sheriff. On Corbin Johnson's property!"

McComber is taken aback by the abrupt change of subject. "A still?" he says, playing for time.

"My English isn't very good," I apologize. "Isn't that what you Americans call a place for making whiskey?"

"Yes, that's right," he concedes.

"I thought you might want to . . . what's that word again . . . inwestigate? Because, as you said," I quote him cheerfully, "'The manufacture or sale of alcohol is illegal.'"

"True, true," he stalls. "I'll definitely look into that as soon as I have a minute." If he imagines I believe him, he must think I'm truly stupid.

"Well," I say, "if you don't have enough time, it's no problem. *Mayn* neighbor told me I could get in touch with—what did she call it?—the Federal Prohibition Unit or I could tell the newspaper."

McComber is silent for a moment, appraising me. I can almost hear the gears in his head grinding. Foreign, he's thinking, but not a fool. Does she know, he's wondering, that all the bigwigs in the county have been getting their whiskey from Johnson since well before Prohibition? Does she know that includes me? Finally he says, "Mrs. Rappaport, I thought you said you didn't want to report a crime. What exactly do you want?"

I've been pondering this question since yesterday. I'm not so arrogant as to believe I can get what I really want: protection for the whole Jewish community from Corbin Johnson and his ilk. And for all the reasons the sheriff just outlined, I don't imagine I'll ever get the satisfaction of seeing Johnson rot in jail for attacking my daughter. In the end, I've decided I'll settle for making sure that man never comes near our property again.

"Well, Sheriff," I say, "I was thinking, maybe *you* could speak to this Corbin Johnson since you go to the same church and all. Maybe you could remind him what the Good Book says about men who rape women."

"I'm sure I could have a word with him."

"And if that doesn't work, maybe you could tell Mr. Johnson I'll forget all what I know about his still as long as he and his Klan *frayndn* never set foot on my farm again. How does that sound?"

The sheriff raises his eyebrows as though he's surprised to have met with a worthy adversary in a woman, an immigrant, and a Jew to boot. "That sounds like a plan, Mrs. Rappaport," he allows.

I slap my hands on my thighs and rise. "I thought it might be," I say, and, nodding curtly, take my leave.

#

Whatever hope I had that Sala would reconsider her decision to marry Morris, I'm soon disappointed. As soon as I get back home, Hodel meets me at the kitchen door. "You can't let her marry that boy. She doesn't love him."

"She told you?"

"Everything."

I'm glad Sala could unburden herself to someone closer to her own age. And it's not that I don't agree with Hodel. I feel like my best hope for Sala—that she marry someone she genuinely cares for—is about to be dashed, just like my hope that she would get an education. But when I hear Hodel saying it, I can't help reminding her that Jewish women have had arranged marriages for centuries, often with men they barely knew. The girls could always say no, but everyone expected that love would grow from the marriage, not the other way around.

"Like it did with you and Sender?" Hodel asks.

Is she being sarcastic? I must be doing a bang-up job of hiding my feelings about Sender if she can ask this question seriously. "Well," I say noncommittally, "marriage is complicated."

"I know you and Sender argue, but I can see the love there."

Surprising myself, I begin to cry. Is it a reaction to the attack on Sala? The idea of her entering a loveless marriage? Or my own unhappy relationship with Sender? Probably all three.

Hodel is shocked. I don't think she's seen me cry since I wept in frustration over braiding her hair when she was three years old. "*Blumele*, what is it?"

"Sender doesn't love me," I manage to squeeze out between sniffles.

"You can't mean that! I've been here more than a year. He's never so much as looked at another woman."

Maybe it's time for my sister to get a glimpse of a real-life relationship, not just the romantic vision she has of what her future would have been like with that no-goodnik Zavel Bercovici. I calm myself. "Sender never loved *me*, Hodel. Sender loves Torah. If the Bible says this and this must a man do for his wife, that's what Sender does. And if that wife can help him run his farm—the only other thing he loves—well, so much the better. It's true I don't have a human rival, but in some ways, my lot is harder. I have to compete with his grand ideas for even a scrap of his attention."

"I'm so sorry, Bluma. I didn't know."

"I'm glad it wasn't obvious, but you see, this is what I don't want for Sala. Morris is another *luftmensch* with his head in the clouds. He only thinks about the Talmud and now Zionism too."

"But he does love her."

"Yes, at least he loves her."

#

After we retire to our bedroom that night, I tell Sender, "I need to talk to you about a match between Sala and Morris. She wants to go forward."

"*Got tsu loybn*! That's wonderful news. I'll go to Gold tomorrow and work out the details."

"Not so fast, Sender. I think Sala is making a rash decision."

"Rash? That boy has wanted to marry her since he first laid eyes on her three years ago."

"But she hasn't wanted to marry him. She's been very adamant."

"Nu, what changed her mind?"

I knew this question would be coming, and since Sala has forbidden me to tell her father about Corbin Johnson, I have a made-up answer ready: "She thinks maybe she was being too picky."

"You mean she's finally seen reason?"

"But Sender, reason is not love. She doesn't love Morris."

"Bluma, marriage doesn't have to be about love. Look at us. We weren't in love, but things worked out between us."

"Ah, but *I* was in love," I blurt out. What can I say? It's the truth. Before Sender came along, I was pretty sure I'd be an old maid. As I overheard my father tell the matchmaker, "A great beauty, Bluma is not." Then a miracle happened. The matchmaker sent us Sender, and oh, was he handsome! And learned—he was a yeshiva boy back in Russia. When we talked, I heard a person with drive and ideas. In my defense, I was only fifteen with no experience of the world, but he seemed like the perfect man. Well, that perfect man is now sitting across from me in awkward silence. Not that I expected him to fib about loving me on sight, but he could have said he came to love me. "Don't worry," I lie, "my love died a long time ago. But why shouldn't Sala have love?"

"Look, Bluma," Sender answers with as much compassion as he has in him, "we have a partnership, which is not such a terrible thing. Morris is a good man—much kinder than I am. Maybe he and Sala will have more than we do. In the meantime, the Talmud says a father must not marry off his daughter until she says, 'I want this one.' I've waited a long time, but now Sala has spoken. If she wants to marry Morris, so be it."

As promised, Sender goes to the Golds the very next morning. If Harold is less enthusiastic than my husband (I'm sure he was hoping for a bride with a bigger dowry), Morris wants the match so desperately that his uncle gives in and offers them his blessing. My daughter asks only for a short engagement, which Morris agrees to happily. Sala seems relieved, like this marriage will close the door she opened when she let Corbin Johnson into the house.

Chapter 13

THE WEDDING DAY DAWNS, muggy and gray, with temperatures that will have us all sweating through our finery. I'm just glad I'm not downstairs, where all the Jewish farm wives are bustling around, though what they're doing, I can't imagine. The ceremony will be at the Golds' house, and Elsie and Hodel have been cooking for days. Still, I can hear the women *patshkeing* in the kitchen.

I'm in Sala's room, where I'm helping her dress. She's so pale, her face is almost the same color as the wedding veil. I asked my cousin Mendel to get me a small pot of tinted face cream from that Jewish immigrant Helena Rubinstein. Now I dab a bit on Sala's cheeks to bring some color. If her eyes were not so sad, she would be a picture. She's wearing the dress Hodel and I made for her, cinched at the waist and embroidered with lilies of the valley down the neckline. We even made it a bit short, coming just above her ankles like the current fashion. Fortunately, Sender will be too joyful to notice.

"Thank you for the gown, Mama," Sala says solemnly. "It's beautiful."

"I wove that fabric two years ago. I figured it wouldn't be long before you needed it. But Sala, is this the day? Because if this isn't what you really want, you can still back out."

Sala looks at herself in the mirror. "Can I?" she says flatly.

"Yes, darling. Just say *I* won't let you go through with it, and *af mir di aveyre*—let the sin be on my shoulders."

"No, Mama. This is what I want. Morris is a smart man, a scholar. And he's sweet. Maybe once I was looking for someone more exciting. But I'm not that girl anymore. I'm going to marry Morris and be grateful he wants me."

I can't help thinking gratitude is not the best foundation for a good relationship, but I don't know that I'm an authority on the subject. I'll just have to help her make the best of things. "Are you ready?" I ask.

She nods, and I hold her by the elbow as we go down the stairs. Waiting at the bottom, Chaia and Reyzel are wearing the new dresses I made them—Reyzel with pride and Chaia with resignation. The pink linen frock with a dropped waist and ruffled bottom suits Reyzel's rosy cheeks and plump little body; on Chaia, it hangs like laundry on the line, no matter all the alterations I made to fit it.

"Oh," Reyzel gasps when she sees Sala, "you look like a princess!" Chaia has always been more perceptive. I know she's picked up on Sala's grim mood over the past few weeks. Searchingly, she looks at her sister before she takes her other elbow. And so we process into the parlor.

As we enter, the women are attaching a large prayer shawl to four wooden poles for the chuppah, the wedding canopy. Dov Fishkin is tuning up his fiddle. When he sees Sala, he says, "The only problem with this wedding? The bride is too beautiful!"

This extracts a small smile from Sala. "Shall we call Morris for the *badekn*?" I ask. This is the ceremony where the groom looks at the bride before she puts on her wedding veil, supposedly so he isn't tricked into marrying someone he didn't bargain for, as Jacob was in the Bible.

If it were possible, I'd say Sala goes even paler than she was before. Grabbing my hand, she whispers in my ear. "What if, when Morris looks at me, he sees into my heart? What if he knows there's no love there? What if he says I'm not his true bride and he refuses to veil me?"

"Sala, that man saw into your heart the day he met you. He knows how good you are. He'll draw the veil over your face with joy."

The other women are smiling at what they assume are the usual pre-wedding jitters. Sala's grip on my hand tightens as she steadies herself. "All right. I guess I'm ready."

I send Hodel out to the barn where the men are waiting with Morris. The women gather in the parlor, and the men join them in a circle around the bride and groom: Mendel and his wife, Dvora; Old Man Kaminsky and Mrs. Kaminsky; the Cohens and their children—all twenty-two Jewish farm families. Morris is dressed in a white *kitl*, a robe which Jewish men wear on ritual occasions from their weddings to their funerals. Because it has no pockets, it's supposed to symbolize that the couple are marrying for love, not money. In this case, Sala doesn't bring a huge quantity of either. We took her dowry from the grape fund, which wasn't a hardship as Morris announced his intention to live with us and help on the farm. I think Sala is committed to learning to love Morris, but at this moment, that's not the feeling she has for him.

Fortunately, Morris is unaware of this. He just figures his persistence finally paid off. When Harold says formally, "Look now on this daughter of Israel. Is this the woman you wish to marry?" Morris, overcome with emotion, breathes, "Oh, yes." He approaches Sala tenderly and lifts the veil over her face. Then he and Harold start off for the Gold farm where they'll wait for the wedding procession.

Sender comes up to Sala with tears in his eyes. Putting his hands on her head, he delivers the traditional blessing:

> May you be fruitful and prosper. May God make you as Sarah, Rebecca, Rachel, and Leah. May the Lord bless you and guard you. May the Lord show you favor and be gracious to you. May the Lord show you kindness and grant you peace.

"To the ceremony, then," he cries out.

The guests all answer with mazel tovs and good wishes. Sender and I flank Sala, who's trembling. With fear? Squelched tears? I doubt she knows herself. Hodel and the little girls squeeze in next to us. I see Chaia put a tender hand on Sala's arm. Then four of the farmers lift the chuppah above our family, while Rozhinkes dances between us. Picking up his violin, Dov Fishkin strikes up *Lomir Ale in Eynem*— Let us be merry and joyful, a traditional wedding song. Never before have I noticed the hint of sadness in the minor key and the slow cadence, like someone might be marching to her doom.

Part II

Chapter 14

MORRIS HAS BEEN A welcome addition to the farm. To make room for the bridal couple, we had to make up a bed for Hodel in the kitchen, but she's always a good sport. Morris is a bit of a klutz when it comes to plowing or planting, but he works hard and he understands how to manage the whole grape-growing operation. Plus, whenever Sender wants to debate a fine point of Torah, Morris is ready, which has improved my husband's disposition.

Most important, Morris is unfailingly considerate of Sala. He brings her little bunches of wildflowers, he praises her skill with a needle, he sings "A Woman of Valor" to her with fervor. And she is always appreciative for these attentions.

Still, there's no baby. A few times, she tried to talk to me about it, but it was slow going: "Whenever he tries to . . . I can't help remembering . . . " This is exactly what I was worried about. If Sala had some passion for Morris, she might be able to get past her memories of Corbin Johnson's attack, but no amount of duty and gratitude is going to erase the image of that beast looming over her. In despair, she even told Morris to divorce her, but he said it wasn't what he wanted. When she breaks down in tears with me, I just pat her back and tell her it will get better with time. I'm not sure I believe it, but there's an old saying, "Where two sleep on one pillow, a third shouldn't mix in."

Anyway, I should be glad we don't have more mouths to feed. The farm that was just starting to support five people is having trouble supporting seven. Our very spartan spring convinced me I had to come up with something to earn extra cash. As luck would have it, the answer came from the Jewish Agricultural Society newsletter, which, with some disdain, described how farmers in upstate New York were using their properties to board city dwellers looking for relief from the hot, crowded summers of the Lower East Side. It wasn't farming, the JAS reporter sniffed.

It *was*—much more importantly to me—a source of income. I talked with Hodel about it, and she was willing to take on the cooking for the extra guests. The girls were open to it, and Morris will do anything Sala wants. Sender, on the other hand, wasn't enthusiastic about this compromise in the pure mission of agricultural self-sufficiency. "Have we gone back to the land just to become petty innkeepers?" he asked indignantly.

"Have we gone back to the land just to starve?" I demanded.

Since Sender didn't have a better idea about how to raise some much-needed funds (and since he'd promised to go along with my plans when I gave him the money for the mortgage), he finally agreed to the boarders as long as they were not his responsibility. So, with help from Morris, I put an advertisement in "The Independent," Cleveland's weekly Jewish newspaper:

> *Notice:* Are you looking for someplace to spend the summer that combines healthy living and economy? Lovely old farmhouse in Geneva, close to the pleasures of the resort town Geneva-on-the-Lake. Sabbath-observant. Kosher cuisine.

We might have been stretching the point with *lovely*; we finally painted the house, but we had to use the cheapest stuff we could find, a shade resembling dried oatmeal. And as good a cook as Hodel is, I don't know that knishes qualify as *cuisine*. Still, the ad did its job. Within a month, we had signed up the Davidov family for July and August.

Where, you might well ask, are we going to put these guests? We have only the three bedrooms and the potential to convert the linen closet. At first, I imagined myself telling the boarders, "Sleep faster. We need the pillows." Then I remembered we have some experience with strangers staying at the farm. Last September, during the harvest, we hired an itinerant picker and put him up in the barn for a week. Of course, I can't put the boarders in the barn, but I can put Chaia and Reyzel there. Reyzel will sleep in one of the unused horse stalls. Chaia is going up in the hayloft, a dream come true as far as she's concerned until she learns she'll be tasked with keeping an eye on the Davidovs' twelve-year-old son, Shmulek, also known as Sylvester.

You can tell from Shmulek's English name, which his mother, Minnie, insists we use, that the Davidovs are what my mother would have called *edlgepatshket*. That's a term of her own invention, a mashup of *edl*, refined, and *ongepatshket*, which means over-embellished to the point of silliness. I guess Americans would say "pretentious." Minnie has already sent me a list of Sylvester's dietary requirements and his schedule, including rest periods, summer homework, violin practice, and, God help us, times to "use the facilities."

All of this is written in English, which, apparently, the Davidovs prefer to use. I suppose they wouldn't be caught dead speaking Yiddish, the language of immigrants. After all, Papa Ephraim was born in the United States (to recent immigrants from Poland, but who's counting?). I will do my best to converse with them in English, though, since they both know our *mame loshn*, this seems like a ridiculous exercise.

Late on the morning of July 1, the Davidovs pull up in a ponderous maroon Nash, with Ephraim driving, his arms extended straight out so that he has to move his whole body to turn the wheel. Minnie is holding on to her straw picture hat, its clutch of dark cherries bobbing dizzily as the car jolts up the drive. Stepping down from the car, she regards our "lovely" farmhouse dourly. In general, they're a stern-looking bunch. Ephraim has a black beard, trimmed so that each hair is precisely the same length. It chimes with his black suit and black shoes and black hat. He looks like what he is: a physician. Minnie, a large woman with an enormous bosom, towers over Sylvester. He may, in fact, be twelve, but you wouldn't know it to look at his scrawny legs and stooped shoulders. So pale is he and so thin, I wonder whether the child has seen sunlight or eaten a real meal in his life.

The first thing out of Ephraim Davidov's mouth is, "Be careful with our bags, especially Sylvester's violin. It's a Scarampella." He says the last with an emphatically rolled R. Chaia, who's been unloading the luggage, ceremoniously hands the case to little Reyzel. Is that a smile I see just barely curling the corners of Sylvester's mouth?

Not long after, we hear some scales on the violin. I'm no expert, but from what I can make out, Sylvester is definitely not a prodigy. Surprisingly, Reyzel has positioned herself on the landing where, unobserved, she can hear Sylvester play. "Oh, Mama," she says as I pass her on my way to change my stained apron, "isn't the music wonderful? It's like the violin is talking to us."

"Yes, Mamele. It's a lovely instrument," I say, leaving out the rest of my thought: when it's played by someone who loves it.

#

For the boarders' first morning on the farm, Hodel has fixed pancakes with syrup made from our wild blackberries. According to Minnie's instructions, Sylvester gets a plate of plain cottage cheese and a large glass of milk straight from Bubale. He takes a big mouthful of the latter and then tries discreetly to spit it back into the glass. "May I ask," he says with the good manners he was no doubt trained to use, "what this drink might be?"

"Milk," Chaia tells him, amazed that anyone over the age of two wouldn't recognize it.

"I don't think so," Sylvester says politely. "Milk comes in a bottle, and it's cold."

Before Chaia can start laughing at him, I intervene. "Actually, Sylvester, milk comes from cows. This afternoon, Chaia will show you how we milk our cow, Bubale."

"That will be fascinating."

"I'm afraid that won't be possible," Minnie breaks in, rising after her second helping of pancakes. "Sylvester has Latin homework."

I see Sylvester's face fall, but he makes no murmur. After Minnie leaves the table, I notice Reyzel spear the rest of the pancakes and slide them onto Sylvester's plate. He digs in gratefully.

After breakfast, Sala and Hodel give everyone a tour of the farm. Sylvester has to stay behind. According to his schedule, he has to both use the outhouse and practice his violin. At nine thirty, he dutifully begins sawing away in the parlor. I'm working at the loom, so I see Reyzel creep into the room and sit cross-legged at his feet. Sylvester gives her one of his tentative smiles, all the encouragement Reyzel needs to ask, "May I hold your violin?"

"Reyzel," I intervene, "Sylvester's violin is very special. I'm sure his parents wouldn't like him to risk breaking it."

"But I'll be so careful! Please, can I just touch it?"

"That's all right, Mrs. Rappaport," Sylvester says. "She can't do anything worse to it than I already have. One time I got so sick of it, I threw it on the floor."

"Oy yoy yoy! You don't like the violin?"

"I'd rather play baseball, but my mother says that's not a pastime for a nice Jewish boy."

"What about Moxie Manuel?" I say, throwing out a name I remember from my cousin Mendel's introduction to the American pastime and its roster of Jewish players.

"Right?" Sylvester says. "But Mother isn't impressed. Anyway, here, Reyzel." He hands the violin to my daughter and shows her how to hold it.

"How do you make it sing?" she asks.

He gives her the bow, and, taking her arm in his, draws it over the strings. There's a hideous screech.

"Oh, no! That's not what it's supposed to sound like," Reyzel gasps.

"I'm afraid your hands may be too little to do the fingering. That's what makes it play notes."

"Let me try."

I'm uneasy about this lesson, which I'm sure Minnie would not approve of, but I'm impressed that Reyzel is able to arch her hand over the frets and sound a few tones. Then, suddenly, we hear the group coming back from the fields. Hurriedly, Sylvester reclaims the violin and starts bowing. He's laboring through some piece when the grownups walk in. "Nice fiddling, Sylvester," Sala compliments him.

"There needs to be more ritardando on the last measure," Ephraim says curtly. Sylvester sighs.

The next day, Morris prevails on Harold to loan him the car so he can drive the Davidovs to Geneva-on-the-Lake for a swim and a picnic. Chaia tags along to navigate and make sure no one drowns. Totally enamored of Sylvester, Reyzel asks to go as well. From what Chaia tells me on their return, I needn't have worried about drowning. Minnie covered Sylvester in a long-sleeved shirt and long pants and then sat him under a beach umbrella with her and Ephraim. While the two adults gazed out over the water, Sylvester did more of the extra summer homework his mother requested from his teacher. Mostly Reyzel splashed around in the shallow water, but when Minnie gave Sylvester a brief reprieve from his studies, my daughter and the boy wandered along the beach together. Apparently Reyzel did all the talking, but Sylvester didn't seem to mind.

On the Fourth of July, the whole family and the boarders trek into Ashtabula for the festivities. Ephraim is not much impressed with the parade; the county's new fire engine pales in comparison to Cleveland's fleet, and he thinks the girls dressed as Betsy Ross are showing way too much leg. And don't even get him started on what passes for fireworks. "Why, you should see the display over Lake Erie!" he brags.

None of us (and I include Minnie and Sylvester) are too sad when Ephraim goes back to Cleveland to attend to his patients. He'll come back for the weekends. Now it's time for the other guests to amuse themselves.

For Minnie, this seems to mean *dreying* poor Sylvester *a kop*—spinning his poor twelve-year-old head around with endless tasks and routines. Occasionally she springs him for an hour or two, and he sneaks off with Chaia and Pasquelino, both of whom have taken to him. He's got a fine sense of humor and a willingness to try anything, despite his lack of physical prowess. I will say the extra food Reyzel has been sneaking him while she watches his violin practice is helping him fill out a bit. In return, when his mother isn't looking, Sylvester has been showing Reyzel more about how to play the instrument. I can hear her humming his exercises as she does her chores.

Chapter 15

AUGUST ROARS IN WITH a heat wave. Minnie brings out her silk fan and sits under the elm tree in the front yard, sweating and fanning. Even she realizes it's torture to force Sylvester inside for hours of practice and study. More and more, he joins Chaia in feeding the animals, weeding the garden, and exploring with Pasquelino.

Then one Monday morning, after a weekend visit from Ephraim, who accused his wife of being too lax, she summons Sylvester to the parlor. She's fanning furiously. "Young man," she says, "you've been slacking off. Today, you will practice violin for two hours in the morning and two hours in the afternoon. And I want to see your mathematics worksheets finished."

This is at least an all-day sentence, as I'm pretty sure Sylvester hasn't looked at his homework for a week. I expect Sylvester to submit meekly.

Then he surprises me. "But Mother, we have plans to go fishing."

"Is fishing on your schedule?"

"But Mother—"

"Is fishing an activity for nice Jewish boys?"

At that moment, Chaia appears to collect Sylvester. "What's wrong with fishing?" she wants to know.

"I wouldn't expect you to understand," Minnie says. "Your parents are farmers." She says the last part as though farmers were lower life-forms.

While I'm debating whether to give this woman a piece of my mind, Sylvester speaks up with an insubordination I didn't know he had in him. "Isn't it enough for you to criticize me all the time?" he demands. "Do you have to insult my friends too?"

Minnie is so shocked, she's speechless—momentarily. It's long enough for Sylvester to rush out the front door, slamming it behind him.

"I don't know what's gotten into that boy," Minnie sputters. "I'm sure you know I meant no insult. It's just that he needs to develop some discipline if he's going to succeed in the more refined world we live in."

Chaia is watching this interchange, so I really can't let this affront pass. "You are thinking it takes no discipline to get up at five in the morning to milk cows? Or to set grape stakes in the freezing cold? Would you like maybe to weed the garden this afternoon with Chaia?"

"Oh, you know what I mean," Minnie harrumphs. "Those are not the skills he will need to be a doctor like his father."

"Will he need to play the violin?" Chaia asks, honestly perplexed.

"Don't be impertinent, little girl," Minnie scolds her. "Now go and find Sylvester and bring him back here for his violin practice."

Chaia looks at me questioningly, but I'm not Sylvester's mother. I nod, and she trots off. Minutes tick by, much longer than I would have expected if Sylvester were just cooling off in the barn or under the elm. Minnie is beginning to get anxious. She breaks the silence. "Where is that boy?" she asks, as if I should know the exact tree he's hiding behind. More minutes pass until Chaia comes back through the front door. Reyzel is with her but not Sylvester.

"I got Reyzel to help me. We looked for Sylvester everywhere. Maybe he went into the woods?"

"Well, go find him!" Minnie demands.

"Now, just a minute," I break in. "My daughters are not servants, and they did not make Sylvester run away. Of course we'll find him, but please don't order us about." With that, I ignore Minnie and every other instruction she undoubtedly has waiting for us. "Girls," I say, "let's make a search party. Chaia, go get your father."

"Don't you remember? Papa took Morris over to the Ponskys. They're studying *Midrash Tanchuma*."

It's probably not fair, but I say under my breath, "May he live long enough for me to kill him!" With the men gone, I tell Chaia and Reyzel to find Hodel and Sala. I figure that between the five of us, we'll find Sylvester soon enough. Minnie has decided that her role will be to sit in the parlor and wait in case her son comes back on his own. God forbid she should tire herself.

The girls and I agree to split up into teams. Chaia teaches us all a special whistle she and Pasquelino use when they want to summon each other in an emergency. Then she goes off with Hodel to check the old shack she and

Pasquelino use for a clubhouse. Sylvester has joined them a few times, and Chaia thinks he may be using it as a hiding place. I shepherd Reyzel and Sala. Both teams are calling Sylvester's name as we go, but there's no answer. Is he hiding? Lost? We fan out farther, but there's still no sign of him.

Suddenly I hear the sound of Rozhinkes barking. "Reyzel, what's the dog doing in the woods?" I ask.

"Could he have found Sylvester?"

"From your mouth to God's ear!" We follow the racket to the path down to the Grand River. Rozhinkes is standing near the bank, woofing like a maniac, but we don't see Sylvester anywhere. The trees here come almost to the edge of the bank, obscuring the view of the river some thirty feet below. I'm terrified of what I'll see there. "Reyzel, go quiet the dog," I say as calmly as I can. "And you two stay away from the edge."

Once Rozhinkes quits yapping, I think I hear a faint noise above the rushing water. I hold out my arm to stop the girls chattering. Yes, there it is again. It's the sound of Sylvester calling, "Help! Oh, please help me. I'm down here."

Gingerly, I approach the steep bank. The hollering grows louder. I lie flat on the ground and hang my head over the edge. There's Sylvester on a shale ledge about six feet below, clinging onto a tree root that's poking out of the bank. The ledge is wide enough, but shale is notoriously crumbly. Every time he moves, a bit of it flakes off and falls into the racing river.

"It's okay," I yell down to the boy. "We're here, and we'll help you. Just stay still." Then I say, "Reyzel, start whistling." In as steady a voice as I can manage, I tell Sala to go to the barn and bring me back a long length of rope.

While Reyzel signals frantically for the other children, I sit near the edge, speaking soothingly. In a few moments, Chaia and Hodel come running. Chaia peers over the edge and says, "Whoo, boy!" I give her the look mothers reserve for foolish children. Chastened, she plops down next to me and hangs her head over the side. "Sylvester," she says as though they were having a conversation around the dinner table, "what are you doing down there?"

"I came to the river to be by myself. I guess I got too close to the edge and my foot slipped. I don't know how much longer I can hold on."

Chaia tries to calm him. "It's not really so bad down there. You have plenty of room. You could even let go of the root."

"No, no. I can't let go."

By this time, Reyzel is also hanging her head over the side. "You'll be okay, Sylvester! We'll get you out in no time."

"Here comes Sala with a rope," Chaia reassures him.

I say a little prayer of thanks when I see my daughter. Like anyone who has spent time on a farm, I have some useful knots up my sleeve. I use a clove hitch to tie the rope to a sturdy oak near the edge of the bank. Then I lower the other end down to the child on the ledge. "Now, Sylvester," I say, "I want you to grab onto the rope, and we'll haul you up."

"No, I can't," he cries. "If I let go of the root, I'll fall."

"Darling, just hold on with one hand to the root and grab with the other the rope"

"No, I can't. I'll fall when you try to pull me up. I'm not strong enough."

"Yes you are," Reyzel tells him. "Just think of all the things you learned to do this summer. You can climb into the hay loft. You can shimmy up an apple tree. And you reeled in that huge bluegill."

"But I'm scared."

"Oh, this is silly," Chaia says. Before I can stop her, she's taken hold of the rope and is using it to rappel down the bank to join Sylvester on the ledge. A gasp goes up from Reyzel, and I can hear Sala praying. I rush to the edge of the bank, lie flat, and peek over. "All right," I hear Chaia say, "I'm bringing the rope to you, and I want you to grab it with your right hand." Miraculously, Sylvester does as he's told. Chaia flings the rope into a loop around the boy's hand. "Now your grip on the rope is safe. Grab it with your left hand too." Although he starts to protest, Chaia talks him through the maneuver, and he follows directions. "Okay, I'm going to take hold of the root, so Mama and the others can pull you up with the rope. It's not very far to the top. Promise me you won't let go."

"I promise," Sylvester says weakly. Hodel and I begin carefully hauling up on the rope. Rozhinkes is whining anxiously. When we've raised Sylvester to the lip of the bank, Sala and Reyzel clutch his arms and help him over the top. "Oh, my God," he cries, "I'm safe! But now Chaia is stuck down there."

"She's not stuck," I insist, though I really didn't like the clumps of shale I saw falling from the ledge as Chaia helped Sylvester. "Chaia, we're throwing you the rope," I call out. Once again, the rope goes over the side.

"Mama," she answers, "I think it will be easier if I just climb the rope instead of having you pull me out. We have a rope swing at school, and one time, the boys dared me to climb it. It was a cinch."

Though I like this even less, my daughter has already started up. She grips the rope with her knees and starts hauling herself up, hand over hand. In a minute, we can grab her by the shoulders as she heaves herself onto the bank, panting from exertion. The dog races up to her and licks her face. Realizing I've been holding my breath, I let out a slow exhale. I say a prayer of gratitude and a special thank you to the dog. Who knew that annoying yapping was going to be a lifesaver some day?

Everyone is shell-shocked. Sylvester has sweat through his shirt and smells faintly of rotten eggs. We head back to the house, where Sylvester spills the whole story to his mother. If she's grateful, she never says so. Instead, she tut-tuts over Sylvester, inspecting his hands for any sign that his misadventure has damaged his bowing fingers.

I will say that since that day, Minnie has eased up on Sylvester's schedule and the supervision of his practices. He's free enough to show Reyzel how to do some pretty fair scales. A few mornings, when his mother isn't paying close attention, Reyzel plays his exercises while he escapes into the woods with Chaia and Pasquelino. We're all sorry to say goodbye to the boy when the summer ends, but I'm hoping we can get by next year without boarders, at least not any as edlgepatshket as the Davidovs.

Chapter 16

Sometime around her birthday last December, Chaia became a woman. You might imagine a twelve-year-old girl budding. Well, by this year, Chaia is in full bloom. She would have been delighted to remain a washboard-thin child, but she's now zaftig, with curves that the boys in her class have started to notice with varying degrees of appreciation or mockery, mostly the latter. Pasquelino's mother has decided the children are too old to be tramping around the woods together unaccompanied. Of course, Sender agrees with her. It's a shame, really, as there's nothing between them other than friendship.

The girls in Chaia's class don't interest her, and they have contempt for Chaia, now not only the teacher's pet but also the bustiest girl in the school. Add to that her being the only Jewish child her age, and it equals a lot of loneliness. When her classmates do pay attention to her, it's usually to make fun of her looks or the "strange food" (like bagels) she brings in her lunch bag.

I wish she got a little respite at home, but Sender is always on her for something: talking back, daydreaming, not being interested in cooking or baking or weaving. He's given her a few licks for forgetting her chores, all the while reciting from the Talmud how we must take care of our livestock even before we feed ourselves, lest we cause the animals to suffer. I do my best to shield her from the worst of his ill temper, but I can't change the fact that he wishes she were someone she's not. I know how that feels.

Does this make me closest to Chaia of all my daughters? No. But I see that right now, Chaia needs me the most. I've already failed at protecting Sala; she was denied an education, and she rushed into a tepid marriage despite all my efforts. I don't know what else I can do for her. Reyzel, on the other hand, has her father's favor, plus she's naturally outgoing, quick to catch the enthusiasms of her schoolmates and mold herself to them. She has plenty of friends, some of them, I'm sorry to say, among Chaia's tormentors.

In fact, Reyzel is not above getting her own digs in. She seems to forget that Chaia is the one who helps her with her homework, who gets her books from the library and reads to her at night. She sees only the smarty-pants that her teacher is always comparing her to. Somehow, she's turned the word "bookworm" into a weapon that she slings at Chaia whenever she thinks I'm not listening.

Tonight, when I'm passing by their bedroom, I hear what sounds like Reyzel jumping on her mattress, singing. I stop for a moment outside the door. I guess I'm just in time for verse two:

> Charlie's nose has a great big hook.
> She's only good at reading books.
> Her clothes are dirty. Her hair is funny.
> She'll probably try to take your money.

I open the door on Reyzel cackling. Charlie is turned away from her, with her nose in a novel. From the way Reyzel's grin collapses, she knows she's in trouble. "Mama," she begins babbling at once, "I didn't make up the song. Honest. It's a jump rope rhyme Gladys Evans made up. She's really mean. I was just showing Chaia what the other kids are saying."

I look at Chaia. "I know what they say. I don't care," she mutters.

I'm so angry at my youngest child, I'm afraid of what might come out of my mouth. I manage to confine myself to a simple, "Reyzel, you come with me."

I stand Reyzel in the hall. Shivering now with her feet on the cold floor this chilly fall evening, she probably thinks I'm going to spank her. Instead, I empty out the linen cupboard again. This time, I don't bother with a feather bed, only a spare blanket. "You don't deserve to share a room with your sister," I say. "You can sleep on the floor in there. When you've thought about what you did, you can come and talk to me."

"But I'm sorry," Reyzel protests.

"About what?"

"I don't know what you want me to say," she whines.

"And that's the problem." I leave her curled up in the blanket with the door open. Her whimpering carries down to the kitchen, where I'm darning socks. If she expects the waterworks to make me relent, she'll be sniveling a long time.

The next morning, Reyzel gives me the silent treatment during breakfast. In fact, she doesn't speak to me when she gets home from school, and she doesn't talk to me at dinner—not exactly a punishment. As bedtime rolls around, though, she apparently decides she's going to have to make a stab at a better apology if she doesn't want another night on the closet floor. She appears at my side as I'm scrubbing the pots. "I'm sorry, Mama. I didn't make up the rhyme, but I shouldn't have repeated it. Can I go back to my own room now?"

"That's all you have to say?"

"I said I was sorry!"

"Did you apologize to Chaia?"

"Not yet, but I will."

"And what will you apologize for?"

"For the rhyme."

"You'll sleep in the linen closet until you can do better than that."

Furious, Reyzel flounces out of the room. I hear her start to complain to her father, who's in the parlor, reading the great rabbinic commentator Rashi. Before she can get up a head of steam, I enter the room, giving Sender a meaningful look that would have made my mother proud. Since he doesn't really want to be interrupted anyway, he composes his face into a mask of severity. "As the Proverb teaches, 'Do not forsake the instruction of your mother,'" he says. "From this we learn, mothers are in charge of discipline. You must do as your mother says." Reyzel turns on the tears, but Sender is already back to his text. She rushes up the stairs and shuts herself in the closet. It must be dark in there, but I guess she's making a statement.

Reyzel repeats some version of this performance for the next two nights. Finally, on the fifth night just before bedtime, Chaia comes with Reyzel to speak to me. "Mama," she says, "I'm not mad at Reyzel anymore. Why won't you let her come back to our room?"

Reyzel turns her defiant little face to me. "See, Chaia doesn't even mind what I said. Why should you?"

"Do you even know what the rhyme you recited was about?"

"It was mean."

"What made it mean?"

"It was making fun of the way Chaia looks."

"What about the way she looks?"

"Her nose."

"And does your sister have a hooked nose?"

Reyzel studies Chaia's face, as though for the first time. "No," she admits.

"Is she dirty? Is her hair funny?"

Reyzel lowers her head and mumbles, "No."

"Have you ever known her to steal?"

Reyzel shakes her head.

"So why do you suppose Gladys said Chaia would take your money?"

"To be mean. I already said that."

"Reyzel," Chaia says with some impatience, "she said it because I'm Jewish, and Jews are all supposed to have hooked noses and be dirty and only care about money."

"But I'm a Jew," Reyzel says, almost in wonderment.

"My point exactly," I respond. "You weren't only making fun of your sister with that rhyme, which is bad enough. You were making fun of yourself and your whole people."

"That nasty Gladys Evans. I'm never giving her part of my sandwich again!"

"That's well and good, but do you have something to say to your sister?"

"I'm sorry. Honest I am."

Chaia forgives her easily. "Besides," she says, "it's hard to fall asleep without the sound of you breathing."

I guess that's as good a basis for a ceasefire as any. I send them off to their room.

#

While Chaia has her struggles with the humans in her life, she's made one important friend. She's taken a liking to our new horse. In fact, she named him: Balagan, or Chaos. That about describes his state when Sender brought him home from the cattle auction.

I should mention that, on the day in question, Sender went to the auction to buy a couple of goats. Hodel and I planned to start making and selling branza de burduf, a Romanian goat cheese that's left to age inside fir tree bark until it becomes spicy with resin. But no goat could compete with Balagan. As Sender tried to explain to me, this animal was so wild—bucking and rearing when the handler brought him into the ring—that no one was bidding on him. That allowed Sender to scoop up the horse for a song (or, I guess, the price of two goats). As an experienced horse trader, Sender knew a beautiful stallion when he saw one, and I had to concede Balagan was a handsome beast, with a coat the color of chestnuts and a white blaze. What we need with a stallion is another question, one that Sender can't really answer.

Anyway, Chaia fell in love with Balagan on sight. She may shirk her weeding, but she never forgets to clean Balagan's hooves, curry him, or comb his mane and tail. Sender has been teaching her how to train him too, which involves a lot of patient circling around the corral. At least it gives them something to do together that doesn't involve Sender yelling at her. He says Balagan is ready to accept a rider. Now we just need a saddle. And a bridle. And stirrups. It may be a while before I get my goats.

Chapter 17

WHILE CHAIA IS PREOCCUPIED with Balagan, Reyzel also has a new passion. A lover of the violin since the summer Sylvester stayed with us, Reyzel became fascinated with Dov Fishkin's klezmer-style fiddling whenever he performed at events for the Jewish farmers. Generous man that he is, Dov offered to teach her how to play. We scrounged up a violin, which was surprisingly easy. I guess every immigrant family wants their child to play like Jascha Heifetz, the famous Jewish musician who was performing on concert stages at age seven. There are quite a few instruments lying around, discarded when the child's playing turned out to sound not like Heifetz but like a cat in heat.

Reyzel, on the other hand, has had an affinity for the instrument since the first time she picked it up. Even the dog likes to hear her play. Now she can master the most complicated tunes Dov throws at her. Sometimes, she goes with him to perform klezmer music at weddings all over the region. They're a popular pair: the comical master of ceremonies and his pint-sized pupil.

I just wish she would devote some of that same focus to her schoolwork. Last week, when I saw Miss Dupont after one of Chaia's elocutionary contests, she told me Reyzel wasn't "living up to her potential."

"You should hear her play the fiddle," I said, trying to put in a good word for my daughter about something Miss Dupont might appreciate.

"I would like to hear that," Miss Dupont replied. "Please tell Reyzel to bring her violin to school next Friday so she can play something for the rest of the children."

Now Reyzel is mad at me. She says the other kids will laugh at the music she plays. "They want to hear 'I'm Just Wild About Harry' or 'I

Dream of Jeannie with the Light Brown Hair.' I play '*Naftule Spilt Far Dem Rebn.*' It's going to be a disaster." I guess it's a mother's job to embarrass her daughters. Anyway, today is the performance, which Miss Dupont has scheduled for the end of the school day—so I can attend, she informs me. Never mind that I hear Reyzel practicing every day at home and that I have challah to bake for Shabbas.

I arrive at the school at a quarter to three sharp. When I enter, Miss Dupont is rapping on the desk with her pointer. "Now, children, we have a special treat today. Reyzel Rappaport is going to play for us on her violin." A groan goes up from Alvin Baker, a big galoot who's been a terror since he was in knee breeches. He used to sit behind Chaia, and before she cut her hair, he would dip her pigtails in his inkwell. Now Reyzel is his favorite target. Either he has a crush on her or he's a budding anti-Semite. Whatever his feelings, his groaning is followed by a gale of titters and guffaws from the rest of the boys. Miss Dupont raps again, a reminder that the pointer can be used on fingers as well as on the desk. The class quiets.

Reyzel has put on her Shabbas dress, a plaid shirtwaist with ruffles at the neck. She wears matching bows at the end of her braids. With her close-set eyes, light brown hair, and a mouth like an archer's bow, Reyzel is a cute little girl. With her violin in her hands, she becomes something else. She puts the instrument under her chin and raises the bow. Then she launches into the most devilish dance tune Dov ever taught her. The music speeds along, winding its way around a basic theme with trills and plucking. When I wrench my eyes away from Reyzel for a moment, I see the students are rapt, thrumming on their desks or tapping their feet in time to the music. At the end, everyone bursts into applause. Not a disaster, it seems. Reyzel takes a modest bow, but I can tell she's pleased. As she returns to her desk, her classmates beam at her.

The one who turns out to be her biggest fan is Miss Dupont. Before I can gather the girls together to head for home, she calls me aside. "Mrs. Rappaport, Reyzel is a real talent," she says as though she's telling me something I don't know.

"She is good, isn't she?"

"Good? She's a prodigy. How did she learn to bow with such virtuosity?"

Prodigy? Virtuosity? These are not words I know, but I gather it's a compliment. "Our neighbor, may he live to be a hundred and twenty, has been teaching her," I say. "He fiddles at all the weddings and bar mitzvahs."

"How does she learn the tunes?"

"She listens. She watches. She plays."

"That's astonishing, to play by ear like that. But with all due respect to your neighbor, Reyzel really must work with a true violin teacher. First, she has to learn to read music. And she must study the classics: Mendelssohn and Bach and Mozart. I happen to know an excellent teacher, retired from the Cleveland Symphony and living right up the road in Unionville. I'm sure I could arrange for her to have lessons."

"Miss Dupont, that's very kind of you, but Unionville? I don't know how we should get Reyzel to Unionville. It's far from our farm, and we have no car."

Chaia and Reyzel have been listening to this exchange, and Chaia decides this is the moment to jump in. "She could ride Balagan."

"Charlie," I say, being careful to use her school name, "So wild is Balagan, even you haven't been able to ride him. How will Reyzel do it?"

"Papa says he's ready to take a saddle. I'll work with him until he's tame enough for Reyzel."

Reyzel is looking up at me with those doe eyes of hers. "Please, Mama."

"Reyzel, my heart, I'm so sorry, but even if you could get to the lessons, we have no way to pay for them."

"Let me see if I can take care of that part of the problem," Miss Dupont says. "I'll speak to Mr. Pendergast, the teacher. He's an old friend of the family. Maybe we can work something out."

#

Word comes from Miss Dupont the next week that her father's friend, Guy Pendergast, will take Reyzel on as a student without charge if she'll also help him organize his music library. Does Reyzel know from organizing anything? Not if the state of her room is any indication. Plus, I don't think the added responsibilities will do Reyzel's schoolwork any good, but if Miss Dupont is for it, who am I to argue?

Everything is set for her to begin lessons except how she'll get to Unionville. Chaia is working diligently to train Balagan, but it's spring planting season, and everyone, including Sender, is too busy to help. Chaia wants to put a saddle on the horse, but we haven't managed to find one we can afford.

Though Reyzel is disappointed, today she serenades us with a fragment of classical music she heard on the Golds' radio. I'm working at the loom, and Sala and Hodel are hand-finishing tablecloths when Sender storms into the parlor, more apoplectic than usual. "Where's Chaia? She was supposed to milk Bubale. The cow is still out in the pasture with her udder so full she's tripping on it."

"She's probably out in the corral with Balagan," Reyzel says before I have a chance to head her off and go warn her sister.

"That nogoodnik! When I catch up with her, I'll give her such a *patsh in tuchus*, it will be a long time before she forgets her chores again."

"But, Papa, she was only trying to get the horse ready for me to ride to my violin lessons."

"There are more important things in this world than your violin lessons." When Sender barks at Reyzel, we know he's really mad. He stomps off, with the four of us trailing him, hoping we may be able to lighten Chaia's punishment.

But Chaia is not in the corral. She's not in the barn, and neither is Balagan. Sala is the first of us to hear her screams for help. She rushes to the back door of the barn and points. "There she is, out near the woods, on Balagan." Chaia is clinging onto the horse's neck for dear life. Balagan is galloping wildly, shifting Chaia's body so that she's practically riding on his flank.

I've never seen my husband move so fast. He leads our workhorse, Barney, out of his stall and smacks his rear until he reluctantly begins to trot. Running alongside, Sender traps a hank of Barney's mane in his fist and hoists himself onto the horse's back. With some fearsome shouts, he gets Barney going at a gallop, heading straight for the trees. The rest is like a dream. We see Sender ride Barney right up next to Balagan until they're going at the same clip. Then, with a shout to hold on, he leaps behind Chaia on Balagan's back. He grabs Chaia around the middle and rights her. Leaning over, he begins patting the horse, whispering in his ear. Gradually, Balagan calms down. Somehow Sender steers the horse with his knees, and they begin the trip back to the barn at a slow trot. Barney, glad to be out of the race, plods along behind.

We're all expecting an explosion from Sender. Surprisingly, he lets Chaia down gently and, still seated on Balagan, walks the horse over to the corral where they do some easy laps. Both are dripping with sweat. We just stare, dumbfounded. Finally, Sender dismounts, leads Balagan to his stall, and begins wiping the horse down with cool water. All at once, he seems to notice us. "Do you have no chores to do that you have time to watch me do mine?"

He's right, of course, but I have to ask, "Sender, where did you learn to ride like that?"

Sender smiles mysteriously. "I had a l life before you knew me."

"So did I, but I don't have any hidden talents like jumping from one horse to another."

He chuckles, but no more information is forthcoming. It takes his favorite, Reyzel, to pry the details out of him. "Please, Papa, tell us!"

"A long, long time ago," he begins, as though he were reciting a fairytale, "before my family came to Falciu, we lived in a shtetl in Russia. One day, a Cossack brigade tore through town."

"Did they start a pogrom?" Sala asks.

"No, that came later, after I'd already left home. But for me, this visit was just as bad. They forced every boy over fifteen to join up. Unfortunately, I made the cut. They yanked me out of the yeshiva and marched me away to join a regiment."

"A Cossack regiment couldn't have been a friendly place for a Jewish boy," I say.

"For four years, I rode with them, every day getting cuffed and sometimes feeling the sting of the whip, every day being fed only enough to keep body and soul together, every day being called a dirty Jew. They were brutes, the Cossacks, but they knew horses, and eventually, so did I."

"How did you get out?" Hodel wants to know. "I heard service in the brigades was supposed to be twenty years."

"I knew I wouldn't survive that long. Then one night, my commanding officer, the ataman, came back to our encampment, drunk as Lot. 'Rappaport,' he says to me, 'I need a shave. I want you to cut my beard.' Well, I'd barely learned to cut my own beard, let alone someone else's. But he insisted—had his batman bring his razor and soap."

This sounds almost comical, like a story Sender made up to amuse the children. Reyzel is hooked. "What did you do, Papa?"

"What could I do? He sat in a chair and threw his head back, showing his neck and chin. For a moment, I thought about slitting his throat and being done with it. Instead, I lathered up the soap and smeared some on his face. Then I picked up the razor and went to shave him. Unfortunately, my hand was shaking, and as soon as I started, I nicked him. A tiny trickle of red blood sprouted in the white lather. The ataman knocked my arm aside and put his hand up to his face. It came away pink. 'Why, you dirty Jew,' he roared. 'You'll pay for this!'"

By this time, we're all hanging on Sender's every word. "Did he send you to prison?" Chaia wants to know.

"There weren't prisons while we were on the march, but the ataman told Pyotr, the next in command, to tie me up. 'I'll deal with him in the morning,' he said and stumbled off to his tent."

"You must have been so scared," Reyzel says.

"Actually, that was the moment I knew God was with me. Pyotr was the man who'd taught me to ride. I think the fact that I was good with the horses gave him a little respect for me. Of all the men in the brigade, Pyotr was the only one who had never hit me. In fact, sometimes, he snuck me some leftover food."

"Did he refuse to do what the ataman asked?" Reyzel wants to know.

"And risk his own life? No, he was too smart for that," Sender tells her. "He led me to the edge of the camp, just like the ataman wanted, and began berating me in a loud voice. He made me put my hands behind my back, wound a length of rope around them, and tied it to a tree. As I pulled at it, I realized the knot was loose and placed so that I could easily free myself. Before he left, he put his mouth close to my ear as if to curse me, but he said, 'There's a Jewish town about two hours east of here. Perhaps they can help you.'"

And so it was that Sender made his escape. He eventually found his way back to his own shtetl.

"What would have happened if they'd caught you?" Sala asks, wide-eyed.

"I would have been shot. That's one of the reasons we moved to Romania—that and the pogrom my parents lived through after I left town. Compared to Russia, Romania seemed like a pretty safe place."

I'm stunned. "So for twenty years we've been married, and this is the first I hear about Cossacks."

"My parents didn't think it would be considered an asset in a potential bridegroom."

There, I realize, is the reason Sender agreed to marry me. He wasn't exactly a prize himself. If my father knew the bridegroom was in danger of being shot by the Cossacks, and me along with him, it didn't keep Papa from going forward with the match. Still, I protest, "That was ages ago. Why have you never mentioned it since."

"It's not something I like to remember."

"Papa," Chaia breaks in, "I'm sorry for what the Cossacks did to you, but whatever it was, you're an amazing rider. You saved my life!"

"That's what fathers are supposed to do," he replies. It's the first kind thing he's said to her in a while. Never one to reveal his true feelings, though, he follows quickly with, "But Chaia, no more bareback riding for you. It's a good thing God protects the simple."

"I was just trying to get Balagan ready to take Reyzel to her music lessons. Mama says it'll be a year before we can afford a saddle, and I thought maybe we could learn to ride without."

That's when Sala speaks up. "I've been talking to Morris about that saddle. We would like to purchase whatever is needed to ride the horse. Morris says perhaps you can teach him to ride as well, and he can use the horse to get to the new grapevines more quickly."

If there's a section of the Talmud on horses, maybe Morris will actually learn to ride. More probably, this is Sala and Morris's cover story for doing something special for Reyzel. With no child of their own, they've become invested in her music education. The truth is, everyone in the family, even Sender, wants to make it possible for Reyzel to study violin with Mr. Pendergast.

And so we do. By the beginning of summer, Sala and Morris have secured the saddle, Chaia and Sender have finished training Balagan, and Reyzel has learned to ride. We all come to see her off the first time she heads out to Unionville, her violin strapped securely behind her. Chaos has been tamed.

Chapter 18

WE HAVEN'T NEEDED TO take in boarders since the Davidovs, but we do host Jewish guests who are passing through and have nowhere else to get a kosher meal or to rest on the Sabbath. Often these people are peddlers, usually immigrant men who crisscross the country, selling notions that farm families like ours can't make or grow ourselves.

In the six years we've been in Geneva, we've had annual visits from Yankel Levine. From tramping across the plains and through the mountain passes, there's not an ounce of fat on Yankel's body. Over six feet tall from his fisherman's cap to his slouchy black boots, he has black eyes and a nose that looks like someone flattened it with an iron skillet. He told me once that he supports a family of four back in Odessa, but I didn't get the feeling he missed them very much. He was born to ramble, and apparently his wife is content to stay in Russia. Maybe Sender needed a spouse like that.

Anyway, Yankel's arrival is always an occasion at our house, with the girls pawing through his trinkets and everyone drinking in the tales of his travels. There was the time he was caught in a blizzard in Massachusetts and the time he crossed paths with a grizzly bear in Montana. We're looking forward to more stories tonight when he returns from his rounds: a hike through the countryside, stopping at whatever farmsteads he finds along the way. Hodel has planned a stick-to-your-ribs dinner for him, with chopped liver, chicken with dried apricots, canned green beans from our garden, and almond cake.

At five thirty, I hear Rozhinkes barking, and a minute later I see the peddler coming up the road, seemingly unwearied by the day's exertions. Reyzel greets him at the front door, where he sets down his pack and fishes out a ribbon for her. While Reyzel is adorning herself, Chaia comes up from milking. For her, he has a postcard of the Grand Canyon. He also doles out a recent copy of "The Jewish Daily Forward" for Sender, a skein of blue embroidery thread for Hodel, a tiny fleck of gold he panned in California for Sala and Morris, and some pressed wildflowers for me—"blooms for Bluma," he calls them. As I said, he's always a welcome guest.

As we sit down to dinner, Yankel takes a deep breath. "Hodel, I haven't seen such a meal since I left Odessa. Thank you, my dear, and thank you all for making me welcome."

"Well," I say, "you know you're going to have to sing for your supper. Tell us the latest from the wide world."

Yankel takes a big helping of chicken and beans, and cuts a hunk of rye bread from the loaf. "Let me see. Well, here's a story for Reyzel. I saw a real princess."

"With a crown?"

"Princess Red Feather's people, the Muscogee Nation, don't go in for crowns, I'm afraid, but she wears a beautiful, beaded headband. And she sings like an angel. I heard her give a concert in Denver. She sang in seven different languages!"

Reyzel is a little disappointed about the crown but intrigued by the idea of a musical princess. I'm guessing Yankel has a violin concert in his future. The peddler has a different story for all the girls. He tells Chaia about the cowboys in Texas, and for Sala and Hodel, there's a tale about a Chinese silk importer he met in San Francisco.

Then he turns to Sender and Morris. "I actually ran into some descendants of your 'Back-to-the-Land' comrades in Texas, of all places. Some big Jewish mining macher settled their parents near one of his zinc mines in a tiny place called Cotopaxi, Colorado. Only trouble—the land was lousy for farming: poor soil, big rocks, no water. The colony only lasted a few years."

"Too many of the early settlements ended up like that," Sender says. "Some people were so discouraged they even went back to Europe."

"Well, these folks moved to Texas. One of them even made his living carrying calves on his back from farm to farm trying to sell them! That's a kind of peddling I have no interest in."

"We farmers are a scrappy bunch," Morris says.

I cover a smile at the idea of my son-in-law carrying a calf on his back, but Yankel keeps a straight face. "That's the truth," he replies. "Anyway, they've collected quite a little community of Jews there. I met one guy from your part of the world—it's Romania, right? He moved to Texas to work in his cousin's dry goods store."

"What part of Romania?" I ask.

"Iassi, I think. He actually had a sad story to tell. Met a girl while he was in the army, who agreed to marry him. He promised to go back and get her, but he got delayed at home, and by the time he came for her, she was gone. He was so broken-hearted, he got on the next ship to America."

A hush has fallen over the table. Hodel's face is white as the tablecloth. So are the knuckles of her hands as she clasps them together, almost as if she were praying. In a whisper, she forces out the question, "What was the man's name?"

"Zavel something. I meet so many people on the road, I don't always remember."

"Zavel Bercovici?"

"Yes. Yes, that was it. Did you know him?"

I've leapt out of my seat and positioned myself behind Hodel as I think she may faint. Instead, she slumps forward. A gasp goes up from the table.

"What? What have I said?" Yankel cries.

Sala, who's sitting next to Hodel, leans her aunt against her side and puts a glass of water to her lips. In a moment, Hodel is revived, but she's too overcome with emotion to speak. I get the job of telling Yankel the sad tale of Hodel's abandonment while she sits frozen at her place, the tears we haven't seen in months cascading down her cheeks.

"Was the rumor she heard untrue? Did Zavel not marry someone else?" I ask.

Yankel shakes his head in amazement. "Not exactly true," he says. Everyone in the family leans forward, anxious to hear the real story. "It seems that when Zavel got home, his family's rabbi came to call on him to discuss a delicate matter. There was a young married woman whose father was a member of the shul. Foolish in the way of young girls, she got involved with another man, so her husband divorced her. Soon enough, though, she found herself"—he looks around the table trying to think of a polite way to put it—"in the family way."

"Yankel," Chaia says, "we have animals. We know what it means to be pregnant."

"All right then, do you know what it means for a married woman to have a child with another man—a man who skedaddled as soon as he learned she was going to have a baby?"

"The child is a *mamzer*," Morris answers. "It's a difficult fate. A mamzer is not allowed to marry anyone but another mamzer, and the prohibition is passed down to any children the mamzer himself may have. Many of them are made to feel like outsiders in their own communities."

"But what does any of this have to do with Zavel?" Hodel demands, finally finding her voice.

"Well, you see, there's a loophole for a woman in this predicament," Yankel continues. "If she marries someone else before her baby is born, the child is not a mamzer. Zavel's rabbi asked if he would marry this woman— just until her baby was born—so the child could be considered legitimate. It was a pure marriage of convenience."

"And Zavel, mensch that he is, agreed," Hodel says with anguish. "Oh, how could I have been so stupid? I knew what a rare soul Zavel was. But our brother-in-law Berel was so sure he deserted me. I just didn't have enough faith, and now Zavel has probably given his heart to someone else."

"Oh, no, my girl," Yankel assures her. "Zavel told me the girl he'd asked to marry him was the love of his life. If he couldn't have her, he would never marry another."

By this point, everyone is crying. Even Sender swats away a tear or two. I guess I'll have to retract my curses. In fact, I'll have to admit that part of me has always envied Hodel for her great love and the fact that she could hold onto it, even in the face of what looked like betrayal. And now, to have her faith rewarded, to learn that Zavel also saved his heart for her—well, it does leave my marriage looking more threadbare than ever. If I were being truly honest, I'd have to confess that I also have had only one great love. I married him. It just didn't have a fairytale ending like Hodel's story.

That very night, Sender helps Hodel write a letter to Zavel in care of Bercovici's Dry Goods Store. Within a month, she has an answer. You can see the marks of Zavel's tears on the writing paper, where he's declared his undying devotion. At the end of the next month, Zavel steps off the train in Cleveland, ready to reclaim his bride.

We can see why Hodel fell for Zavel, so striking with his auburn hair and broad shoulders. We're entranced by his Southern accent, which we've never heard before. Chaia, especially, is spellbound as Zavel recalls his army days and shows her the bullet wound through his upper arm.

The wedding is at our farmhouse. I'm ashamed by the contrast between this joyous celebration and Sala's modest wedding, though my daughter wanted as little fanfare as possible. For Hodel, we're making a big *tzimmes*. Of course, I'm happy for my sister, but I can't help wishing I saw more of Hodel's kind of joy in Sala's lukewarm relationship with Morris. Still no babies.

Even so, Sala, selfless person that she is, throws herself into the preparations. She gladly gives Hodel her wedding dress. She helps me make six double-braided challahs for the occasion. And she joins in when the Jewish farm women come to dance with Hodel on the afternoon before the wedding. Each also comes with a piece of advice:

"Don't expect him to change," Clara Fishkin offers.

"As the proverb goes, 'Only love gives us the taste of eternity,'" says Edith Cohen.

Sala offers her advice in practically a whisper. "You don't marry someone to make you happy, just happier."

The ceremony itself takes place in our parlor. Since the bride and groom's parents are back in Romania, Morris and Sala accompany Zavel to the chuppah, and Sender and I escort Hodel. The starved, pallid girl who came to live with us three years ago is now a strong young woman. As is the Jewish custom, she circles Zavel seven times to symbolize how she will build their private world. They sip wine from the same glass. Zavel consecrates Hodel to himself according to the laws of Moses and Israel, and he gives her a plain gold band.

The ceremony ends with Zavel stomping on a wine glass. Why destruction to conclude a happy occasion? The rabbis say it's to remind us of the destruction of the Temple in Jerusalem. Some jokesters say it's the last time the groom will put his foot down. To me, it says something about how men have the capacity to smash things, but I have to trust that Zavel won't use that power.

Jewish weddings traditionally include a feast, but Hodel's is definitely not traditional. At Zavel's request, we introduce the Geneva farmers to a new delicacy: barbecue. Zavel came from Texas with what he called a "ristra," a string of dried peppers, like a fiery red flower. These he put in a pot with tomatoes, onions, garlic, and spices. On the day before the wedding, we dug a pit in the backyard and filled it with logs. When those burned to embers, we wrapped chicken and beef in leaves, laid them in the pit, and covered the whole thing with soil. Now we have some of the tenderest meat I've ever tasted doused in Zavel's spicy sauce. Barbecue—who knew?

That night, Reyzel and Dov Fishkin play dance music on the fiddle until the stars poke through the night sky. It's such a happy occasion that the green-eyed monster of my jealousy retreats into his lair. I will certainly regret losing my sister to Texas, but who could lament so undeniable a love match?

What a wild coincidence that Yankel should bring this story of Zavel Bercovici to us all the way from Texas. Or maybe a better way to think of it is to say Hodel and Zavel were *bashert*, fated to be together. According to the Talmud, before we are fully formed in the womb, a heavenly echo rings out the name of the person we are intended to marry: our *basherter*. Certainly, someone up above knew that my sister and the young soldier were meant for each other.

Chapter 19

COMING UP IS OUR fifth Passover on the farm. While the holiday is supposed to be about telling the story of the Exodus from Egypt, for women, it's mostly about crumbs. The girls and I started cleaning two weeks ago, sweeping every floor, turning out every pocket, shaking every eiderdown to make sure there were no remnants of *hametz*: the five types of grain prohibited on the holiday. Not for the first time, I really missed my sister. We even flipped open every book in the house. You wouldn't believe the number of crumbs we found in *Jo's Boys*.

The night before Passover, Sender led the girls in a search for any stray crumbs that theoretically escaped our notice. (In fact, as is traditional, I left a few ritual crusts of bread for them to find.) Sender was armed with a beeswax candle to light the way, a turkey feather to sweep up the crumbs, and a wooden spoon to catch them in. In order for the ritual to be completed, the crumbs were transferred into a paper bag along with the feather and the spoon. On Passover morning, Sender will burn the hametz, the final step in making our home ready for the holiday.

The next morning, the kitchen is a *balagan*, and I'm not talking about our horse. I'm making my Passover almond cake, which, because it has no leavening, will fall like a pancake if anyone opens the oven door while it's baking. Sala is starting on the brisket, which needs to roast and rest before we slice it and reheat it in its own juices. Up in the attic, Morris is getting the Passover dishes. And, of course, Sender is reading a commentary on the prayers we'll use tonight at our Seder. Given how much we have to do, he might as well be contemplating whether a flea has a bellybutton, but then, I never did win an argument with Sender about the need for study. In the middle of all this, Reyzel and Chaia are darting around, stuffing their lunch bags with anything they can find that's not hametz, which we stop eating well before the holiday begins this evening.

At eleven o'clock, Sender decides it's time to burn the crumbs from last night's search. He picks up the brown paper bag on the table, but it's suspiciously heavy for ten crusts of bread, a feather, and a wooden spoon. When he opens it, he cries, "This is not our hametz!"

I take the bag from him and peer inside. An apple, a piece of salami, and some walnuts. "It's Reyzel's lunch," I tell him.

"Gevalt! What are we going to do?"

"Can't you just burn that and call it even?"

"Bluma, this is no time for jokes! If we don't get our hametz back and burn it by noon, our house won't be kosher for Passover."

Actually, I wasn't joking, but I can see Sender is not going to take any shortcuts. Someone is going to have to drop what they're doing and get over to the grade school to trade bags with Reyzel. Since the school is two miles from here, the only way this will work by the deadline is on horseback. Sender will undoubtedly say he's too busy, and anyway, I don't want him to be the messenger. I can't imagine the difficulty he'll have explaining to Miss Dupont why he has such an urgent need for a bag full of breadcrumbs.

That leaves Morris, who, true to his word, has been learning to ride. This is still a work in progress. I've seen Morris seated on Balagan, walking around the corral, his slim body herky-jerky as the stallion paces. Still, we send Morris to the school like a soldier off to battle. After he mounts up, Sender gives Balagan a good swat on his hindquarters, and off the horse goes at a trot, with Morris valiantly clinging on to the reins and the pommel.

I don't know how Morris stayed in the saddle or what he told Miss Dupont when he finally arrived at the school, but somehow, he comes riding up to the house at about a quarter to twelve, gripping the precious bag of crusts. When he surrenders it to Sender, I can see his hands are shaking. Sender has already prepared the wood for a fire in the yard. He tosses the hametz on top and lights it with a fireplace match. We all stand around and watch till the breadcrumbs burn to ash, just a few minutes before midday. The holiday is saved.

Now that we've removed the hametz, I can bring the boxes of matzo from Cleveland into the kitchen. You would think we could make matzo at home. The recipe is easy enough: mix flour and water; bake. But, according to the Talmud, for matzo to be kosher, it must be finished—from mixing to rolling to baking—before it could possibly rise. How long is that? The rabbis say the time it takes to walk a *mil*. Now, no one is sure exactly what a mil was or how long it would have taken to walk it, but the rabbis settled on eighteen minutes.

For the matzo to be fully kosher, the flour must also be minded before the baking begins to make sure it doesn't come into contact with water or too much sun, which also might cause it to ferment. If this weren't strict enough, for the first Seder, Sender insists on having *shmure* matzo. For this special "watched matzo," even the wheat is guarded from the time the seeds are planted. No one ever accused the rabbis of the Talmud of being careless.

With the matzo squared away, there's still the matter of the kosher-for-Passover wine. Ordinary kosher wine will not do for this purpose. For the five years Jewish families have been farming in Geneva, Passover wine—in fact, all kosher wine—has come from Cleveland as well.

But not this year. Last fall, just before the grape harvest, Morris got Sender and Harold together to talk. "How much sense does it make," he asked, "for Concord grape growers such as ourselves to be buying wine? We should make it."

"What about Prohibition?" Sender wanted to know.

"It's perfectly legal to make wine for sacramental purposes." Morris had done all the research on the Eighteenth Amendment—of course. He also knew the rules that make wine kosher for Passover. He found a source for the proper yeast and a rabbi who would certify that our wine met all the requirements. Then he cleared out a space for the job in the cellar. The operation would pay for itself if we made enough to supply the other Geneva Jewish farmers as well.

So we are now, you should excuse the expression, vintners. Morris purchased a big wooden tub, and in batches, we put the grapes in it and stomped on them. Even Chaia enjoyed this chore, although our feet were stained purple for days. Miss Dupont was concerned that we'd bruised Reyzel's legs with some strange, foreign punishment. Teetotaler that she is, I'm not sure the true explanation made her feel any better, but we assured her that the resulting wine would only be used in religious ceremonies. After the grapes were crushed, Morris added some sugar and allowed the mixture to ferment for ten days. There followed several rounds of filtering over a period of three months.

The best part of the whole process was watching Morris and Sala grow closer as they worked together to make the wine. Suddenly Morris's pedantic tendencies turned out to be useful. You should have seen them taking the temperature of the juice, weaving new and better cloth for straining it, and, toward the end of the three months, sampling and giggling. One time I went down to the cellar to retrieve some potatoes, and I caught them kissing!

Finally, the wine was ready. We picked a Friday night dinner for the tasting. As a tribute to all her hard work, I had Sala light the Shabbas candles. I wish Sender had let Morris say the Kiddush, but he wasn't letting anyone usurp "his" blessing over the wine. He lifted his glass: "Blessed art Thou, O Lord our God, King of the universe, who creates the fruit of the vine."

It tasted delicious. I know some people think Concord grape wine is too sweet, but to me, this is what wine should taste like. Once, Marta Giordano gave me a shot from her secret stash of Chianti, and it was all I could do not to spit it out. Who wants a drink that tastes like tobacco and sour plums?

When Passover neared, we had more orders for our wine than we could fill. There was even money left over. I'm thinking about the saga of the winemaking as I retrieve a bottle for our Passover table. All the cooking and cleaning are done. We're all dressed in our best. We gather and begin to tell the story of the Exodus.

It's traditional for the youngest child in the family to chant "The Four Questions," which begin, "Why is this night different from all other nights?" Usually, a little boy gets this honor, but since we don't have one of those, the task has been Reyzel's since she was about four. After she finishes, Sender looks meaningfully at Sala and Morris. "Nu, my children, Reyzel is getting a little old for this job. When are we going to get someone to take it over?"

Sala's fair skin turns crimson, but Morris looks even prouder than he did when we tasted the wine. "We expect a new addition to the family in the fall."

"*In a mazldike sho,*" we all cry at once. "May it come to pass in a happy hour." Much hugging and jubilation has to happen before we can get back to the Seder. Between the four cups of our very own wine and the wonderful news about the baby, it's the most joyous Passover I can remember.

Our own exodus from Romania has started to feel like a good decision. Not that the American versions of the Egyptians have disappeared. The Klan is still going strong, with millions of members, especially in the Midwest. Morris read me an article about it in *The Ashtabula Star Beacon.* They threw a "konclave" at Buckeye Lake—a sort of picnic for bigots. Seventy thousand people attended. Of course, many of their events are not so peaceful. We still hear of Black people being lynched. And one day, Marta Giordano came to visit me in tears. The Klan had set off twelve bombs at the University of Dayton, a Catholic school not too far south of here.

At least Corbin Johnson is giving our place a wide berth. And we've found a community, not only among the other Jewish farmers but also with some of our neighbors like Marta and Ethel. With the success of the vineyard, the farm is beginning to make money. Even the match between Sala and Morris has turned out better than I ever expected. In all, I feel like we're coming out of the wilderness.

Chapter 20

SALA AND MORRIS'S BABY has names in three languages. To carry on the memory of Morris's father, his Hebrew name is Yitzkhak. At home, we call him by his Yiddish name, Itzik. The proud parents also wanted him to have an English name, so out in the wider world, he will be Isidore. Very fancy. We also have baby news from Hodel: Rosa Chava Bercovici, named for our mother of blessed memory. It seems 1924 has been a vintage year.

Speaking of vintages, Itzik was born in early September, just before the grape harvest. Our first winemaking experiment was so successful, that we decided to expand it and make wine for Shabbas as well as Passover. We set aside two hundred bushels. This put Sender in good spirits, you should excuse the pun. With the proceeds from the wine, he bought his new prized possession, a Victrola. There's a recording of the famous cantor Yossele Rosenblatt playing now.

"*Oy, a mekhaye*—such a pleasure—to hear Yossele Rosenblatt sing '*Eli, Eli*,'" Sender sighs. "Children, did you know that the great conductor Cleofonte Campanini begged Cantor Rosenblatt to sing for his opera company, but Rosenblatt told him he would only use his voice in the service of God?"

"Yes, Papa, and when Enrico Caruso heard Rosenblatt sing, he ran right up on the stage and kissed him. We've heard those stories ten times since you bought the record player," Chaia says cheekily.

"And you'll hear them another ten times if it pleases me to tell them. Do you have any idea what a miracle it is to hear a voice like this in the comfort of your own home?"

"Rosenblatt is a genius," Reyzel allows. "Now just imagine how wonderful it would be if we could also hear a great Jewish violinist like Leopold Auer."

"That will be our next record," Sender says. Reyzel plays her father even better than she does her violin.

I jump in and ask Sender a question I admit I've asked before. "Are you sure we can afford a record player and all these records? And what about that cantor you're bringing here for Yom Kippur? Isn't that going to be expensive?"

"We finally have almost forty Jewish families in Geneva, and you want Shloimie Ponsky to lead services again? May God forgive me for speaking ill of a pious man, but Ponsky sings through his nose. He sounds like a duck. Besides, what self-respecting Jewish community doesn't hire a cantor for Yom Kippur?"

Gone are the days when I could hold Sender to his promise to follow my plans for the farm and save money for new grape vines. As far as he's concerned, we're in the black now, and all previous agreements are canceled. I sigh.

"Bluma," Sender reassures me, "we've had, *Borukh Hashem*, a good year. Now we've got the whole north side of the hill in production, and the crop looks great. Money's coming in. Why even Chaia has her own little business tutoring children with more money than brains. I just set up a bank account for her."

It's true. Miss Dupont got the idea that Chaia could help some of the students who were struggling with their schoolwork. Chaia has made it into a going concern. "How much money have I got, Papa?" she asks.

Taking a bankbook from his vest pocket, Sender flips it open and answers, "twenty-six dollars."

"By the time I finish high school, I'm going to have enough money to go to college. Miss Dupont said if I keep doing well in school, I can get a scholarship for part of the tuition, and I know I can raise the rest of it."

"So you see, college *and* cantors. We're rich as Rothschild," Sender pronounces.

Sender doesn't really have the slightest interest in Chaia going to college. We don't know many young people who've gone on to higher education and certainly no girls. In fact, Sender made noises about pulling Chaia out of high school like he did with Sala—until I threatened to do what I've been contemplating off and on since I arrived in Geneva: leave and take the girls with me. That did the trick.

But college and cantors, records and record players—none of these are my real worry. "Okay," I allow, "a cantor is one thing. But buying Old

Man Custer's car? Sender, what do we need with a car? I think you're just trying to impress Harold Gold."

Surprisingly, it's Chaia who jumps to her father's defense. "Oh, Mama, it would make our lives so much easier. Papa could pick me up from the houses where I tutor, and it would save me hours on horseback."

I think but don't say: car or not, Sender will not be doing that. Now, Reyzel might be able to charm a few rides out of her father, as she tries to do now. "Papa could take me to my violin lessons," Reyzel adds. "By the time I get there on Balagan, I'm tired, and sometimes I have to come back when it's getting dark."

Even Morris piles on in his own gentle way. "We could use a car to start selling our wine in Cleveland."

"But Sender doesn't know how to drive a car," I protest.

"I learned how to drive a tractor. How hard can a car be?"

"Famous last words."

"*Genug Shoyn*," Sender snaps, his typical way of shutting down a conversation. "I'm going to buy Custer's Model T, and that's the end of the story." He marches out of the room, slamming the door and waking Itzik, who howls louder than Yossele Rosenblatt.

"Did you really need to spoil his fun?" Reyzel demands. "Papa says we have the money."

"As my mother, may she rest in peace, used to say, 'Don't sell the skin off the bear while he's still in the forest.'"

"Reyzel's right, Mama," Chaia chimes in. "You can't be so worried about money all the time. We're doing fine."

When Chaia and Reyzel, who usually fight like cats, are on the same side of an argument, I know I don't stand a chance. With another sigh, I get up and go into the kitchen. Handing Reyzel the still-squalling baby, Sala follows me. I remove a bowl from the oven, where my bread dough has been rising and start pummeling it on the kneading board.

Sala begins, "Don't be mad at them, Mama. They're too young to understand how things work around here." I grunt as I push on the dough, but she continues. "Reyzel still thinks Papa knows best about everything." I grunt and push. "Chaia doesn't realize that the money is coming in now because you had the idea to plant more grapes." Grunt. "Neither of them understands that you do the books and make sure the bills are paid."

I stop kneading for a moment. "Sala, do you know why I've always liked to bake bread?" I ask.

Sala is puzzled by this turn in the conversation, but she says, "Because it's a mitzvah?"

True enough. In Judaism, there are 613 mitzvahs, only three of which are special to women. One of those is to separate an olive-sized lump from the rest of the challah dough in memory of the sacrifices that were offered in the ancient Temple in Jerusalem.

I do take that pinch and burn it in the bottom of my oven. But to be honest, that's not the real reason I bake bread. More important, it gives me a way to work things out. I gather all my frustrations—a husband who's too busy studying the Talmud to pay attention to the bills, daughters who think I'm a scold—I take all that and hurl it at the bread.

When I explain this to Sala, I think she's a little shocked, especially when I tell her, "There are days when it doesn't hurt that the dough feels a lot like flesh. Better, I've always thought, to wallop flour and yeast than your family, however much they might deserve it." Scandalous, maybe, but true. In my mind, I yell at the dough: Oy, push; vey, fold. When I'm done, I take the ball and divide it and braid it and bake it, and all the anger turns into something beautiful.

#

True to his word, the next week Sender goes with Harold Gold to buy the old Model T from Frederick Custer. As he told me later, he and Gold did some serious negotiating until Custer gave in and sold the car for fifty dollars. Sender handed over the money and told Gold he could leave. Then he waited for Custer to return to his house before he tried to start the car.

"You didn't ask Mr. Custer to show you how it worked?"

"I should tell a *goy* I don't know how to drive?"

"And you didn't ask Harold?"

"That blowhard?"

Sender might have gotten away with his pride intact. He did know how to crank the engine from watching Harold. As he'd reminded me, he drove a tractor, and the car wasn't all that different, except for one thing: stopping. Sender knew that the way to stop a tractor was to take your foot off the gas. Our Fordson tractor is a huge beast, and without fuel, it slows down pretty quickly. Cars, we were all to find out, don't work that way.

All we saw at first was Sender's grand entrance in the Model T. He started beeping the horn as he drove up the dirt drive toward the house.

He'd cleared a space for the car in the barn, and we all ran toward it to see his triumphant return. Grinning and waving, he rode toward the barn and took his foot off the accelerator. The car didn't slow. As he approached the barn door at speed, we heard him yelling, "Whoa, you bastard. Whoa!" Unfortunately, the car didn't understand English. It ran right through its designated space toward a pile of farm equipment, where it was finally slowed down by a spike-toothed harrow.

Once more, Morris put his research skills to good use. At the Geneva public library, he found a book that explained how to brake and also how to fix four flat tires. He tried to pound out the dent in the grill and fix the fender, but the car still looks like an old man with broken teeth and only one eyebrow.

When Sender is finally up and running again, I can't contain my curiosity. I risk his ire and ask, "Why did you yell at the car in English instead of Yiddish?"

"Bluma," he says with total seriousness, "that car is definitely not Jewish."

#

Sender's other investment—in the circuit-riding cantor—is about to bear fruit. It's Yom Kippur, and the house is so full of people, it feels like the walls will bow. We're hosting the service that gives voice to our hope we may be forgiven for the sins we committed over the past year.

Our kitchen has been crawling with women, each one bearing a platter of some delicacy we'll eat when the fast of Yom Kippur ends tomorrow evening. There are bagels and cream cheese, kugels, bowls of herring, honey cakes, and—my contribution—three huge, coiled challahs studded with raisins. Many of the women just drop off their dishes and head home. We're not required by Jewish law to attend the service, so anyone with young children will be taking care of them today. We'll also look after the farm animals, who don't know from Jewish holidays; they still have to be fed and milked.

The men are milling around in the parlor, where we've replaced the furniture with borrowed, mismatched chairs. The men will occupy these. The women who stay will stand in the back or sit in the kitchen. By tradition, men and women don't pray together, lest the men become distracted by some lovely ankle or stray curl of hair. To my mind, that's a problem the men ought to be able to deal with, but nobody asked me.

At one end of the room is a portable ark, made by Marvin Lev. The cabinet is fashioned from oak with the lion of Judah inlaid on the front in cherry wood. While we all know Marvin is a rumrunner, bringing whiskey from Canada across Lake Erie into Geneva, we figure it's a minor sin. Besides, Marvin is a maven when it comes to carpentry. As the saying goes, if you need a thief, you might be willing to take him off the gallows.

From the *tararam* in the kitchen, I can't really hear what's going on in the parlor until Harold Gold's voice rises above the others. "Do you know anything about this Cantor Kolowitz that Rappaport is bringing out to lead the service?"

"He came to my Cousin Morty's shul for the High Holidays last year," Mr. Kaminsky answers. "Morty said the '*Koyl Nidre*' was the best he'd ever heard."

"Best he'd ever heard? Your cousin must have grown up in Cleveland. He should have heard the cantors we had back in Europe."

"Well, whatever kind of cantor this Kolowitz is, he and Sender better get here soon, or they'll end up traveling on the holiest day of the year," Shloimie Ponsky adds. "Of course, in a pinch, I could always lead the service."

"That won't be necessary," Morris says quickly. "I hear them coming up the drive now."

From the sound of it, Sender is approaching at his usual breakneck clip. We all crowd onto the porch to greet them. There's a screech of brakes, and Sender hops from the driver's seat. Much more slowly, Cantor Kolowitz struggles out. Burly, with the kind of barrel chest that makes for fine, resonant chanting, Kolowitz has ginger hair and, at least at the moment, a pasty white complexion. He's not an old man, but his legs buckle, as if they're too weak to hold him. He drops to his knees and, much to our surprise, puts his lips to the earth.

"I always thought the first time I'd kiss the ground would be when I finally got to visit the Holy Land," he says shakily. "With that driving, I'm just grateful to arrive in Geneva in one piece!" He staggers to his feet.

"Oh, come now, Cantor. It's true, we tipped over when that *yuts* blocked my way outside of Madison, but we were easily righted. We just had to wait for another car to come by and help. That's why we're a little late."

"We only tipped over once, but what about that time you got lost and drove through a wheat field to get back on the right road? I might have to settle here in Geneva, because I don't think I'll survive the ride back into Cleveland with that mishugener."

Harold jumps in. "Don't worry, Cantor. I'll drive you back in my roadster when the holiday is over. In the meantime, please, let's start the service. It'll be sundown soon."

Kolowitz still seems short of breath, but he obliges, with Harold leading the way into our house and the rest of us trailing like ducklings. Sender, however, is not to be upstaged in his own home. "Before the holiday starts," he says, "I'd like us all to raise a glass to celebrate the visit of the fine *khazn* I brought to Geneva, Avram Kolowitz of Berdechev. We make this schnapps from our own peaches."

All of the men take a small glass from a table in the corner. Kolowitz says the blessing quickly and gulps down a grateful snort. "Ah!" he says, seeming steadier. "Let's begin." He stands at a small table facing the ark and, opening his book, begins to chant, his singing as magnificent as Kaminsky promised. It sounds like the ancient voice of longing itself:

"Koyl Nidre, Ve'esare, Ush'vue—"

Suddenly Cantor Kolowitz stops and listens intently. The women begin whispering, but no one can figure out what might be the matter. In a moment, he begins chanting again, *"Koyl Nidre, Ve'esare—"*

Once again, the cantor stops mid-phrase and cocks his head. We hear only Bubale mooing from the barn.

"Rappaport," the cantor demands, "what is that sound?"

"That, my dear Cantor Kolowitz, is a cow. You were expecting maybe Yossele Rosenblatt?"

#

Cantor Kolowitz has been at it for hours, with just a short break this afternoon and no water to ease his parched throat. Other peoples may have champion athletes; Jews have heroic *daveners*. We've reached the final service of the holiday, when the gates of heaven are supposed to be closing, and we rush to squeeze in one last prayer for forgiveness. Kolowitz and the men are chanting *Avinu Malkeynu*. Over and over, they repeat the refrain: "Our Father, our King, have mercy on us, answer us, for our deeds are not enough." The music sounds like it's hammering on the doors of the Almighty himself.

From my seat in the kitchen, I'm thinking about my deeds. I scrub and pump, mend and iron, bake and hoe. These seem like very small accomplishments to throw into the balance against my misdeeds: the sharp tongue, the stubbornness, the jealousy. For hours, I've been trying to atone, but the whole machinery of Yom Kippur feels too daunting. I'm hungry and more cranky than repentant. "Our Father, our King," I scoff. Who goes to their father when they need forgiveness? Suddenly I have a vision of my mother reciting the women's devotions she used to say while she waited for my father to come home from shul. One comes to me now: "God, grant me a good heart and good thoughts so that I may be at peace with my sins."

"Amen," I say.

Chapter 21

SENDER AND I ARE sitting in our usual places on the porch, looking out at the farm. We can just see the oldest grapevines beginning to set fruit, the immature globes green and spiky like bottle brushes. Over the past year, Sala and Morris have turned the vineyard into a thriving business, providing kosher wine to all the farmers in Geneva, and through Cousin Mendel, to many of the kosher markets in Cleveland. Sender is anxious to show the property off to Reuben Pincus, a representative of the Jewish Agricultural Society, who's touring the farms the JAS has supported in Northern Ohio.

"You're sure that applesauce cake will be out of the oven in time?" he demands nervously.

"Already done."

"And the girls have weeded the back garden?"

"Yes, Sender." As it happens, I was out there to pick early peas this morning, and the vegetables were flourishing, the silver-gray carrot fronds and pepper leaves trembling in the breeze.

But Sender is not through worrying. "Did Reyzel tie up the dog?"

"Sender, we aren't expecting a visit from the Messiah, only Mr. Pincus."

"May God forgive me for saying so, but Reuben Pincus is almost as important to us as the Messiah. He can teach us some new methods. It's 1925, Bluma. Time to modernize."

"Are you sure you don't want Morris to be part of this tour? He knows more about the vineyard than anyone."

"Morris is a good boy, but he's still a *pisher*. He hasn't been here from the beginning like I have. Do you think maybe Pincus will write something in his newsletter about me?"

"Well, he's already crowned Harold Gold the Grape King. Maybe he could make you the Grape Tsar."

"Shah, now! Pincus is coming."

Reuben Pincus is huffing up the drive, his suit dusty from the cuffs to the knees. Why he's wearing a suit to tour farms, I cannot guess. And he's carrying a briefcase!

Sender bounds down the steps to shake his hand. "You must be Mr. Pincus. *Sholem aleykhem.*"

A portly man, Pincus is panting and has to wait a moment before he speaks. "*Aleykhem sholem*, Mr. Rappaport. Glad to be here. I decided to walk from the Cohen's place, but it was a little farther than I imagined."

"Of course, of course."

I can see that Sender isn't going to introduce me, so I speak up. "I'm Sender's wife, Bluma. You must sit a minute and have a glass of iced tea with maybe a *kleyn shtikl* applesauce cake. The apples are from our own trees."

"That sounds lovely."

Pincus takes the chair I've vacated while I pop into the house for the cake. The kitchen is thick with the fragrance of cinnamon and clove, and the cake, with its dusting of sugar, looks, if I do say so myself, like it came from the bakery. When I return to the porch, Mr. Pincus is reminiscing. "I remember when you bought this place, Rappaport. It was in pretty rough shape. I'll be frank. In the beginning, I wasn't sure you'd make it. Now I understand you're supplying Shabbas wine for the whole district. You've done wonders."

I'd love for Sender to give a little credit to the rest of the family, especially Morris, but instead he says, "The Fordson tractor helped with that, thanks to the loan from the JAS."

Pincus is happy to join in the mutual congratulations. "And you've helped the JAS," he says. "I understand there are now fifty Jewish families in Geneva."

My mother, may she rest in peace, would have warned them, "Don't break your arm patting your own back."

At this moment, Reyzel peeks her head out the door. She's just back from school, still wearing her shirtwaist, and of course, a pair of matching bows.

"Come, come, Zisele," Sender says expansively. "Come and meet Mr. Pincus from the Jewish Agricultural Society. A very important man. Mr. Pincus, my daughter Reyzel."

"What a very lovely daughter she is!"

"And talented. A budding violinist. Reyzel, play a little something for Mr. Pincus."

"Oh, no, Papa. The gentleman doesn't want to hear me perform," Reyzel protests, clearly for form's sake.

Like a jovial uncle, Pincus insists. Always thrilled to have an opportunity to show off, Reyzel ducks into the house and comes out with her violin. She's decided to play the piece she's been working on—very flashy and very long. Raising her bow, she jumps in, her braids flying. Pincus's smile is broad, but as the piece goes on, the edges begin to sag. Sender is oblivious, but after a few minutes, I interrupt.

"All right, Reyzel, enough with the violin. Mr. Pincus has come on important business. He doesn't have time for little nudniks."

"Not at all, Mrs. Rappaport. She was charming," Pincus says, but I can see the gratitude in his eyes.

"Well, now she's done being charming. Reyzel, go do your homework."

Reyzel, her feathers ruffled, retreats into the house, with Sender smiling benevolently after her. Pincus has finished the last of his snack. Reaching into his briefcase, he digs out a leaflet and hands it to me. "Mrs. Rappaport, your applesauce cake was delicious. Perhaps you'd like this information about the many things you can do with fruit peelings and seeds."

"Thank you," I say trying to sound enthusiastic.

"The JAS is anxious to support the ladies in our farm communities. I always say, every successful farm has a woman in the center of it, making the house a home."

"A lot of the farms around here have women in the fields," I protest.

Ignoring me, Pincus goes back to talking with Sender. "Now that I'm fortified by that excellent cake, I'm ready for a tour. I have some new methods that'll make your farm outproduce anything you've ever seen."

"Wait just a second," I say. "I'll get my boots."

Sender gives me a look. "We won't need your help with this."

"Men's talk you know," Pincus says, "about fertilizer and yields—boring topics for a lady such as yourself." His ruddy face breaks into a patronizing smile.

"I assure you, I won't be bored."

"Bluma, don't you have work to do in the kitchen?" Sender asks pointedly.

I know when I'm licked. Watching Sender and Pincus stride off toward the vineyard, schmoozing happily, I return to the kitchen, not so happily.

#

Washing Mr. Pincus's dishes, I ignore the daggers Reyzel is staring at me. Finally, I make a peace offering. "Here, Mamele, have some cake."

Grudgingly, Reyzel takes a slice. As she eats, she softens. "Mmm. You are the best baker."

"A shame to waste it on that *shmegege*, Pincus."

"Why do you think he's silly? Papa was excited about him coming. He's supposed to teach us how to get higher yields."

"There, even a twelve-year-old girl understands yields. But Mr. Pincus is only interested in talking to men, like your father, who's as much of a maven about yields as our horse is about music."

"Mama! How can you talk about Papa that way? He knows everything about farming."

I can see I've done too good a job protecting Reyzel from the realization that Sender knows a lot more about the Talmud than he knows about grapes. Well, I suppose it's proper that a girl should respect her father, so I say, "Don't mind me, Reyzel. What's that you're reading?"

She flips to the cover: "*The Girl's Reading Book* by Mrs. L.H. Sigourney."

"Nu, read me a little."

In her best declamatory style, Reyzel begins: "'A good education is that which prepares us for our future sphere of action.'" I nod my head judiciously. "'A warrior or a statesman requires a different kind of training from a mother or the instructress of a school. A lady who has many accomplishments, yet is deficient in the science of housekeeping, has not been well educated. A good education makes us contented with our lot and helps prepare—'"

"Oy! Mrs. L.H. Sigourney is worse than Mr. Reuven Pincus," I break in. "Reyzel, I don't care what the book says. Being contented with your lot in life means never trying to make it better. That's something everyone should do, not just warriors and statesmen."

At that moment, the front door slams, and Sender strides into the kitchen, full of purpose.

"So, what pearls of wisdom did Mr. Pincus have for you?" I ask.

"Well, first he told me they've started a branch of the Women's Christian Temperance Union in Geneva. Just what we need—a bunch of meddling yentas preaching against drinking. If they really get going, that'll be the end of our vineyard."

"Don't make such a big deal. Our wine is strictly for sacramental purposes, like Kiddush. And Mrs. Giordano's priest bought some for Mass. That's totally legal."

"That won't hold much water with the yentas."

"Oh, I don't know," I say. "I happen to be a member of the union."

Sender and Reyzel look at me like I've lost my mind. "You joined the Women's *Christian* Temperance Union?" Sender says. "What do you want with that *goyishe meshugas*? Don't we Jews have enough craziness of our own?"

"Joining didn't cost me anything, and it made the neighbors happy," I say placidly. The truth is, I signed on because Miss Dupont is the president of the local chapter, and she's been so good to the girls. Also, I understand the problem. There isn't much alcoholism in the Jewish community, but I've seen women and even children in Geneva trying to haul their menfolk out of the saloons. Miss Dupont told me a few horror stories about students in her class who come to school hungry because their fathers spend everything on drink. But Reyzel doesn't need to know all that. To change the subject, I ask, "What else did Pincus tell you?"

"He said we have a lot of unused acreage on the south side of the hill. If we put some new vines there, they'll get more sun and fruit earlier. We could extend our growing season. All the vintners in California are doing it."

"Sender, I think we should ask the county agricultural agent. Ohio is not California."

"So what? What difference could that make?

"I don't know. Maybe the plants will fruit earlier, but they could also be in danger from our earlier frosts."

"Bluma, Reuben Pincus is an expert on farming. I trust his advice more than yours. He also told me he knows a man who has some cuttings to sell. If we refinance the farm, we'll have enough to plant the whole hillside."

"Oh, Sender, no! Record players and Model T Fords we can maybe afford, but taking money out of the farm?"

"What no? You have to spend money to make money, Pincus says."

"And I say we still haven't paid off what we already owe. You can't do this."

"Since when do you make the decisions? I'm the head of the house. As soon as I get the loan, I'm going over to buy the vines."

"It's too late to plant this year. The vines won't have a chance to root before the cold weather sets in. I'm telling you, this is not a good idea."

"I didn't ask you."

Sender turns on his heel and leaves the kitchen. To his retreating back, I holler, "But you should have."

Chapter 22

USUALLY I CAN PERSUADE Sender that my plans were actually his ideas in the first place, but I lost the battle of the vines. In the end, maybe he was right. The new plants are thriving. In fact, everything is humming along on the farm. Our Shabbas table offers a bounty of spring produce: lettuces and peas, even lamb from our neighbors, the Cohens. As Sala opens the door to bring in the challahs, the smell of bread rushes through the parlor, and along with it, a powerful memory of my mother setting her braided loaves on the Shabbas table with great ceremony. The challah cover she wove is one of the few possessions I managed to bring with me from Europe. In the center are the Hebrew words, *Zakhor es yom haShabbas l'kodsho*. Remember the Sabbath day to keep it holy. I think this is a very astute Commandment. Remembering is actually what makes something holy, passing it from one generation to the next.

Morris pours some of the new batch of wine into the glass decanter he bought for Sala on their last anniversary. Always oblivious to whatever work is going on in the house, Sender is spoiling Reyzel. They're going to play cards right up to the moment the Sabbath begins.

"Gin!" Reyzel shouts, laying out her hand. When Sender puts his cards down and she begins to count points, she realizes he could have won himself, probably several drawings from the pot earlier. "But look, Papa, you also have a hundred points. Why didn't you gin?"

"I guess I just forgot how to count!"

"Sender, what are you teaching the child with this narishkayt? That it's okay to cheat as long as it's in her favor?"

"That her papa loves her more than winning."

"Funny, you never taught me that lesson," Chaia mutters.

129

"Maybe because you never thought you had anything to learn from me."

"I think so much love is maybe not good for Reyzel," I venture.

Sala laughs. "Mama, stop pretending to be so stern. We all spoil Reyzel; that's just how it is." She lifts Itzik onto her hip, something of a feat as she is pregnant with her second child. "Time to put away the cards. Come to the table and let's welcome the Sabbath before this one faints from hunger."

We take our places. We've all brought a few coins to the table, which we slip into our charity box. That's the last we'll have to do with money until the Sabbath is over. Now, covering my head with my shawl, I light the candles. Extending my hands over them, I make three circling motions to invite the Sabbath into myself and my home. I close my eyes and say the blessing.

As we raise our wine glasses, Sender intones the Kiddush, and we all say amen. Last, Reyzel uncovers the challahs and lifts them up. Sender draws a knife over them in a cutting gesture and prays: "Blessed art Thou, O Lord, our God, King of the Universe, who brings forth bread from the earth." He breaks and passes the challah.

Happy with his crust of bread, Itzik is ready to climb onto his mother's diminishing lap and have dinner. But before the meal can start, Sender says, "Reyzel, Ketsele, sing to us that song I like from the Yossele Rosenblatt album— 'A Dudele.'"

Chaia, who'd just been reaching for the lamb, sighs loudly. Reyzel smirks at her and then stands primly at her place. She launches into "A Dudele" in a twelve-year-old's imitation of high cantorial style.

> Ruler of the Universe
> I want to sing a little song for You.
> You, You, You, You, You.

This a song with many verses, each of them about the search for God: further, closer; east, west; heaven, earth. Every time Reyzel seems to be winding down, Chaia starts to pass the food but has to put it down when she realizes the song isn't over. Finally, Reyzel gets to the climax:

> Wherever I turn
> Wherever I look
> You—You!

"Ot azoy, Reyzel." Sender compliments her. "Your singing brings tears to my eyes."

"Mine too," says Chaia. "Let's eat."

No sooner have we finally begun passing the food when there's a sharp knock at the door.

"Who could that be on a Friday night?" Sender harrumphs, annoyed at being disturbed on Shabbas. He approaches the door with a scowl on his face, but it turns into slack-jawed surprise. Standing on our porch is Sheriff James McComber. I thought McComber was a big man when I visited him in his office, but because I'm so short, most men seem big to me. Seeing him next to Sender, I realize he's Goliath, and the tall fedora he wears only makes him more imposing. He removes his hat, ducks a little, and enters the room.

"Good evening, folks. I'm James McComber, the sheriff of Ashtabula County. How's everyone doing tonight?" We all murmur some version of a polite "fine" except for Itzik who is fussing with hunger.

I stand at my place. "Sheriff McComber," I say calmly. "*Borukh Habo*, as we say in our language. Blessed is the one who comes. Just now we sat down to our Sabbath meal. We would be honored you should join us." The rest of the family are staring intently at their plates. Knowing what they do about the sheriff's refusal to do anything after the cross burning, I'm sure none of them can imagine anyone they'd less like to share Shabbas dinner with. I can hear their thoughts shrieking, What in the name of all that is holy can Mama be thinking?

McComber takes a leisurely look around, his eye lighting on the decanter of wine. "As it happens, Mrs. Rappaport, I've already eaten. But I hear rumors that you make some fine wine here on your farm. I wouldn't mind having a glass of that."

"But . . . but what about Prohibition?" stammers Sender.

I'm not sure why McComber is here. To try to shut down our winemaking operation by finding us in breach of the law? To pay me back for refusing to be a pushover last time we met? To harass the Jewish complainers? I can't guess, but I decide to play along. "Don't mind my husband, Sheriff. Of course you will have some *vayn*." Fetching an extra chair from the side of the room, I squeeze it in between mine and Sender's. Then I pour a large beaker of wine. Everyone stares as I place the beaker in front of the sheriff and he begins to lift it. But before he can put the wine to his lips, I break in. "Just one minute, Sheriff. Maybe you don't know this, but I am a member of the Women's Christian Temperance Union." Clearly this is news. He leans back in his chair, folds his hands over his chest, and smiles warily. I continue, "Our *vayn* is only for *secrementl* purposes. Before you should drink, you have to say a blessing."

The sheriff is momentarily dumbstruck. Then he grins broadly. "You mean like 'Good bread, good meat, good Lord, let's eat'?"

Again, he lifts the glass, and again, I stop him. I take a leather-bound book from Sender's place and put it in front of him. Pointing at a passage, I say, "What a lovely prayer you said, Sheriff, but for this *vayn*, you have to say this blessing."

McComber peers at the text. "What are these squiggles, Mrs. Rappaport?"

"Those squiggles are Hebrew, Sheriff. Before we drink *vayn*, we say those Hebrew words."

McComber gives me a long look. Then, bursting into laughter, he says, "Mrs. Rappaport, I can see I'm going to have to study up before I visit you again." He hands me back the beaker of wine and tips his hat. "I'll just say goodnight. You folks have a blessed Sabbath." Then, like a hobgoblin in a fairytale, he disappears out the door.

Chapter 23

SALA IS SO PREGNANT now, her belly arrives in the room before she does. Labor can't be far off, a day Sala has been dreading since Morris got involved in it. While generally Morris is a much more reasonable man than my own dear husband, he's still a man, with a man's tendency to assume he knows best about everything. Including childbirth. Despite the fact that I've given birth to three children and Sala to one, all at home with the help of a midwife, Morris has decided that for this baby, Sala must go to the new Memorial Hospital in Geneva.

You see, Morris is a man of science. Though some might say that's incompatible with being a religious person, Morris begs to differ. God made the universe, but it operates according to scientific principles. The customs Jewish women have practiced for centuries to insure a safe labor he pooh-poohs as mere folk superstitions.

For her first pregnancy, Sala was attended by Dov Fishkin's wife, Clara, a midwife who has delivered scores of babies. Weeks before Itzik came into this world, Clara gave Sala a *kimpetbrivl*: a small parchment inscribed with the names of the angels Senoy, Sansenoi, and Semangalof, who protect women in childbirth. She was supposed to hang it above her bed. When Morris saw it, he took it down and threw it away. This amulet, he insisted, was not Judaism but heretical nonsense that seeped into our religion during the Babylonian exile. I'd say anything Jewish women have used for two thousand years might have some value, but what do I know?

Whatever Morris thought, when Sala went into labor with Itzik, Clara was in charge. A strong woman, with the forearms of a wrestler and the voice of a town crier, Clara started her reign by barring the men from the premises. Then she had us undo all the ties and knots in Sala's clothes and

133

open all the doors in the house—good omens for a speedy and easy delivery. With charcoal, she drew a circle around the birthing room to guard against the evil eye. Finally, she slipped Sala a new kimpetbrivl, which Sala held on to until it disintegrated in her sweaty hand.

Do I believe these charms and talismans actually work? Probably not, but I'll tell you what I do believe: when a woman goes into labor, she enters a dangerous world, one men never experience. Everything narrows down to the agony her body has become. Time pulsates with every contraction of her womb. All the terrible stories she's heard about women and infants dying in childbirth retell themselves in her pain-addled mind. At such a time, if a woman wants to hang on to a kimpetbrivl, I don't see why her husband would stop her.

But now that we have a little money, Morris is determined the newest addition to the family will have all the benefits that the shiny, new, *scientific* hospital can offer. Sala has already seen the baby doctor there, Henry Entwistle. No matter that having a man other than her husband see her naked body had her blushing for a week. Dr. Entwistle has given Morris strict instructions that once Sala's contractions begin, he is to time them and wait until they are no more than four minutes apart, each one lasting at least a minute. "Only when that pattern has been maintained for an hour should you come to the hospital," he decreed.

I'm sure this is very good advice for women who live in Geneva proper. We live ten miles outside, a twenty-five-minute drive on the best day. Also, I try to explain to Morris that second babies can come much faster than the twelve hours Itzik took to make his appearance, but I'm not a doctor, so my opinions hold no water. Neither, apparently, does Sala's desire to give birth at home with Clara Fishkin by her side. Could she put her foot down? On many issues, yes, but Morris has decided this one is a test of his love. The hospital, he argues, will give her ether to put her to sleep during labor, so she won't feel any pain at all. She and the baby will have access to all the most advanced procedures, like forceps delivery. How could she say no?

For the weeks prior to her due date, Dr. Entwistle prescribes lots of rest. Even Morris realizes this is a fantasy. It's August, the peaches are in, the cucumbers have to be pickled, and the farm stand is seeing its heaviest traffic yet. Chaia and Reyzel take on as much extra work as they can, but Sala is still standing over pots of simmering fruit or brining dill pickles, no matter how her ankles swell. In addition, every few days, she and Morris go inspect their grapevines, monitoring them for late-season rot.

It's on one of these trips up the hill to look at the grapes that Sala goes into labor. It begins with such a sharp pain that Sala wants to go back to the house to lie down. Patiently, Morris reminds her that they need to wait for the next contraction to see how far apart they're coming. Morris has been carrying a pocket watch for just this purpose. He reassures her, "Dr. Entwistle said walking is very good exercise in the early stage of labor." Taking her elbow, he guides her up to the next row of plants. In fact, the next contraction doesn't come for another ten minutes, but when it does, it knocks the wind out of her. She slumps to the ground for the thirty seconds it lasts. "Sala, you're doing well," Morris cheers her on. "Let's see when the next contraction comes." She struggles to her feet, and they continue down the row for six minutes, when the next labor pain makes Sala double over. Now even Morris is ready to concede that it's time to go back home. They're about a ten-minute walk from the house, though they have to stop on the way back for Sala to wait out a contraction.

Chaia and I are in the garden picking tomatoes when I see them coming. Sala is the color of paste. As she approaches, she crumples and lets out a sharp gasp. I've seen labor before, and I know we're already past the early stage. "Let me get Clara Fishkin," I plead with Morris. "It won't be long now."

"No, we're going to Geneva Memorial." His voice is full of confidence. "We should get there just in time for the birth."

"Then we're going with you." Morris can tell from my tone that this is not a matter for debate. He brings the Model T out of the barn. Chaia and I help Sala into the back seat, where she can lie against my shoulder and put her feet across Chaia's lap. Before we're even down the dirt road from our house, Sala has another contraction, contorting her body. Her water breaks while we're barreling toward Geneva, soaking herself and Chaia. Her contractions are now lasting a minute or more. We're barely four miles from the farm when we hit a deep pothole and hear the telltale hiss of air going out of a tire.

By now Morris's voice sounds more desperate than confident. Pulling off to the side of the road, he promises, "I'll have the tire fixed in a minute, and we can go on to the hospital."

I'm done humoring him. "Genug shoyn!" I declare. "This baby is not going to wait for you." From that point on, I ignore Morris and concentrate on my daughter. "Don't you worry, Sala. We're going to deliver this child together. Chaia, you take my place here behind Sala's back." There's some scrambling as we exchange places and I position myself between Sala's knees. I slip her a little kimpetbrivl I had Clara make for her weeks ago. She places it under her dress, next to her heart. "All right, sweetheart, you've done this before," I tell her. "When the next contraction comes, we're going to start breathing together."

The grunts and screams coming out of Sala have chased Morris down the road, where he sits with his head in his hands. Chaia and I are completely focused on Sala. Chaia takes off her petticoat and uses it to wipe the sweat from Sala's face and shoulders. I've got mine ready to catch the baby whenever he or she decides to join us.

For three hours, we're stopped by the side of the road. Fortunately, Morris came to a halt under a large maple tree, or the three of us would probably have fainted from the August heat. I alternate between cajoling and commanding as Sala takes what, ultimately, is a solitary journey. Near the end, she says, "Mama, I can't do it anymore. I'm dying."

"You only wish it were so," I say, smiling as I remember that point in all three of my labors. In another minute, the baby's head crowns, and from there, things happen fast. With a final push from Sala, the baby emerges, slick and bloody. I give her bottom a patsh, and she lets out a healthy cry. "Yes, yes," I croon as I wrap her in my slip and give her to her mother, "I understand. It's hard to be a woman in this world."

Chapter 24

THERE REALLY WAS NO warning. September was mostly balmy—temperatures in the sixties and even the seventies. The first days of October brought the same Indian summer weather. The apples were so bountiful, the branches drooped. We were harvesting every day, enjoying the sweetness of corn on the cob and squashes, their taste as variable as where they grew in the garden.

And the grapes! Big, thick clusters swelled on the vines. Morris was tasting them every day, just waiting for the perfect moment to begin picking them. Even the new vines Sender put in were doing well. We wouldn't get a crop from them for three or four years, but the stock was healthy. We had one day of cold, but nothing remarkable. Afterwards, the thermometer climbed back into safe territory.

That's why it's such a shock this morning when I pad down to the kitchen and notice frost crazing the windowpanes. I run back upstairs and shake Sender awake.

Grabbing a kerosene lantern, we rush to the vineyard. Even in the weak light, we can make out the damage. The leaves on the vines are curled and pale. A coating of rime clings to the grapes. "Vey iz mir!" Sender cries. "We've got to wake Morris and the girls and get them out here picking. We'll harvest as much as we can before things get worse. I'll grab a few baskets and start harvesting at the top of the hill."

I don't know if we'll be able to get any help. All the other farmers will be in the same boat, and there won't be enough pickers to go around. Racing back to the house, I get everyone out of bed. "We need to bring in the grapes," I tell them. "The temperature dropped last night, and we can't leave the crop out in this weather." Someone has to watch Itzik and the baby, Rifka, so I assign Reyzel to childcare and tell everyone else to wear their warmest clothes. In a few minutes, we're all assembled on the porch. Dawn is just breaking, though it's hard to tell because of the clouds. It's begun to snow, the flakes blowing onto the porch in a wicked wind. The ground is already dusted with white.

"Go meet your father at the top of the hill and start working," I tell them. "I'll get the wagon and set the rest of the baskets."

I coax Barney out of his stall and hitch him up. Steering with one hand, I reach into the back and throw a basket at the end of each row. The horse nickers in the cold, his breath condensing into a little cloud around his muzzle. It's a hard pull up the icy hill, but Barney is a trooper. He waits patiently at the top while Sender and the girls fill the wagon with the grapes they've managed to pick so far.

We fan out over the rows, hoping to save as much of the crop as possible. I can tell where everyone is from the steam that rises from their breath. The girls and I wear fingerless gloves; Sender and Morris are bare-handed. Everyone's skin turns red and chapped. With numb fingers, we detach the grape clusters and place them in the baskets, which we then ferry to the end of the rows to be picked up by the wagon on the trip back down to the barn. The snow is still whirling around us, not thick but mean.

We pick for four hours. At lunchtime, Sender gets on the driver's box of the wagon, and we all crowd into the back. As we ride down to the barn, Morris jumps off at each row and retrieves the full baskets. The pace is excruciatingly slow, but finally we make it. We gulp down the cream cheese sandwiches Reyzel has prepared for us. Then we return to the vines for another five hours of misery.

The next day, the snow is heavier. We had hoped to get some help today, but the pickers refuse to even come out in this weather. This time, Sender hitches Barney to the bobsled, and the horse gamely hauls it up the hill. We all grab baskets and begin the task of picking again. Popping a grape in my mouth, I bite down. It's like chewing flavored ice. "Frozen," I say, trying to keep the desperation out of my voice. The white-frosted globes are beautiful but unnatural. They ping as they hit the baskets.

"This can't be good," Chaia says to me as the bobsled jounces the clinking fruit.

"No, *Hartsele*, it isn't good."

As the day wears on, it gets harder and harder to see. My breath condenses on my shawl, which holds the cold wetness against my mouth; it's as if the storm itself were smothering me. The tips of Morris's ears have turned crimson. We'll be lucky if he doesn't have frostbite. Sala, still not back to her full strength after Rifka's birth, pushes herself until she collapses in the snow. We send her back to the house, and Reyzel comes to replace her.

"Mama," she says when she reaches us, "what's that noise? It sounds like marbles rolling around."

"These cold temperatures came so early, the grapes have frozen. You're hearing them bounce around in the wagon."

"Frozen? Are they spoiled?"

I don't want Reyzel to be as frantic as I am. "No, Mamele," I say. "Don't worry. Frozen grapes can be made into ice wine. They did it back in Romania. It's special—sweet like candy." Chaia looks at me, disgusted by my attempt to protect Reyzel, but she holds her peace. She's busy managing Balagan, whom she's recruited to help bring in the fruit. The stallion whinnied indignantly when she hitched him to a cart this morning, as though such work were beneath him.

Morris busies himself with the baskets. He's already brought Sender and me a grim report from the far side of the hill. I notice Chaia listening as he tells us that most of the new vines are lost. Morris, of course, has the scientific explanation: because of the alternating heat and cold of the last week, the water in the soil has expanded and contracted, pushing the plants and their roots out of the earth. With the roots exposed, the cold has killed the young plants.

This hopeless harvesting is our life for four days. Worse than that, no one wants to buy our fruit. Finally, a purchasing agent shows up at the barn, where we negotiate the paltry price of twenty-nine dollars a ton. As Sender and I make our way back to the house, I paste on my best smile. The girls and Morris are waiting at the door. "How did it go?" Reyzel wants to know. Sender's answer is to wearily mount the steps to our bedroom.

"We sold six tons and made $174. Not bad," I tell her with as much enthusiasm as I can muster.

That's the last straw for Chaia. "Mama! You have to stop babying her. She's twelve years old. She'll know soon enough that this turn in the weather has been a disaster."

"But Mama said we could make ice wine from the frozen grapes."

"Maybe we can make ice wine, though it's not what people use for Kiddush, so who will buy it? Then we also have to sell grapes. And because of Prohibition, no one but us is interested in grapes for any kind of wine. They want table grapes, and frozen grapes aren't table grapes."

"But somebody bought them," Reyzel protests.

"Yes. Today, someone finally bought six tons for $174," Chaia scoffs. "If we don't make at least $80 a ton, we don't break even. I know Miss Dupont taught you enough arithmetic to realize that doesn't add up."

By this time, Reyzel is sobbing. Sala breaks in. "Chaia, that's enough."

"I wish that were all. The frost took most of the new vines Papa put in this summer. They're dead."

"Mama was right! It *was* too late to plant," Reyzel cries.

"She usually is, but you're such a daddy's girl you never see it," Chaia carps at her.

"Chaia, you have to stop now," I say softly. "This is not Reyzel's fault." I draw my youngest to me and wipe a tear that's drifting down her cheek. "Reyzel, don't cry anymore. Chaia isn't angry at you. It's just been a hard few days. In the end, everything will turn out okay. You'll see. The women in our family know how to make cheesecake out of snow."

Chapter 25

Sometime later, I run into Ethel Blankenship on the road. She commiserates with me about the early frost. Because she and Walter had fewer acres in grapes, most of their cash crops had already been harvested before the weather turned. But for me and Sender, the storm was a calamity: there will be no income from table grapes or Kosher wine. "Why don't you get the old sugar bush restarted?" Ethel suggests. "The Mortons, the family who used to own your place, made some extra cash from that."

"Excuse me, Ethel, but a sugar bush? This is a special kind plant?"

As these conversations often go, Ethel laughs. "No, Bluma, a sugar bush is a stand of sugar maple trees. You tap them for their sap and make maple syrup—a sweetener. I'll get Walter to come by and show you how it's done."

During the time I've lived in Geneva, I've found that the people who really know how to live off the land are like the Blankenships, whose folks have farmed here for generations. She told me once that both her family and Walter's, who were fervently anti-slavery, settled here in the early eighteen hundreds because Geneva was a hub on the Underground Railroad. We Rappaports, on the other hand, don't have the right lore to subsist off this land; I don't know from sugar maples.

Walter shows up the next day with some maple syrup for us to taste. It's a little like caramel but nutty, too. We're instant fans, especially Itzik, who cries when there's no more syrup to dip his slice of challah in.

As it turns out, we're not far from sugaring season. We'll have to make some preparations if we want to start producing maple syrup this year. Morris's wine-making operation is at a standstill, so we decide he will become our maple syrup maven. Walter leads Morris and me to the sugar bush, which is out beyond the meadow. Of course, we've noticed this little forest before. Right now the trees are bare, but in summer, they make a lovely shade. In fact, that's what I assumed they'd been planted for—that and the brilliant orange they turn in the fall. Now I understand that early spring is the magic season for maple syrup.

Walter begins by explaining how the Iroquois discovered the secret of the trees when they saw squirrels chewing off twigs and licking them. When the Iroquois tried it themselves, they discovered the sap was sweet. Later, white settlers learned from the tribe how to boil down the sap to make syrup. "The trade really got going," he tells us, "when the Abolitionists urged everyone to switch from West Indian sugar, which was harvested by slaves, to maple sugar, which small farmers could make for themselves." He launches into a detailed explanation of when and why the sap runs in the trees, how we tap it, and what goes into making syrup.

Obscure historical details? Botany? Engineering? Morris has met his soulmate. By the end of the afternoon, he and Walter are fast friends. For a modest share of the profits, Walter has agreed to help us set up our sugar bush. This involves fixing up the derelict shack that Chaia and Pasquelino used to claim for a clubhouse. In the corner are the slats of an old collecting barrel, which the men take to the cooper to reassemble. There's also a tin tub for boiling that only needs a couple of patches to be serviceable. Walter informs us that we're going to need lots of firewood for the boiling process. For each gallon of syrup, we'll need forty gallons of sap! Every member of the family takes a few minutes out of their usual chores to cut and split logs or find twigs for kindling.

At the appointed time, Morris, Sender, and Walter insert the spouts into the trees and hang the pails. The sap runs like blood from a cut. After two days, when the pails are full, I build a fire in the center of the shack. Sender takes over as many of our other chores as possible, and everyone else comes to help. Sala, with Rifka in a sling, begins stirring the first batch, and the heady smell of maple perfumes the air all the way to the farmhouse. Chaia feeds the fire whenever it begins to die down. We have to keep Itzik out of the shack because of the flames, but Reyzel "helps him" wash out the spouts and pails at the pump in the yard.

In all, we collect almost four hundred gallons of sap. We have to run ten batches, each for about three hours. That's a lot of stirring, especially as the syrup thickens, so we all take turns with the wooden paddle. Night and day, we keep the sap boiling. Chaia ladles the finished syrup into quart Mason jars. The steam coming off the tub contains tiny bits of sugar that stick to our clothes and skin. Our hair is lank from sweat and steam and sugar.

At the end, we have thirty-eight quarts of amber liquid. We put aside a jar for ourselves to eat with matzo meal pancakes on Passover, and we give Walter his share. The rest, we'll sell at the farm stand. The proceeds won't come near what we were making on kosher wine, but they'll help. Every time I see Ethel and Walter, I bless their names.

#

Once sugaring season is over, Morris is at loose ends. Planting keeps us all pretty busy, but after that, he has time on his hands until the grapes start to come in. In true Morris fashion, he decides he will teach himself a new trade. Since he learned how to fix Sender's car out of a book, he goes to the Geneva Library and brings home several tomes: *The Handbook of Automobiles*; *The Boy Mechanic, Volumes I and II*; *A Study of Automobile Clutches*.

Every evening after his chores are done, Morris sits at the kitchen table, studying. At first light, he's out in the garage with the hood of the Model T propped open, taking out and examining various parts. The whole project makes Sender uneasy—the car is his most prized possession—but I've threatened him with selling the blessed thing if he interferes. Then, after Morris cleans the spark plugs, resets the timing, and aligns the front wheels, Sender warms up to the effort. He even appreciates the bit of extra money that comes in when Morris fixes the axle on Shloimie Ponsky's car.

But when Morris comes home from a trip into Geneva with an offer of part-time work at Mitchum's Garage, Sender is not pleased. Sala and I are in the room when Morris announces what he thinks is good news.

"Work as a mechanic? You're a farmer!" Sender objects.

"I would still do my work here."

"That's not the point. What happened to going back to the land? What happened to being a free farmer on your own soil?"

Morris realizes he's on dangerous ground here. There are many reasonable answers to this question. First, the farm is not Morris's soil. Second, we've all seen that the farming part of going back to the land is not Morris's strong suit. Setting up a winemaking operation, managing a sugar bush, fixing a car—mechanics are his strengths; plowing and planting, not so much. But Sender is such an ideologue that he can't accept this about his son-in-law. So Morris treads carefully. "The family has gone back to the land. That's the important thing. But we could use the extra income from one of us working on the outside, at least until we recover from this past year."

"Are you saying I can't provide for my family?" Sender huffs.

"Of course not," Sala hurries to say. "But Morris has some special skills. Why not let him contribute what he's best at?"

"If Morris wants to contribute, let him re-stake the new vines that survived the frost."

"All five of them?" I butt in.

"Bluma, no one is talking to you."

Morris tries another tack. "We wouldn't be the only family with someone working outside the farm. Fishkin runs a garment factory in Madison. Edith Cohen is a seamstress. And we couldn't get along without the income from Bluma and Sala's weaving."

Now Morris has stepped in it. "A few dollars, they bring in," Sender practically yells. "We are farmers. That is what we do. If you don't want to be a farmer, take your family to Geneva and work for the goyim. We don't need you here."

Sala flees the room, the angry tears already starting. Morris rushes after her.

I stare at Sender. "Let me remind you," I say ferociously, "this isn't just your farm, and you won't be throwing anyone out of it."

"Oh, really? Whose name is on the deed? Whose name is on the mortgage?"

"And who helps you pay it? Before I came with the girls, you were in default. Maybe we should all leave. Then you can meet the payments by yourself without compromising your precious 'Back-to-the-Land' philosophy."

"Maybe you should!" Sender snaps back and flounces out of the room.

#

It's a frosty few days at the Rappaport house. Sender will not exchange a word with Sala and Morris. I have nothing to say to him. Poor Chaia and Reyzel know something is off, but they can't guess what. It isn't until Sala and Morris go into Geneva to see about renting an apartment that Sender realizes he's gone too far. One evening after Sala has put her little ones to bed and our two younger girls are upstairs in their room, Sender comes into the kitchen where Sala and I are cleaning up.

"Sala," he says abruptly, "bring Morris here. I want to talk to you both."

"She's not your servant to order about," I protest. "If you want to talk to Morris, go find him yourself."

"It's all right, Mama. I'll bring him down."

When they return, Sala and Morris stand in the kitchen doorway as if ready to escape should Sender start yelling again.

"Well, my children," Sender begins calmly enough, "I understand you're looking for a place to live in Geneva."

"Isn't that what you told us to do?" Sala replies coolly.

"*Khas vekhalile*! God forbid I should turn my daughter and her husband away from my door. You misunderstood me."

I want to say he couldn't have been clearer, but I recognize this is going to be Sender's version of an apology, so I hold my tongue.

"What did you mean to say?" Morris asks, clearly open to repairing this rift for Sala's sake.

"I meant you could work for the goyish mechanic part of the time, but we need you also on the farm, especially when the grapes come in next year."

"So, you'll allow Morris to work two jobs. How generous," Sala says, her feistiness on full display.

"I thought that was what he wanted," Sender returns, starting to get angry.

Morris jumps in. "It is what I want, and we'll be happy to stay. I'm glad we could come to an understanding."

That man is an angel. I only wish mine were.

Chapter 26

GENEVA HIGH, A THREE-STORY brick building with a central spire and narrow, gabled windows, is either imposing or intimidating, depending on your perspective. When I first watched Chaia walk through its arched front door, it was intimidating. Miss Dupont decided Chaia had learned everything she could at the one-room schoolhouse and sent her off to high school when she was still thirteen. Now, as she becomes the first Rappaport not only to graduate from secondary school but also to win a pile of honors, it's a more welcoming place.

The gymnasium is decked out in bunting. A spray of white flowers decorates the podium where the seniors will receive their diplomas. Dressed in their finest, the Rappaports take up most of the third row. Even Itzik sits as quietly as you can expect a four-year old to manage, and Rifka sleeps agreeably in her mother's arms.

Somewhere in the bowels of the school, the graduates have been getting ready, putting on their black robes and mortarboard caps. As they march in, even Pasquelino Giordano looks like a serious student though his mother says she imagines the Latin on his diploma actually reads, "By the skin of his teeth."

Chaia's diploma will list a slew of awards. At a ceremony last night, it was almost embarrassing how many "bests" she won: the history prize, the algebra medal, the best essay on English literature. The faculty named her salutatorian, which, she explained to me, means she will make the first speech at graduation. Although she's been working on it with Dolores Dupont for the past month, none of us have been allowed to see it. As she rises from her seat and approaches the podium, I flash back to that first week of school, when Miss Dupont rapped her knuckles with a pointer—how cowed

Chaia was by the new school and the new country. Today, that girl begins to speak with the confidence born of all those elocutionary contests.

"Principal Lewis, members of the faculty, fellow graduates, friends, and family, welcome to the Geneva High School Class of 1926 graduation, and thank you for the honor of addressing you." A roar of applause goes up from the gymnasium, punctuated by a few whoops from Alvin Baker, who, to everyone's surprise, is finally managing to graduate. Chaia continues, "As some of you know, I was born in Falciu, a little town in Romania. My family left Falciu because Romania—much of Eastern Europe, in fact— had become a dangerous place for Jews. Anti-Semitism was on the rise, with nationalistic leaders calling for the seizure of Jewish property. There weren't any government-sponsored educational institutions for Jewish girls, so you see, even my going to high school is a bit of a miracle."

I sense some fidgeting in the audience. They haven't come to their kids' graduation to hear about the trials and tribulations of the Jews in Romania. Chaia pays the rustling no mind. "That was eight years ago," she continues, "and things have only gotten worse in Romania. One of the most popular political parties has called for depriving Jews of all their rights. Their goal is to eliminate all Jews from Romania."

I know this doesn't seem like an unreasonable goal to some of the parents—for Romania or for the United States either. They've begun to murmur among themselves. It's not the whole audience, but enough to create a hum. Again, Chaia ignores them. "My family is so grateful to have settled in a country that welcomes strangers. When we sailed into the New York harbor, we were greeted by the Statue of Liberty, where the words of the Jewish poet, Emma Lazarus, are inscribed: 'Give me your tired, your poor, your huddled masses yearning to breathe free.'"

An outright boo comes from somewhere in the crowd, but Chaia will not be silenced. She continues, "At school, we start every day with the Pledge of Allegiance, which proclaims 'liberty and justice for all.' But it's important for us not to be complacent. Even here in the United States, we face the problem of bigotry. In recent years, the Ku Klux Klan has gained new strength, terrorizing Black people, Catholics, and Jews. Some of our Geneva neighbors had a cross burned on their property just because they were Jews."

"A good enough reason," someone mutters, but he's shushed by Ethel Blankenship. Chaia soldiers on: "There may even be people in the audience tonight who are sympathetic to the Klan. I think I understand why. It's not always easy to welcome people who speak other languages, eat strange foods, wear different clothes, and have new ideas. But that is the history of our country. Successive groups of English, Scottish, Irish, African, German, Chinese, Japanese, and other nationalities have come and made America what many call 'the greatest nation on Earth.' I'm proud to live in this great nation, and I thank you for letting me address you tonight."

When Chaia finishes, our whole row jumps to our feet, clapping. There's enthusiastic applause from several pockets in the gym. Others are sitting on their hands or whispering angrily to each other. I don't care. Chaia gives me *nakhes*, the particular kind of pride you take when your child does something really fine.

#

After the ceremony, some of the students and their parents come over to congratulate Chaia while others give us cold looks as they pass by. Walter Blankenship pumps Chaia's hand. "How did you get that barn-burner of a speech past Principal Lewis? The last Geneva graduation I was at, the salutatorian just told us how the youth of today will be the leaders of tomorrow. Who else would be the leaders of tomorrow?"

Chaia smiles. "I told the principal I was working on the speech with Miss Dupont. I'm sure he assumed she wouldn't let me say anything too controversial."

"Well, he was wrong about that! It's a good thing you're graduating," Ethel says with a wink.

Finally, we shepherd the family into the car, followed by most of the Jewish farmers, the Giordanos, Miss Dupont, and the Blankenships. As we approach the house, we hear the sound of Dov and Reyzel tuning up their fiddles. The parlor is hung with paper chains that Sala helped Itzik make. Reyzel created a big sign saying "Mazel Tov, Charlie." Marta Giordano contributed a sheet cake, with "Congratulations Graduates" inscribed in blue frosting.

The minute Chaia and Pasquelino enter, Reyzel and Dov strike up the old song, "Mazel Tov." We hold hands and circle around the two of them. Everyone joins the dance; even Miss Dupont stumbles along. Chaia is still wearing her robe and mortarboard and clutching her diploma.

When the music ends, Sender says, "All right, Chaia, we're all very proud of you, but I think now you can take off the cap and gown."

"She's the first person in the family to graduate high school. Let her enjoy it!" I reply.

"And she's the salutatorian!" Sala says proudly.

"What's that?" Reyzel wants to know.

Miss Dupont explains, "It means Charlie got the second highest ranking in the class. That's why she gave the first speech, the salutation. And I'll tell you the truth," she continues conspiratorially. "If Charlie had been a boy, they would have named her the valedictorian, the highest honor for a graduate."

"That's all right, Miss Dupont. Now Reyzel can be the first valedictorian in the family." Sender says the new word with care.

"She'll have to put in a lot more effort on her schoolwork than she does now if that's her goal," Miss Dupont replies tartly.

"I'm just impressed that Chaia made it through school at all," says Clara Fishkin. "After that horrible winter in '25, my son had to drop out and help at home."

Chaia begins to tear up. "Everyone worked so hard to pull me through. Mama and Sala wove till their fingers ached. Morris had two jobs. But I'll make it up to them once I graduate from college and have some money coming in."

Sender is strangely eager to change the subject. "Yes, well, we can worry about that later," he says. "Right now, *es, khaverim*. Eat, eat!"

Gathering around the table, we feast on rugelach and mandelbroit and Ethel's rhubarb custard pie. Mrs. Giordano cuts and distributes the cake, with a little cheek-pinching for all the young ones. There's so much good feeling going around that Chaia actually asks Reyzel to play something on the violin, and Reyzel actually chooses a piece that only lasts a few minutes.

Then Sala asks everyone to raise a glass of Rappaport's best concord grape wine in a toast to the graduates. It's not exactly a sacramental event, but we hope the Federal Prohibition Unit will forgive this one exception to the rules for consuming alcohol. Glasses clink, "*Le khayim*" rings out, and we all drink to the sweet moments life sometimes hands us.

In the hubbub that follows, Pasquelino and Chaia are chatting for the first time in a long time. In fact, everyone is conversing happily when Mr. Giordano says, "Tell us, Chaia, about college. Which one did you choose?"

"I'm going to the Western Reserve University College for Women in Cleveland. I start in September," she announces proudly.

"Well, maybe not September," Sender interrupts. If he was hoping the party would provide enough cover for him to dump this bombshell into the conversation without anyone paying too much attention, he doesn't know his daughter very well.

"What do you mean, Papa? That's when the school year begins."

"I mean, maybe you won't go to school this fall. You could help us another year on the farm."

By this time the party chit-chat has died down, and everyone is listening to this exchange.

"No, Papa. I'm sorry you don't want to part with me, but I'm going to college next year. I saved the money myself, plus I got a scholarship."

"Chaia, you and I should maybe talk about this some other time."

"There's nothing to talk about. I'm going to college."

Sensing something brewing, Miss Dupont breaks in. "And we all know you'll make a tremendous success of it. But I'm afraid I have to be going."

The atmosphere has become so tense that the other guests also begin to make leaving noises. "Yes, we have to go too. Clara and I are so happy for you," Dov says.

"We're kvelling to have a girl from the Jewish community go to college, whenever she starts," Clara adds.

All the guests start to file out, their good wishes a little more hearty than strictly necessary. When they've left, there's a moment of silence. Everyone in the family looks to Sender for an explanation. He's sitting at the table, studiously eating a cookie.

Having guessed what the problem may be, I say gravely, "Sender, what have you done with Chaia's money?"

He's obviously been practicing his defense, as he rushes to answer. "I just borrowed it when I bought the Model T. Doesn't the Torah say, 'You shall not harden your heart, and you shall not close your hand from your needy brother'? How much more so when the person in need is your father?"

"How were you needy?" I demand. "Because you wanted a car?"

"The car was for all of us. Chaia wanted it too, remember?" Using the words of a child who had no idea where the money to buy it was coming from is a new low, even for Sender.

Sala looks at him reproachfully. "This is your excuse?"

"You have to understand. We were already a little bit in debt because of the new grapevines, but our crop looked so good, I figured it would be easy to put the money back after the harvest." He looks at us almost belligerently, as though everyone should understand the justice of what he did.

Even Sender's pet, Reyzel, is shocked. "You didn't ask Chaia if it was okay to borrow her money?"

"I was going to pay it back before she even knew it was gone," he wheedles. "Then the crop froze, and the vines died, and we ended up owing more than we brought in. I tried everything to make some money. I sold the phonograph. I even tried to sell the car, but with the busted-up grill and fender, I couldn't get a decent price for it." No one, not even Morris, will meet his eyes.

More conciliatory now, he turns to Chaia. "But Chaia, we're doing better now. I've already put"—he takes a bank book from his vest pocket—"seven dollars back in your account. With a little more tutoring, you should have enough to go to college in a few years."

"Papa, how could you?" Sala demands.

I shake my head. "As my mother, may she rest in peace, used to tell me, 'One mourns for the dead seven days, but for a fool, a lifetime.'"

Chaia says nothing. She carefully removes her cap and gown, and lays them on the table. She gives her father a long, hard look and starts up the stairs without speaking.

Calling after her, Sender tries, "Chaia, it was a bad time. Everyone lost something. Should you not have contributed to the family?"

"I think you've said enough," I tell him.

Itzik has fallen asleep on the sofa. Morris retrieves him, and he and Sala take him up to bed where Rifka is already tucked in. I head into the kitchen. Maybe washing some dishes will keep my hands busy when what I want to do with them is pound on Sender's chest. Reyzel, despondent at getting a glimpse of her idol's clay feet, follows me with her violin and begins furiously going at one of her more demanding pieces. Only Sender is left sitting at the table, stubbornly eating rugelach.

Chapter 27

I'VE BEEN THINKING A lot about Chaia's graduation—the party where her dream was crushed, of course, but also the speech she made. She talked about how proud she was to be an American, but the truth is, she's not a citizen. Right now, I can't do much about the money Sender took from her; our finances are still too tight. But I can make her a bona fide American.

According to the law, any minor becomes a citizen when her parent is naturalized, and Chaia won't be eighteen until December. I filed a declaration of intent to get my citizenship with the clerk of courts in Ashtabula several years ago. But there's a test, and I never seemed to find time to study for it. At least, that's what I told myself. It's probably more honest to say that I wasn't sure I could pass it. It's one thing to learn history when you're a teenager, another when you're thirty-eight. But enough excuses now. Chaia is still seventeen, and I'm going to get naturalized in time for her and Reyzel to become citizens with me.

These days, Chaia is pretty sullen (and who could blame her), but I've enlisted her to help me. Every night after dinner, we practice from a textbook we got from the Bureau of Naturalization. At first, I try to remember every detail, like the list in the Declaration of Independence of the King's "injuries and usurpations" against the colonists. The going is very slow. We realize we'll never be ready if we don't pare down our reading list. Chaia believes the judge will focus on the most important points: the three branches of government, how a bill becomes a law, and the preambles to the Declaration and the Constitution.

I don't find this part difficult—far from it. For a woman raised in a country ruled by a king, it was inspiring to learn how a group of men, most of them younger than I am today, came up with a new idea about how free people should govern themselves. I was so impressed I had Chaia read me the introduction to the Declaration of Independence over and over till I learned it by heart.

Reading for myself has been more of a challenge. Goodness knows Chaia has plenty of experience teaching children, but their brains are more flexible than mine. I'm struggling through the McGuffey Reader, the same book the girls used in school: "The dog ran." "Come with me, Ann, and see the man with a black hat on his head." "Your parents are very kind to send you to school. If you are good, and if you try to learn, your teacher will love you, and you will please your parents."

I do think my mother, may she rest in peace, would be pleased. She herself was illiterate, her father being of the opinion that females didn't need to know how to read. If that sounds familiar, it was a widespread belief among men in Eastern Europe, both Jews and non-Jews. Sender is practically a freethinker by comparison. College for Chaia was going to be a rare accomplishment. A university education for men in Romania was unusual, and don't even ask about women. To be fair, I've noticed the same thing is true here in Ohio.

Well, my mind is wandering, and I have homework to do: "All through Halloween night, Ann laughs at the ghosts." How am I supposed to figure out a language where *gh* makes an *f*, a hard *g*, or no sound at all?

#

I won't say I'm going to earn the history prize, but, ready or not, the time has come for my citizenship test. I'm to appear before a judge at the Ashtabula County Courthouse. With me are Sala, Chaia, and Reyzel, as well as Ethel Blankenship, who is my witness. She'll testify that I've lived in the United States at least five years and that I possess a "good moral character."

To me, the courthouse looks a bit like a proper old lady, the tall central windows staring down at me in disapproval, the spires and dormer windows like the creation of a very extravagant milliner. We troop through the front entrance, flanked by columns that make me feel more daunted than ever. I know these immigration judges can ask whatever questions they want and use their own discretion to decide if an applicant passes. Some of them believe there are already too many immigrants in the country, and they make the exams as difficult as possible. Ethel catches my involuntary shiver. "Bluma Rappaport," she says, "you're going to become an American citizen today. Nobody can stop you."

Nobody except Judge Herman Alexander, I think as we enter our assigned courtroom. Judge Alexander sits above us on a dais behind a mahogany desk, each of its spindles carved to a fare-thee-well. Over his starched white shirt and silk cravat, he wears a severe black robe. Whatever hairs he's missing on his head (and that would be many), he makes up for with a full, drooping mustache, which does nothing to hide the look of irritation on his thin mouth.

We take our seats. Barely looking up from the papers on his desk, the judge says, "Bluma Rappaport?"

"Yes, sir."

"And whom have you brought with you as your character witness?" His nasal voice is full of impatience.

"That would be me, your honor, Ethel Blankenship." I see Judge Alexander look Ethel up and down. I imagine he doesn't understand why a person so obviously a native-born American would be standing up for the likes of me.

"You can testify to Mrs. Rappaport's residency in this country for at least the past five years?"

"We've been friends for almost ten."

He purses his lips. "Very well. And what have you to say about Mrs. Rappaport's fitness to become a citizen?"

"Well, sir, I know that Mrs. Rappaport is a very hard worker. She and her husband have totally transformed the old Morton place back into a working farm and sugar bush. Besides, she's a talented weaver and," Ethel says triumphantly, "she's a member of the Women's Christian Temperance Union."

The judge's eyes widen in surprise, but he recovers himself and asks sternly, "Has she ever been a burden on the public weal?"

I have no idea what that might mean, but Ethel assures the judge that we've never taken charity.

"Very well. Mrs. Rappaport, I'm now going to give you a literacy test. This paper has a paragraph I want you to read out loud." He glowers at Ethel and the girls. "And there's to be no helping from the spectators or I will have you removed."

He hands me a paper that's been smudged and wrinkled from passing through the hands of many people like me. I find that comforting. Even more comforting are the first words I see on the page, which are easy for me to make out. There's nothing I can do about my Yiddish accent, but I read in a strong voice: "We hold these truths to be self-evident, that all men are created equal, that they are endowed by their Creator with certain unalienable Rights, that among these are Life, Liberty and the pursuit of Happiness."

Maybe the judge selected this passage because he hopes to trip up immigrants with difficult words, or maybe he just loves it as much as I do. Either way, I'm pretty sure I just passed the literacy test. I can almost feel Chaia beaming at me.

But Judge Alexander isn't through with me yet. "I'm now going to ask you ten questions," he tells me. "If you miss more than two, your application for citizenship will be denied." He looks only too happy for that to be the case, so I'm surprised at how easy his first few questions are: "What are the three branches of the United States government?" "Name four rights that are guaranteed by the Bill of Rights." "When was the American Revolution?" By question five, I'm thinking Chaia was right: the judge just wants to be sure I'm familiar with the basics every citizen should know. But question six is a ringer: "Which branch of government has the power to punish counterfeiters?"

I wrack my brain, but this is not a detail I remember. Straining to come up with a logical answer, I venture, "The judiciary?"

A smirk edges up the corners of Judge Alexander's mouth. "That is incorrect. The correct answer is Congress. That is one incorrect answer. You can only miss one more." With a certain gusto, the judge pulls out what he imagines will be another hard one: "What is the subject of the Third Amendment to the Constitution?"

"Soldiers cannot be quartered in a house without the consent of the owner or in a manner prescribed by law," I quote back to him. I imagine many Americans don't see this as a particularly important law, but in the part of the world I come from, armies are always taking up residence in people's homes, wanted or unwanted, so this is one I memorized.

The judge plays with the corner of his mustache for a moment. Then he asks, "How long is the term of a United States senator?"

Has he softened toward me since I knew about the Third Amendment? Why else would he lob me such an easy one? "Six years, your honor," I reply gratefully.

I soon realize he was only toying with me. "On what date was the first session of the United States Congress?"

The first session? Who remembers? I know the Constitution was ratified in 1788, and I know each new Congress convenes on January 3, so I guess, "January 3, 1789."

"That is incorrect. The correct answer is March 4, 1789. If you get my final question wrong, you will not pass the test." I can hear the hint of satisfaction in his voice.

Ethel gets up from her seat and intervenes. "Judge, can you explain what the opening date of the first Congress has to do with American citizenship? You can see that Mrs. Rappaport knows the important elements of our system of government. Why try to trip her up with trivialities?" The girls nod their heads vigorously.

"The United States government formally began on that date, and I think it is entirely appropriate to expect a new citizen to know it," Alexander intones.

"And to know what branch of government is in charge of punishing counterfeiters?"

"Sit down, Mrs. Blankenship," he thunders. "This is my courtroom, and I will ask the questions I deem important. If you think these interruptions help your friend, you are mistaken."

Reluctantly, Ethel takes her seat. The girls squirm. And now Judge Alexander comes in for the kill: "Mrs. Rappaport, please name three usurpations perpetrated by the King of England against the American colonists."

I pretend to hesitate. "Of course, your honor," I stammer. Number one is really easy, so I start with, "He taxed the peoples without their consent." Judge Alexander nods. I purse my lips and scrunch up my eyes. "He broke up their legislatures," I say though I struggle a bit with the pronunciation. Judge Alexander nods grudgingly. Now I furrow my brow as if I'm searching my memory, though the truth is, the Declaration of Independence, which was the first thing I studied, lays out multiple reasons, all of which I know. I pick one that seems right for the moment. "The king tried to keep new people from settling in the colonies by changing the laws how they could become citizens," I say as a smile spreads over my face. "Can you imagine?"

Part III

Chapter 28

FROM THE PARLOR, WHERE I'm weaving, I can hear Chaia and her beau, Sanford Margolis, on the porch talking about politics. To me, it's not a romantic conversation, but I guess this is, for Chaia, what qualifies as a date.

He: "I don't see how you can deny Marx's logic. 'From each according to his ability; to each according to his needs.' Imagine a world where that was true. People like us wouldn't be working our fingers to the bone and still just barely scraping by." Sanford is right about scraping by. He's a cutter at Joseph & Feiss, one of the largest garment manufacturers in Cleveland. They make everything from rompers and knee pants to uniforms and suits, not that you'd know it to look at Sanford's clothes with their fraying collars and shiny knees. Everything droops on his skinny body like it was still on the hanger.

Even so, Chaia seems to find him—and his style of wooing—appealing. But if Sanford expects her to bow to his superior powers of analysis, he has another think coming. She: "Sanford, you talk as if the world runs by logic. You have your ideals, but I come from a country that knows something about how Communism works in the real world. During the Great War, Romania and Russia were supposedly fighting together, alongside the allies. But when the Russian Revolution broke out and the Bolsheviks took over, it was chaos. The Bolshevik troops turned into looters who destroyed everything in their path."

Sanford is silent. In fact, they both are silent. Are they enjoying the moonlight? Are they holding hands? I suspect they're honing their next argument. All I know is that the matchmaker Sender insisted on hiring for Chaia sent over information on several eligible young men. Sanford is the first and only one Chaia consented to meet.

Sender is disappointed that she chose the man with the dimmest prospects: a tailor and a Communist to boot. It's true he has more in his brains than in his pockets, but that doesn't bother Chaia. "Love is like butter," Sender tells her. "It's good with bread." As if he had room to talk. Anyway he's forfeited any chance he had to influence her. I don't even try. This is her life now, what we haven't ruined for her. Sanford may be a luftmensch—an air-man, a dreamer—but I like the way they are together.

The silence is broken suddenly by howling. Sala and Morris's newest addition, two-month-old, Ruthie, up for her ten o'clock feeding. She manages to wake Rifka, who wakes Itzik, who wakes Rozhinkes, and a great cry goes up, like the multitudes at the Wailing Wall. It's time to bring in the reserves—in other words, me. By the time I'm finished helping Sala settle everyone back to sleep, Chaia is in her bedroom and Sanford has disappeared into the night.

#

Sanford has become a fixture at our Friday night dinners, reliably exasperating Sender with his rough-shaven face, his lack of a yarmulke, and his talk of the utopia that is the Soviet Union. Every time her father goes red in the face with irritation, I think Chaia likes Sanford a little bit more. He's definitely growing on me, despite the Communist nonsense. Radicalism is not such a bad thing in the young. Let them change the world; God knows we need it. The sisters mostly approve of Sanford. Sala, who likes everyone, thinks Sanford is a "fine man," and Reyzel pronounces him "a bit of a flat tire, but nice."

Other than *shnoring* dinners, Sanford's idea of a good time is to take Chaia for a ride in a rattletrap Ford he borrows from one of his organizer pals. They're trying to bring the Amalgamated Clothing and Textile Workers Union to Joseph & Feiss, but it's been slow-going since a recession hit the Cleveland garment industry. So Sanford drowns his troubles in talk. He and Chaia go to Geneva-on-the-Lake, sit by the water, and talk. They drive across the county's nineteen covered bridges—and talk. They also get together with Sanford's Cleveland friends, a motley bunch of Communists, Socialists, anarchists, even some free love champions, though I gather the main activity at these parties is also talk.

I've been wondering when the talk will turn to marriage when I find it already has. After dinner tonight, when Sanford has left in that way he has of evaporating, Chaia comes into the kitchen, where the girls and I are washing the dishes. "Well," she says shyly, "Sanford proposed."

"I knew it!" Reyzel cries. "He was shaking his knee and tapping his foot even more than usual."

Sala embraces Chaia with her soapy hands and says, "I'm so happy for you!"

"What about you, Mama?" Chaia asks. "Are you ready to have Sanford for a son-in-law?"

"It would have been nice if he'd asked your parents first," I reply, "but more important, what do you have to say about it. Are you ready to have Sanford for a husband?"

"I'd love to have Sanford for a husband. I'm just not sure I want to spend my married life in Russia."

"Russia?" the rest of us exclaim together.

"Chaia, I know you think I'm a nudnik, but you don't have to move all the way to Russia to get away from me," Reyzel protests.

"We'd never see you again!" Sala cries.

Then I pile on. "Russia! What narishkayt is this? Sanford lives in Cleveland. His parents live in Cleveland."

"Yes, but he was born in Odessa. Now that the Tsar has been overthrown and the Bolsheviks are in power, Sanford feels it's his duty to go back and help build 'the workers' paradise.'" Chaia says this last bit with enough scorn that I'm relieved she hasn't bought into Sanford's airy-fairy fantasies.

Still, I'm not sure what she'll do for love. I try again to dissuade her. "All I know is that Russia is no paradise for Jews. Just ask your father. Besides, it's as cold as a mackerel and run by that meshugener, Stalin."

"Do you think I don't know this? It's why I haven't made up my mind about going there. I want to live with Sanford, but I don't want to live with Stalin."

As always, Sala is the most kindhearted of us. "Chaia, what a hard choice!" she sympathizes.

That's the moment I realize that Chaia, my fierce, decisive, strong-willed daughter, is on the verge of tears. As she breaks down, her whole body sags. We haven't heard Chaia cry for years, not even when she found out that Sender spent her college money. I take her in my arms, and we wait until she regains her composure.

When Chaia can speak again, she tells us, "Ever since Papa broke up my friendship with Pasquelino, I haven't had a friend who was a boy. To be honest, until I met Sanford's circle, I didn't really have any friends—just my sisters. You've been my whole world." Now Sala and Reyzel are tearing up too, and I might as well confess, I'm choked up myself. "I can't imagine going so far away from my family. Plus I don't really believe in this idea of Sanford's, that everyone in the USSR is living in plenty and harmony. It's a nice dream, but everything I read tells me it's not reality."

"Then you must talk Sanford out of going," I declare, like I don't know from experience that talking a man out of a dream is a lost cause.

"Don't you think I've tried? But Sanford says he'd be no fit partner for me if he didn't act on what he believes is right."

"What about what you believe is right? Doesn't that count?" Reyzel demands.

"I just don't see a way to compromise on this," Chaia replies. "Either his life loses meaning or mine does."

"I don't know," Sala ventures. "When I met Morris, he was set on moving to Palestine to build the Jewish state. But after we were married and Itzik was born, he realized that his life was here."

"I'm afraid I don't have the luxury of time. Sanford has already talked with the Russian consul in Cleveland. He's going to leave at the end of the summer, whatever I decide." We all gasp.

"You would go with him, even knowing it's crazy?" Reyzel pushes.

"I'm thinking about it. He's the only person I've ever met that I can really talk to."

"You can talk to us," her little sister protests.

"Yes, but you're not interested in politics or literature or the other things I care about. Sanford is, and he really wants to know what I think. We may not always agree, but he respects me. Where will I find that again?"

There's a long silence. In the end, I realize the best thing I can do is to let my daughter come to her own decision. "Chaia," I tell her, "you've always been a person who reasons things through. You'll spend some time thinking about this, and whatever you choose, we'll be behind you. You know we love you whatever happens." Sala and Reyzel are nodding wholeheartedly.

I continue, "Maybe, though, don't share this with your father just yet. You're of age, so he can't keep you here if you want to go to Russia. But there's no point getting him riled up if you don't end up by leaving."

#

Weeks pass, and no one speaks of Chaia's big decision. First of all, we don't want Sender to know before he has to. He'd have trouble accepting Sanford even if the boy was willing to move to Geneva and toil away on the farm. Russia? *Nisht do gedakht*. Don't even think about it.

Though we don't harangue Chaia, we do what we can to make staying in America look like the right choice. Reyzel goes out of her way not to be irritating. Sala takes over Chaia's turn at the milking whenever she can. I have so many arguments with Chaia in my own head about why going to Russia would be a terrible idea, but I keep them locked behind my tongue. And every Friday night, Sanford shows up for dinner while we try not to give him the evil eye. In the meantime, the endless streams of talk roll on between the two lovebirds, his prominent Adam's apple bobbing up and down and her mop of curls bouncing.

One Sunday, Sanford has a special outing planned. They're going to Cleveland to hear William Z. Foster, the Communist Party's candidate for president of the United States. It's clear Foster has no chance of being elected, but he's declared that his campaign will raise the consciousness of the entire working class. Oy.

Sanford comes to pick Chaia up at three o'clock. They're even going to have dinner in a restaurant, the New York Spaghetti House, next to the theater where Foster will speak. Chaia comes down wearing a dress Sala made for her, a drop-waisted blue wool with a flounced hem and a spray of embroidered flowers at the shoulder. Her hair is molded into a finger wave, thanks to Reyzel, who learned how to do it from some women's magazine she cadged from a friend. I'm not sure those humorless Communists will appreciate it, but I think she looks lovely.

It's after ten when the Ford rolls back to the house. I'm honestly not waiting up for Chaia. Today was laundry day, and I happen to still be folding clothes in the kitchen when they arrive. I'm ready to give them a decent interval for a goodnight kiss, but I hear Chaia run directly from the car up the front stairs. There are no footsteps behind her. When I appear in the parlor, she's just taking off her wrap.

"So, how was William Z. Foster?" I ask hesitantly.

"I've broken things off with Sanford—that's how William Z. Foster was!"

Chaia's eyes are dry, but she's obviously upset. "I'm so sorry, my heart, sorry that things didn't work out with Sanford. But what does that have to do with William Z. Foster?"

"Do you know what that man's speech was about? He was explaining Stalin's decision to break off any collaboration with Western Socialist parties. He called them 'social fascists'!"

I have no idea why this would break up a relationship. "And this is bad, why?" I ask.

"We have many friends who belong to those parties," Chaia tells me. "And Sanford wants to move to a country whose leader thinks his friends are fascists? Worse than that, he's ready to cut those friends out of our lives right now. He spent the entire ride back to Geneva trying to explain this betrayal." Chaia has grown more and more heated as she talks until her voice cracks on her final verdict: "Well, if he wants to go live under Stalin, he'll have to do it without me."

Inside, I'm hugely relieved, but I know that's not how Chaia feels. "Darling, you must be heartbroken," I say.

"Honestly, Mama, I've known for weeks I didn't want to go to the USSR. Tonight was just the deathblow, especially when Sanford started defending Stalin. It's one thing to admire Karl Marx and the original ideals of Communism. It's another to shut off your own brain when an oaf like Stalin tells you to disavow your friends."

"I guess when you take ideas seriously, like you and Sanford do, it's hard when your thoughts don't match."

"It's like we're from two different religions. His is Communism. Mine is common sense and decency."

"I can imagine how disappointing it is to find that the person you love isn't the man you thought he was." This, I can say from experience.

She sighs bitterly. "Once, I believed Sanford and I had a true marriage of the minds. Now I can't imagine anyone who thinks like I do."

"Darling, don't give up hope so easily. We'll ask the matchmaker to find you another suitor, maybe someone who's not so political."

"You mean someone who doesn't understand what I think and doesn't want to? A match like yours and Papa's? I think I'll stay an old maid."

I'm stung. Of course, Sender and I are hardly a love match, but our marriage produced a few good things, like Chaia herself. But this is no time for me to get my feathers ruffled. "Nonsense, Chaia," I say. "There will be other men."

"I don't think so, Mama. All the love I had is spent."

164

Chapter 29

IT'S BEEN SIX YEARS since Reyzel started studying the violin with Guy Pendergast. We've rarely met the man. At the recitals he's organized for Reyzel and his other students, he's a distant figure, usually seating himself on the far end of a row, where his pupils can't see him. Reyzel says it's because he doesn't want to distract them. I suspect it's because he's mortally shy, one of those people who's spent his life devoted more to his work than to anything human. When I've come up after the recitals to thank him for everything he's done for Reyzel, it seems to pain him to meet my eye. When Sender claps him on the back, he actually recoils. His shoulders are so hunched and his paunch so protruding, it's like he's placed a physical barrier between himself and the world.

That's why I'm surprised when Reyzel brings home a note from him. I may have learned to read a little English, but his script is so full of curlicues, I can't make it out. I hand it to Reyzel, who reads, "Dear Mr. and Mrs. Rappaport, I wonder if you might stop by my home sometime in the next week to discuss a new opportunity for Reyzel. Would Wednesday, right before her lesson, be convenient?"

"Do you have any idea what this is about?" I ask her.

"None, but it sounds exciting."

Something about the way she says this—a little tremor in her voice— makes me suspicious. "Really?" I probe.

"Maybe he wants me to play a concert somewhere," she says airily.

"Maybe, but you've performed before, and he never asked to talk to us about it. Remember last year when you did that concerto at the Little Youngstown Symphony? He just announced that you'd be playing, and so you did."

"Well, I guess there's nothing to do but go to Mr. Pendergast's house next Wednesday and find out what he has in mind."

#

The following Wednesday, Sender and I show up with Reyzel fifteen minutes before her lesson is to start. Mr. Pendergast's housekeeper meets us at the front door and shows us into the music room. The only place I've seen more books is the Geneva Public Library. Now I understand why Mr. Pendergast needed Reyzel's help organizing. All the shelves are lined with musical scores, their bindings giving the room the scent of leather. A grand piano sits in one corner, with sheet music ranged along the top of it. If English was hard for me, I can't imagine reading these lines and notes, like little birds flying across the page. I feel a surge of pride that my Reyzel knows this mysterious language.

Mr. Pendergast is studying a score and doesn't turn around when we come in. The housekeeper motions us to some chairs, which look like they've been dragged in for our visit. Not at all surprised by this lack of a greeting, Reyzel goes over to a stand next to the piano and sets out her music. Taking her violin from its case, she begins warming up. She starts off playing long tones, moving her bow slowly for four strokes on each string. Mr. Pendergast is still looking at his score, but I can tell his ears have perked up and he's listening. "Rose," he says with a hint of impatience, you can make that bow change at the frog much smoother. Do it again."

I'm amazed to hear her begin again—no kvetching, no arguing. I'm also surprised that she seems to have adopted the English version of her name, but I guess there's precedent for that. Anyway, this obedient Rose is not the Reyzel I know. Finally, after Reyzel/Rose has played the exercise to Mr. Pendergast's satisfaction, he turns in our direction. More accurately, his body is facing us, but he seems to be directing his comments to the wastebasket under his table.

"Welcome, Mr. and Mrs. Rappaport," he says rather formally. "I wanted to talk to you in person about an opportunity that has arisen, which I think may be highly advantageous for young Rose." Reyzel has stopped practicing and is looking at him eagerly. I'm anxious to hear what this opportunity may be, but, from his rigid posture, I sense Sender has adopted his usual skepticism about all things outside the little world of the farm.

Mr. Pendergast continues. "Perhaps you know about the famous Swiss violinist and composer, Ernest Bloch? You may have heard his magnificent 'Schelomo'?"

Of course, we recognize the name Schelomo—it's Hebrew for Solomon—but we've hardly heard any classical music beyond what Reyzel practices at home. We shake our heads.

"Ah. Well, you see, Maestro Bloch is, like you, an Israelite. He has composed several pieces on Jewish themes."

I still don't see where this conversation is going, but I nod as if I do. Sender seems to have let down his guard a bit; if there's a Jew involved, he figures it can't be all bad. We wait patiently for many seconds until Mr. Pendergast has geared himself up to go on. "I got to know Maestro Bloch when I was in the Cleveland Symphony. He was at that time the director of the Cleveland Institute of Music. Now, of course, he's moved on to the San Francisco Conservatory, a very fine new school for serious music students."

He stops again, as if everything has now been explained. Only when he glances at our puzzled faces does he realize he's left something out of the conversation. "Maestro Bloch is going to be in town next month for a performance of his symphonic poem, 'A Voice in the Wilderness.' When I learned he was coming, I wrote to him about Rose, and he has consented to hear her play. He will give her a critique, which, in itself, is an amazing gift from so famous a musician. And if he thinks she's as talented as I do, he can open many doors for her."

Reyzel looks like she's about to swoon. She's dropped her bow and her violin to her sides and stands like she has just heard the original voice in the wilderness. Sender, who would usually mistrust any such proposal, seems intrigued. "You say Bloch is a Jew?"

"Oh, yes. Somewhere here I have an interview he gave to the *Boston Post*." Pendergast searches among the scattered papers on his desk, finally scooping up a newspaper clipping. "Ah, here it is. Bloch says, 'A tree must have its roots deep down in its soil. A composer who says something is not only himself. He is his forefathers! He is his people! Then his message takes on a vitality and significance which nothing else can give it, and which is absolutely essential in great art. I try to compose with this in mind. I am a Jew. It is my own belief that when I am most Jewish, I compose most effectively.'"

My suspicion that Reyzel had an inkling about the purpose of this meeting is growing stronger. I can just hear her suggesting that Mr.

Pendergast be ready to forestall any objections from us with a deluge of information on Ernest Bloch's Yiddishkeit. If I'm right, I'd say she knows her father well. He responds, "Well, of course she should play for this Ernest Bloch. What harm could there be in showing him Reyzel's talent?"

Reyzel is smiling triumphantly when I decide I have to inject a little realism into this conversation.

"Mr. Pendergast, so generous of you to arrange this audition for Reyzel. I mean, that's what it is, right? An audition?"

"Well, Mrs. Rappaport," Mr. Pendergast says carefully, "if Maestro Bloch is impressed with Rose's playing—and I think he will be—he could arrange for her to attend the San Francisco Conservatory when she finishes high school."

There it is. I suppose San Francisco is not as bad as Russia, but it's two thousand miles away. Besides, as I tell Mr. Pendergast now, "I'm sorry, Sir. You should excuse me for saying so, but it's not possible we could afford such an education for Reyzel . . . I mean, Rose."

To which Sender adds, "And even if we could, where would she live in San Francisco? She's not a cowboy." As far as my husband is concerned, any part of the country past Indiana is the Wild West. By this point Reyzel is both pouting and rolling her eyes.

"Mrs. Rappaport, Mr. Rappaport," Pendergast says, finally meeting our eyes, "I think we're getting ahead of ourselves. Right now, it will just be a marvelous educational experience for Rose to play for Maestro Bloch. He will give her valuable advice on her technique, emotional expression, stage presence. That may well be as far as things go. Let's just take it one step at a time. If there's more on offer, you can always decide then whether you want to pursue it."

I recognize this as the flying wedge of a campaign Reyzel and her teacher have concocted to get her into music school. I look at Sender. I think all that talk of "deep roots" and "Jewish forefathers" has won him over, and he likes to think of his daughter playing for this famous musician. If it comes to Reyzel moving to San Francisco, he imagines he will just put his foot down. Maybe, but that child has him wrapped around her little, violin-playing finger.

\#

Three weeks later on a Sunday morning, we find ourselves in front of a mansion on Euclid Avenue in Cleveland, the home of the Institute of Music. I know it was once the residence of a single family, which is hard to believe as the building takes up a full city block, with enormous bay windows and huge, oak doors.

There's no one else at the institute so early on a Sunday. We're greeted at the door by Ernest Bloch himself, a dapper man in a three-piece suit. His hair has receded so far up his forehead that his face looks like it was pasted in the wrong place. When he shakes my hand, he has as many calluses as I do, except his are on his fingertips, from pressing down the strings, I imagine. Despite the fact that Maestro Bloch is a famous composer, he's very *heymish*, like someone from the old country. He's especially kind to Reyzel, who's been so nervous on the way to Cleveland that Sender had to pull over so she could throw up in the bushes. Her usual cockiness is completely sapped.

"Well, Rose," he says when the introductions are over, "shall we go into the practice room and hear you? Guy Pendergast tells me you're going to play the Bach Chaconne." Reyzel's voice in answer is uncharacteristically timid. This does not seem like an auspicious start.

Sender and I are left in the reception area, what must have been the home's enormous front parlor, which is furnished with some overstuffed, straight-backed chairs. Trying one, I decide I cannot spend the audition sitting on one of these unfriendly seats. I move close to the practice room and listen intently. The sound is muffled, but if I actually put my ear to the door, I can make out what's happening.

Waving me away, Sender stage whispers, "What if someone comes in and sees you?"

"Then they'll see me. Shah, now, she's starting to play." In a few seconds, Sender can't stand the suspense either and he takes his place beside me at the door.

Reyzel is playing the opening. From the many, many, many times I've heard her practice, I can tell it's note perfect. Still, there's something missing. She's too careful, and the music is almost lifeless.

Bloch listens for two or three minutes before he stops her. "That's very good playing, Rose. Your technique is excellent. Not many young violinists even attempt the Chaconne."

Oh, no, I think. There's obviously a "but" coming. This is where he lets Reyzel down gently and sends us on our way. Although I'm thankful that means Reyzel won't be going off to California, I know she'll be crushed.

But Bloch surprises me. He says, "Mr. Pendergast tells me you started playing violin in a klezmer style."

"Yes, but I've left all that behind me," Reyzel says quickly. "Now I concentrate only on classical music."

"Do you think you could remember some of your klezmer music? I'd love to hear a dance tune, perhaps something that starts off slowly and builds with variations."

"Of course," Reyzel replies, more polite than enthusiastic. She takes a minute, almost as if she needs time to adopt another personality. Then she begins a *freylekh* she and Dov used to play to get everyone up and moving. The notes leap easily from her instrument, twining and spiraling.

When the piece is over, I can hear Bloch get to his feet. "Brava!" he cries. "That was wonderful. Now, you know, Rose, Bach's Chaconne is also a dance. Its essence is very much like the piece you just played. Do you think you could play the Chaconne again, but in the spirit of this klezmer tune?"

"Yes, Maestro," Reyzel says uncertainly, "I can try."

"Good. Let's move the music stand to another part of the room, so you can get a completely fresh start. Remember, now, make the piece dance."

When she lights into the Bach again, her old verve is back. In my unschooled opinion, the piece is even better than in any of her previous runs at it. When she finishes, Bloch says, "Well, Rose, that was a delight. Shall we go and talk to your parents about where we'll go from here?"

Sender and I race back to our seats and try to seem like we've been waiting there patiently. When Reyzel and the maestro emerge, they both look exultant. Bloch draws up two chairs across from us and begins. "Mr. and Mrs. Rappaport, as I'm sure you know, your daughter is a remarkable musician." Sender grins happily, but I'm nervous to hear what Bloch means by "where we'll go from here." I don't want the answer to be San Francisco, but when Bloch speaks, I see that what I want doesn't matter.

"I would be delighted to welcome Rose into our program at the San Francisco Conservatory when she finishes high school at the end of next year. We have a very fine violinist on our faculty, and of course, violin is also my instrument. As you may know, Jewish music is a passion of mine, so I think this would be a very good fit for Rose."

I'm sure the maestro notices my face fall. Sender isn't too happy either. "You may be interested in Jewish music," he says, "but, besides you, are there any other Jews in San Francisco?"

"Actually, Mr. Rappaport, San Francisco has the second highest number of Jews in the country, behind New York City. And what's even more significant, there's virtually no discrimination in San Francisco. The dreamers who came out to the West Coast were self-made men. They didn't bring the old prejudices about Jews with them. In fact, some of the great businessmen of the city, like Isaac Magnin and Levi Strauss and Adolph Sutro are Jews. I'm sure we can find accommodations for Rose with a Jewish family and that she will feel very comfortable there."

I recognize my cue to be the wet blanket one more time. "Maestro Bloch," I say, "I'm sure everything you tell us about San Francisco is true, but there's just no way we could afford to send Rose to your school. For a train ticket, we wouldn't even have the money." I'm hoping this frank admission will end the conversation because I really cannot face losing Reyzel. Looking over at her apologetically, I see a tear make its silent way down her cheek. Clearly, she's been nursing this dream of going to California since Mr. Pendergast first mentioned playing for Maestro Bloch. My words have crushed something essential in her.

"Mrs. Rappaport," Bloch replies, "I understand your situation. Fortunately, I think I may have a solution. A very prominent lawyer and banker I know has a particular interest in classical music education. After I heard such wonderful things about Rose from Mr. Pendergast, I took the liberty of contacting him, and he's agreed to fund her tuition and any other expenses if she chooses to attend the conservatory."

I've never seen such a look of longing on anyone's face as I do on Reyzel's at this moment. As I predicted, she has conquered Sender, who's nodding vigorously. I think about sending Reyzel across the country to a city where we know no one. I think about how I would miss the strains of violin music floating through the house and even the sounds of her and Chaia bickering. I think that even after her schooling is finished, she may stay on the West Coast for the rest of her life. I think about the fact that we may hardly ever see her, the cost of travel being so high. Then I look at Reyzel again, and I say, "That sounds like a wonderful chance for Reyzel . . . I mean Rose. How can we ever thank you?"

Chapter 30

REYZEL GOT HER GOOD news in August of 1929. The stock market crashed two months later. Although Ernest Bloch sent a letter reassuring us that Reyzel's scholarship to the San Francisco Conservatory was still on offer, that didn't help with the pickle the rest of us were in. We hadn't quite recovered from the blizzard of '25 when grape prices began to fall again.

Now, almost a year into the Depression, no one is buying anything that isn't absolutely necessary. Our weaving and wine aren't bringing in their usual stream of extra money. Maple syrup is a luxury, which most people have replaced with sugar water. As for Chaia's tutoring income, well, the parents have decided that, with money so tight, their little darlings will just have to study by themselves—or not. In other words, we're back to our earliest days on the farm, trying to live off the land, which has been even harder since our Fordson tractor was repossessed. Sender is back to plowing with Barney, who's really too old for this kind of work, or Balagan, who's too overbred.

We can't afford to heat the whole house, so we do most of our living in the kitchen. This Sunday afternoon, Sala and I are cooking schav, a soup made from sorrel, which grows wild on the farm. We take turns bouncing Sala and Morris's latest addition to the family, Mordechai, otherwise known as Motke, otherwise known as Marcus. The other little ones are ranged around the Franklin Stove, playing with some blocks Morris made them. What this really means is that Itzik builds a tower and Rifka and Ruthie knock it down. Also with us is Chaia, studying her book, *The Russian Tragedy*, by somebody named Rosa Luxemburg.

Reyzel, who's been out foraging, comes into the kitchen with two brimming baskets. Her cheeks are rosy from the September wind. Cold and rain have come early this year. "That storm was a godsend. It shook down so many hickory nuts, I filled both of these."

"Oh, goody," Chaia says sarcastically. "The last batch only took me two hours to shell."

"It's the hickory nuts and the mushrooms Reyzel finds that are giving you a break from grape jelly sandwiches," Sala reminds her.

"And for that, I do thank you, Reyzel. Once we get through this Depression, I will never eat anything purple again."

Chaia's kvetching is beginning to get to me. "Go, girls," I tell her and Reyzel. "Get your clean aprons. I put them in your room. And when you're through shelling the nuts, please put them through the grinder to make hickory butter."

Truth to tell, I've sent them off so I can have a minute alone with Sala. We've all been crammed in the kitchen for days, and I haven't had a chance to have a real conversation with anyone. "I'm telling you, Sala," I begin, "every day Chaia gets more *farbisene*."

"Can you blame her for being bitter? She had such plans. She was going to college. She was going to marry Sanford. Instead, she's stuck here, doing work she never had any interest in."

"Hunh! Or talent for." I know I'm being harsh, but it's hard to put up with Chaia's constant grousing, which threatens to set off a chorus of everybody else's complaints. "Besides," I add, "you're also stuck on the farm. Is this the life you would have chosen?"

"It isn't what I thought I wanted. Morris isn't what I thought I wanted. You know that better than anyone. But here I am, four children later, and when I look at my life, I'm content." She glances over at her brood, playing happily. "What would be a better place to raise the little ones, especially right now? I read the stories in the paper about soup lines and men riding the rails. At least we have a place to lay our heads."

"*Keyn en hora*. May it only continue!"

"And Morris is bringing in a little money—may God bless Cousin Mendel for giving him a job after Mitchum had to let him go. I hate that he has to stay in Cleveland during the week, but at least he comes home with some chicken backs or the end of a brisket. I know we keep adding hungry little ones to feed."

"Every one of them is a blessing. It's just we don't have enough to cover the mortgage for the second month in a row now. I'm trying to figure out what else we can sell."

173

"Don't worry, Mama. We'll get by."

"Of course we will. As the saying goes, 'When you lack butter for the bread, it's not yet poverty.'"

#

Less than a month later, poverty arrives. We've just come from Madison where we tried to sell the last of our crop. I told Sender to just let the grapes rot on the vine. With the price per ton at twenty-eight dollars, it was costing us more to pick them than we were earning. The last few days, no buyers at all stopped by the farm. That's why we lugged the grapes as far as Madison, but still there were few takers. The grapes are starting to turn, their winey smell pushed toward us on the wind. Sender drives the wagon onto the old bridge over the Grand River in Harpersfield.

I jump down from the box and look over the side. Below us, the river, swollen from recent rains, rushes by. Reflected in the churning water, the trees, orange and yellow, make a crazy quilt. Soon the surface will be marred by thousands of grapes falling into the water. Sender joins me at the railing, a bushel of grapes in his hands. "I don't understand it," he says. "Reuben Pincus from the JAS told me I should put half my acreage in table grapes. Even in a depression, he said, the rich buy table grapes."

I could remind Sender that Reuben Pincus's advice has never been particularly good, but why beat a dead horse? Instead I say simply, "Who is rich anymore?"

"It's true. Even Harold Gold has been dumping his crop. Pretty soon, there'll be so many fermenting grapes in the Grand River, anyone who drinks the water will get *farshnikert*."

He heaves his bushel up to the rail and empties its contents. The sound is like hail. I go to the back of the wagon and get a bushel. At my height, it's a trick to heft it over the railing, but, when one must, one can.

#

Though no one feels much like celebrating this year, Sender and Morris are banging the last nails into the frame for our sukkah, hanging the fabric walls I wove myself from white and blue linen. This is the booth we put up each year during the holiday of Sukkoth to remind ourselves that for forty years in the desert, our ancestors had no permanent homes.

By Jewish law, the sukkah shouldn't have a closed roof—just branches through which we can see the stars. In the Promised Land, they use palm fronds, but those are in short supply in Ohio. Instead we cover our sukkah with dried cornstalks and a few pine branches mixed in for fragrance.

The holiday also marks the end of the harvest season. In honor of that theme, Itzik, now a very grown-up six-year-old, has been put in charge of stringing apples and grapes and gourds to hang from the branches. Since it's been a rough year, we've given him only the misshapen and wormy fruit, hoping God will understand we need the rest to get us through the winter. We do have a beautiful banner for the wall, embroidered by Sala with a passage from Ecclesiastes: "A time to plant and a time to pluck up that which is planted."

During the holiday, we'll eat all our meals in the sukkah, by custom with guests who may be poor or homeless. On the first night of Sukkoth every year, my father used to read to us from the great Jewish philosopher Moses Maimonides: "Anyone who sits comfortably with his family within his own sukkah walls and does not share with the poor is performing a good deed not for joy but for the stomach." This year, we'll have Dov and Clara Fishkin, who just lost their farm. They'll stay with us until they can arrange for a place in Cleveland, where there are rumors of work. We, ourselves, are hanging on to the farm by our fingernails. We took out another loan on the property, but a second year of miserable sales has just about eaten through what we borrowed. Still, as long as we have a place to call home, we'll invite our less fortunate friends.

Clara and the girls are in the kitchen, putting the finishing touches on the meal. The Fishkins brought us the last of their chickens when they had to vacate their farm, so we'll have the luxury of soup with kreplach, little dumplings filled with ground chicken. There will be potato kugel and cabbage stuffed with rice. For dessert, I bring up a dozen apples from the root cellar. Traditionally, I would serve them with honey, but this year, it's going to be our own maple syrup, another work-around dictated by necessity. I have to say, I hold God partly responsible for the uncertain state we're in, so if everything is not exactly as he likes it, he'll have to forgive us.

On Sukkoth, as is true before any Jewish holiday meal, we're seriously hungry until we eat because there are so many rituals to perform. Each night, we formally invite the biblical patriarchs to take up residence in our booth. On the first night, we focus on Abraham, who represents love and kindness. Sender intones:

Enter exalted, sacred guests!
Enter exalted, sacred ancestors!
Be seated, exalted guests!
Be seated, faithful guests!

It's all a little spooky. Itzik, Rifka, and Ruthie huddle around Morris as their grandfather chants. Chaia is unmoved, but Sala closes her eyes in concentration, and Reyzel is at least enjoying the music. As for me, well, for many years now, in the privacy of my own mind, I've invited my own exalted guests to the sukkah. I summon Abraham's wife Sarah, who suffered even more than I do from a husband whose faith led him to ridiculous lengths. (Sender may have sacrificed Sala and Chaia's education, but at least he wasn't willing to sacrifice the children themselves.) After Sarah, I invite my mother, may she rest in peace, who taught me everything I know, and my sister Hodel, who's having her own struggles surviving these hard times. For a while, the dry goods store she and Zavel invested in was doing well. Then, more and more of their customers bought cars and started to do their shopping in the nearby big city, Fort Worth. They've been bleeding money, and the Depression certainly hasn't improved matters.

Despite all my worries—for my sister, for myself—once we finally sit down to our meal, a mysterious peace descends over me. It's a crisp fall evening, and the stars are winking through the branches of the roof. The little booth fills with the smells of apples and pine, chicken soup and challah. The little ones aren't crying, and the big ones aren't arguing. For one night in this lean, hard season, I remember how our ancestors wandered and that eventually, they found their way home.

Chapter 31

WE EKED OUT A living that winter, partly by not paying the mortgage. In my defense, ignoring the cries of hungry children is much harder than ignoring statements from the bank.

When I spot a black Cadillac making its way up our still-snowy drive late one afternoon in March, I have a pretty good suspicion about what's coming. And when a well-fed man in a wool coat and a tweed hat climbs out, I can easily guess his errand.

Sender, who's returning from the barn, heads the man off on the porch. My husband isn't dressed for the weather. He'd just gone out to check on Barney, whose right hind leg has been wobbly. I quietly crack a window to hear the conversation.

Taking an envelope from his coat pocket, the man looks at the address and says, "May I speak to the head of the household, Mr."—he hesitates a moment over our last name—"Rappaport?"

"I'm Sender Rappaport."

"Mr. Rappaport, I'm Oscar Dalton from the Unionville Savings and Loan. It seems you've been ignoring our mailings, so I came to speak to you in person. May I come in?"

"You're from the bank?"

"As I indicated."

"Then no."

The March wind is still in its "like a lion" phase. In a sudden gust, it blows Mr. Dalton's hat off his head. Dalton tries to maintain his dignity, but I get a certain enjoyment from watching it snag on a blackberry bush. Sender must be freezing, but he stands completely still.

"Very well," Dalton says through thin lips. "As I'm sure you know, Mr. Rappaport, your mortgage has gone unpaid for six months."

"And I'm sure you know, Mr. Dalton from the Unionville Savings and Loan, we're in the middle of a depression."

The banker taps his foot impatiently. "I sympathize," he says without a trace of sympathy, "but the bank is a business. We'll fold if everyone who's having money troubles doesn't pay what they owe."

"I'm not everyone," Sender insists. "For fourteen years I've lived on this land and paid every month my mortgage." (This is a bit of an exaggeration, but it's true in spirit. I'm proud of my husband for standing up to this macher.) He goes on. "I'm good for the money. I'll pay you back when things get better. In my life, I've never cheated anyone. You can check and see."

I recognize the iron set of Sender's jaw, but Dalton isn't deterred. Obviously, he's had many versions of this conversation before, and he has a practiced answer. "Because we understand the difficulties of the current moment, the bank has been patient. But we ourselves can't afford to extend your credit any further. This is your official notice that Unionville Savings is foreclosing on your loan, effective at the end of this month." He tries to hand the envelope to Sender, but my husband throws it over the porch railing. "Mr. Rappaport," Dalton says wearily, "you may toss the notice in the snow, but it doesn't change the fact that the bank will own your farm at the end of the month. You need to vacate the premises by April 15."

"You would put my family out on the street at such a time?"

Dalton smiles blandly. "Despite the rudeness you've shown me," he says, "the institution I represent has a heart. You can stay on the farm as a tenant, as you will see described in the tenancy agreement, also in the envelope. Of course, under that arrangement, a reasonable share of your proceeds would go to the bank."

Sender calms down a bit. In fact, he's beginning to look interested. Dalton picks up on this change and urges him, "Think about it, Mr. Rappaport. I'll bid you good day."

Making his cautious way down the icy steps, Dalton retrieves his hat and motors off. Sender, shivering, watches him go. Only when he's disappeared down the drive does Sender go into the yard and rescue the envelope. Dusting the snow from it, he enters the house.

#

I've stolen back to the kitchen, where everyone is huddled around the Franklin Stove. Reyzel is doing her math homework, with a lot of help from Chaia.

"I don't see why anyone has to prove that if a triangle has two equal sides, the third side will also be equal. It's common sense," Reyzel is protesting.

"It's also geometry, and if you don't learn how to do proofs, you're not going to pass it. So, let's assume—"

Sender enters the kitchen with the envelope still clutched in his hand.

"Who was at the door?" I ask innocently.

"A Mr. Oscar Dalton from the Unionville Savings and Loan."

Sala gasps. Clasping Itzik to her and covering his ears, she says, "It's finally happened, hasn't it? They're going to foreclose on the farm. Tell us the worst. When do we have to leave?"

"We don't." Sender smacks the envelope down on the table. By this time, Itzik has squirmed out of Sala's arms, and he peers intently at the letter.

The girls are well aware of our unpaid bills, so Chaia asks skeptically, "We don't need to leave? How would that work?"

"You're so smart," Sender shoots back. "You read it and tell them."

Taking the envelope from the table, Chaia opens it and studies the documents inside. It takes what feels like an hour for Chaia to read through them while we're all frozen in place, like people in a painting called "Poor Family Awaiting Eviction." Reyzel has begun unconsciously shredding her math paper. Even Rifka, Motke, and Ruthie are quiet, sensing that something important is happening. Finally, Chaia throws the whole megillah back on the table. "Papa," she says, unsmiling, "I don't know what the man from the bank told you, but we've lost the farm."

"But we can still live on it. Mr. Dalton says Unionville Savings and Loan has a heart. They'll let us stay on as tenants."

"A heart?" Chaia sneers. "Papa, times are so bad the banks can't find buyers for all the farms that are going under. That's why they've come up with these tenancy agreements—so they can get some income from the properties they're stuck with. They're so magnanimous, they'll take 'only' 25 percent of our proceeds."

"Ach! You and your big words. You always look at the dark side. We Rappaports are strong. We can produce enough to give a share to the bank, and little by little, we'll buy back the farm. The Jewish Agricultural Society will help us."

It's Sala's turn to be skeptical. "The Jewish Agricultural Society? The Jewish Agricultural Society couldn't even save Harold's farm, and he was 'the Grape King.' Morris told me they have to move in with their daughter in Poughkeepsie."

"Sender, look," I say, trying to temper my exasperation, "we simply can't manage if we have to pay the bank a quarter of what we bring in. Once we've paid for our expenses, we won't have enough money left to feed ourselves."

"Money, money, money," he retorts. "That's all you're interested in. What about the land?"

"As my mother, may she rest in peace, used to say, 'Money may be dirt, but dirt is not money.'"

"Your mother?! Who cares what your mother used to say? This is what I say, and I am the *balabos*. We're staying here." His voice has risen to a roar.

Chaia looks at him coldly, but she doesn't stoop to answer. She just leaves the room. Shocked by this display of fury from her father, Reyzel slips out after her. Quietly, I help Sala herd the children up to bed. I've already said my piece, for all the good it did.

#

The next morning, when I come downstairs to light the stove, I see an envelope on the kitchen table, addressed to me. It's in Chaia's hand.

> Dear Mama,
>
> Last night was the end for me. It was bad enough that Papa took my college money, but I'm just not willing to give up the rest of my life for a farm I hate, one that you don't even own anymore. I'm truly sorry for the effect this will have on you and my sisters, but I've decided to leave Geneva—

I put the note aside for a moment. Covering my mouth with my hand, I try to hold back the sobs, which escape as ugly grunts. I dash away the tears and pick up the paper again.

> I'm going to stay with a Cleveland friend I met through Sanford. She wrote to me that there was a job at her office and invited me to room with her. I didn't intend to move, but now I'll accept her offer. I'm going to take the car since it was purchased with my

money. When I'm settled, I'll send you my address and whatever money I can spare. Please know that I love you and I wish it could have turned out differently.

Chaia/Charlie

Sender finds me at the table, the letter clutched in my hand and the tears streaming down my cheeks. "What now?" he demands.

I hand him the letter. Really, I know better than to expect any remorse from him, but his reaction is even fiercer than I imagined: "That little thief! But then you never did teach her to honor her father. If she were here right now, she'd get a lesson from the back of my hand."

In a choked voice, I manage to spit out, "I'm glad she's gone. At least one of us has escaped from you!"

"Well, good riddance. She never was much use anyway."

As Sender storms off, I whisper, "But I will miss her. I will miss her every day."

Chapter 32

WE'VE COME TO CLEVELAND for the day so Sender can say Kaddish for his mother, who died a year ago this week. There are no longer enough Jews in Geneva for a minyan. I'm sure he realizes I've come along so I can see Chaia, but we don't discuss it. In fact, we're mostly silent with each other these days. I see his misery as we try—not very successfully—to make a go of the tenancy agreement. I'm even sorry for him. After all, the farm is his life's work. But to lose your daughter over it, well, that's way beyond my comprehension.

Chaia and I have been corresponding by letter. She's working for an outfit that auctions off repossessed household goods; there have been heaps since the Depression started. Her job includes typing up the lists of items for sale. There's a trick to it, though. The typewriter has a broken letter J, and the auction house can't afford to replace it. So Chaia must think of a synonym for any word with a J in it. A Chinese jar is a pot. A jewelry box is a container for necklaces, earrings, and bracelets.

Today, Chaia is treating me to coffee at Mills Cafeteria, an unprecedented luxury, as we've never eaten out, even when times were good. Of course, there were no kosher restaurants in Geneva, and Mills is not exactly following Jewish dietary rules either, but if that's where my daughter wants to meet me, that's where I'm going. Taking the Rapid Transit downtown, I descend from street level into a cavernous, two-story restaurant with grand chandeliers and ironwork balconies. I could not look more out of place, my shapeless brown wool like a smudge among the blue, green, and red coats with their cinched waists. I'm lost until Chaia waves me down from a table for two and shows me how to go through the line. Since she insists, I have coffee *and* dessert—a piece of lemon cake. Chaia takes only tea, evidence of what a stretch this outing must be for her budget.

Unlike the cheery tone of her letters, Chaia's manner today is subdued. She asks after her sisters and Morris (conspicuously leaving out Sender), but she seems disconnected.

"How's work?" I ask, trying to get a conversation started.

"Oh, fine. I don't mind the tasks I have to do. I just don't like to think about where all the items we sell come from. Yesterday I logged a gold locket with a picture of a young man still inside. Last week, we sold some child's dollhouse."

"That must be hard for you."

"Not as hard as it was for the owners."

The conversation stalls. I poke at my cake, gummy and sharp with imitation lemon flavor. I try another tack. "And your apartment?" I ask. "Everything is going well with your roommate?"

"She's fine."

This is not like Chaia. While she may sometimes have been brooding at home, she always talked to me. Is she angry? Does she think I should have done more to talk Sender out of staying on the farm? I decide to be direct. "Chaia, something is wrong. I can feel it. Won't you tell me what's going on?"

Immediately, she looks stricken, and a few unbidden tears start to make their way down her cheeks. "I knew this would happen if I tried to talk to you about it," she says. "I don't want to be crying in the middle of Mills Cafeteria."

"Well, then, let's leave. Maybe there's a place we could sit together outside?"

Chaia leads me a few blocks away to Willard Park, an expanse of green lawn. The weather is blustery, so we practically have the place to ourselves. I plop down on a bench. The cold penetrates my coat and travels up my spine. Giving an involuntary shiver, I begin, "Nu, Chaiale?"

However much she clenches her eyes shut, the tears start to fall again. She begins tentatively, "You know I've been corresponding with Sanford?"

I didn't, but it doesn't shock me. I always thought he was her basherter. "He's doing well in Russia?" I ask, reaching over to dab at her wet cheeks with my hanky.

"Ukraine, actually, and no. He's working in the Almazna Coal Mine."

Of course, Sanford chose the job he was probably least suited for. The boy has the strength of a flea.

Chaia continues, "The letters I've been getting are heavily censored. It seems like every third word has a black bar through it. Still, I gathered he was putting in long hours and that conditions were difficult."

"So, is that schlimazel ready to come home?"

"They won't let him, Mama. No one can leave the USSR without an exit visa from the government, and those are practically nonexistent."

"Oy! Can he at least get a different job?"

"No, he's stuck. I've been really worried, especially since I sent him my new address before I left the farm, but I never got anything back. Then a few days ago, an envelope arrived with a postmark from Persia."

"Persia?" My brow wrinkles.

Chaia opens her pocketbook and hands me the letter. I have to shield it from the wind as I read:

> My Dearest Charlie,
>
> I don't know if you'll ever get this message. I've given it to a comrade who's being transferred to Baku in Azerbaijan. He'll try to get it over the border into Persia so it won't be censored.
>
> Things in the mine have gotten worse. We've been given a quota to fulfill and told that if we don't meet it, we'll be charged with treason. Since there's no way we can dig that much coal, I assume we'll be sent to the Gulag soon. That's why I'm running the risk of writing, since the Bolsheviks will kill me one way or another.
>
> I was reckless not to listen to your warnings about Russia. It's not the workers' paradise Marx envisioned. Now, as I face paying the price for my foolishness, I wanted you at least to know that you are in my thoughts and that the memory of you keeps me from despair.
>
> All my love,
>
> Sanford

What can I say about this letter? If it breaks my heart, I can only imagine what Chaia must feel. I fold it and put it carefully back in its envelope. Chaia returns it to her purse. "I really loved him," she says, her voice quivering.

"I know."

"So why couldn't we be together? Why did he insist on following some crazy ism? He's just like Papa with his Back-to-the-Land fantasies. Their dreams just take over and ruin everything. I should be mourning Sanford. I should be mourning what's happened to Papa. But I'm just so angry."

"I understand. I'm angry too." We're silent for a long time. Finally I tell her, "I don't know why, but Chaia, some people are caught up in the winds of history, like that scrap of paper flying across the lawn. Of course, we don't always have a choice. Sometimes it feels like we have no say in our own destiny. But remember: you understood what was happening in Russia, and you decided not to go. You saw that the farm was lost, and you decided to leave. Of all the Rappaports, you've had the clearest eye."

"What good has it done me? I see clearly that I'll end up by myself." She's stopped crying, but there's no mistaking the desolation in her voice.

"You will always have your sisters and me. And in the meantime, you're making a life for yourself. You're not dependent. You're not beholden to anyone. I hope you know how much I admire you."

"But does it have to be so lonely?"

"Sometimes, my heart, I'm afraid it does."

Chapter 33

JUNE 1931

SINCE CHAIA DECAMPED TO Cleveland, the mood around the farm has been sober. We carry on as though it were plausible that three women could manage a farm with one man who is only here on the weekends and one man whose idea of morning chores includes strapping on tefillin and praying till somebody else has finished the milking. We manage to put in a garden that I hope will feed us over the summer, with jarred fruits and vegetables carrying us through the winter.

When he's home, Morris does what he can to keep the vineyard in reasonable shape. Then one day, he comes back from a tour of the grape-vines with a leaf, trembling in his hand as though the wind were whipping it about. He meets us in the kitchen.

"What's wrong?" Sala asks. Wordlessly, Morris holds out the leaf. Peering over Sala's shoulder, I notice tiny orange circles on the surface and white spots on the underside.

"It's powdery mildew," Morris says frantically. "I told Sender he should get rid of the trimmings from when we pruned the vines, but he never did. I think the fungus must have grown in the debris."

"What's this you're blaming me for?" Sender demands, clomping in from the parlor where he's been studying *Daf Yomi*.

"Not blaming," Morris rushes to conciliate. "I know how busy you are. It's just that the grapes have been infected."

By this time, Reyzel has heard a quarrel brewing and come in from the garden. She studies the leaf for a moment. "Isn't there something we can do?" she wants to know.

"We could treat it with copper sulfate and lime," Morris says. He looks at me hopefully.

Why am I always the one who has to say we don't have the money? "Morris, I'm so sorry, but we're barely putting food on the table. I just don't see how we can afford the chemicals."

"But we'll lose the crop," Morris practically moans.

"Well, that's your fault," Sender says curtly. "You're in charge of the vineyard, and now there won't be any income from the grapes. Just what we needed."

This is too much for Sala. For years, she's held her tongue. Not this time. "Morris's fault! He's working a full-time job to bring some money into this house *and* spending his weekends tending the crops while you're in here studying Talmud. Do you think Morris wouldn't also like to read a book some time?"

"Sala, hush. Your father is just worried about the farm," Morris tries to quiet her.

"I won't hush. You asked him to do a simple thing—burn the vine trimmings—which he forgot all about. And now he's trying to hold you responsible for the consequences? No. You've been slaving away here since we got married, and my father dares to blame you for this disaster? Let him lie in the ground and bake bagels!" That Sala would wish evil on anyone, let alone her father, is a sign of just how far she's been pushed.

She takes Morris by the hand and practically drags him upstairs to their room, with Sender shouting after her, "A child who curses her father shall be put to death. It says so in Torah!"

"Papa," Reyzel says, scandalized, "You don't mean that."

"She's dead to me," Sender bellows. "And I do mean that." He flings open the kitchen door and marches off toward the barn.

Reyzel and I are speechless. At dinner, no one has anything to say. Sender won't even ask Sala to pass the potatoes. The little ones are strangely quiet. When I think the tension can't last a minute longer, Sala stands up at her place. She speaks as though she's been rehearsing: "I'm sorry I lost my temper earlier. I should not have spoken to Papa as I did. But this situation can't go on. No matter how hard we work, the farm is failing. Morris and I have discussed it, and we've decided that it's time for the children and me to move to Cleveland with him."

"Oh, no!" Reyzel cries out.

"We'll send you as much of what we earn as we can. Maybe with our help, you can ride out this bad patch."

"Bluma, tell your daughter we don't need her money," Sender says frostily.

"She's standing right here. She heard what you said, even if it isn't true." Chaia has been sending me money for months, which we couldn't do without, and Sender knows it. With Sala and Morris gone, we'll need even more support to hang on.

But Sender isn't about to admit that. "She thinks she and that husband of hers are so important? She thinks we can't get by without them? Hah!"

"Please, Sender," Morris breaks in, "you and I have worked shoulder to shoulder for ten years. Don't let this come between us. We love you all, but we have to do what's best for our children."

Sender has turned his back to the table. His silence is as loud as his words were last night.

"Don't try to reason with him," Sala says bitterly. "The only person he cares about is himself."

Truth is truth, even though it's hard to hear coming from Sala, who's always tried to see the best in everyone. She gathers her family together, and they leave the table, now almost completely deserted, with just Reyzel, Sender, and me left at our seats.

I don't try to get Sala to change her mind. In fact, I'm happy she and Morris will be free of us. Everyone but Sender knows our ship is foundering, and I don't want them to go down with it. In three days, they've packed up their belongings, and Cousin Mendel comes to get them. They'll room with him and his family. Reyzel and I stand on the porch, waving and weeping as they pull away. I can hear Sender in the parlor. He's reciting the prayer for the dead.

#

The first piece of good news I've had in a while comes from Cleveland two weeks later. Morris has a new job as a mechanic. It seems that a good customer at Mendel's grocery is a supervisor at White Motor Corporation. He and Morris had frequently compared notes about, well, whatever car fans find interesting about automobiles. Anyway, when one of the very rare mechanic jobs at White opened up, he thought of Morris. The position pays enough for Morris and Sala to rent their own apartment. They've found one with an unheard-of two bedrooms and a park down the street for the children. There's even a shul in walking distance, so Morris can once again take up his Talmudic disputations.

Sala, who'd been watching Mendel's grandchildren in exchange for a room in his house, has agreed to keep taking care of them in the new apartment. He'll throw a few dollars her way every week. I remember that once Sala wanted to be a teacher. Keeping an eye on six children under the age of six may not be exactly what she had in mind, but, as the saying goes, *nifter shmifter, a lebn makht er*—dead-shmead, as long as she makes a living.

The truth is, Sala sounds happier than she's been in a long time, maybe because the childcare doesn't come on top of staking grapes and boiling maple syrup. I should be happy too. I have a gainfully employed son-in-law, two gainfully employed daughters, and one more daughter with an all-expenses-paid scholarship she'll be taking up in September—all nearly miraculous in these hard-luck times. And I am happy for them. They don't have everything I wanted for them, but then, who gets everything?

But as the girls take up their own lives, I can't help wondering what I'll do with myself. So many of the people I know are pulling up stakes as their farms fail (and they're too sensible to accept the kind of *farkakte* tenancy agreement Sender has enslaved us to). Am I doomed to work this unworkable farm that I never wanted in the first place? After all, I'm only forty-one—not dead yet.

Chapter 34

OUR MEETING IS PLANNED with all the secrecy of a spy mission. Chaia will drive Sala and the children from Cleveland to Geneva-on-the-Lake. I'll tell Sender that Reyzel and I are taking the wagon over to the Cohens to pick up some items they can't take with them when they leave their farm. They're the latest of the Jewish families to go bust.

And we will go to the Cohens, but only after we meet the others at the beach. Part of me thinks I should just inform my husband I'm going to see my daughters and let him stew. But the other part of me has to live with an increasingly gloomy man, and I can't bear the vast silences that will greet me if he knows I crossed him.

Anyway, the day is mild, and the children are delighted to play in the sand. Itzik has brought a collection of tin cans and mason jars he uses to build a castle. Rifka helps by gathering shells and stones to decorate the battlements, and Ruthie gleefully smashes whatever they manage to construct. Baby Motke snoozes in his mother's arms while the four of us sit in the shade of the trees and schmooze.

"How is Itzik liking school?" Reyzel asks.

"He loves it. And it's Isidore, if you please," Sala replies. "Now everybody seems to have an English name. I think I'll be Sally. How about you, Mama?"

"It's true Bluma never suited me. I'm not much of a flower."

"How about Rosalind?" Chaia suggests. "Like in Shakespeare's *As You Like It*."

I almost choke on my iced tea. Shakespeare is a little high-flown for me. "I'm afraid I've never read it," I tell her.

"I just saw it for class." Chaia drops this juicy bit of information into the conversation as if we all knew she was going to school.

"What class is this?" Sala asks, her interest piqued.

"I'm taking a class at Fenn College," Chaia answers, trying to seem nonchalant.

"All right," Reyzel prods her. "What's the story?"

Chaia flashes us a grin that I haven't seen for too long. She explains that Fenn is a new school, founded by the YMCA, for students who can't afford traditional higher education. "At first it was only a technical school, but they recently added a junior college for liberal arts. I decided to take a night course on Shakespeare this summer just to see if I could manage it and work at the same time."

"And?" I say.

"I got an A-plus on my paper."

This surprises no one. "Chaia, that's wonderful," Reyzel says. "So you'll be continuing in the fall?"

"Yes, the school is set up for working people. I should be able to finish an associate degree in three years."

Nothing could make me happier than this news. I've always felt we failed Chaia, Sender because he took her college money and me because I didn't realize what he was up to and stop him. But Chaia has figured out how to recover her dream on her own.

As we all congratulate her, Rifka and Ruthie traipse up to our blanket, kicking sand into the food and demanding a snack. Sala produces a special treat—black and white cookies—which the girls take happily back to the sandcastle to share with their brother.

I'm still kvelling about Chaia's accomplishment, so I'm not prepared for her question to me. "How are things on the farm, Mama?"

There's a long pause. Finally, Reyzel speaks for me. "Pretty glum. The grapes are all infected with mildew, which probably doesn't matter since the price per pound is so low, it's not worth picking them. Papa's been hiring himself out to the Blankenships, who don't really need the help, but they feel sorry for us. Then he comes home and broods. Even Rashi isn't giving him much comfort these days."

"He's still mad at us?" Sala asks gingerly.

To give myself time to think about how to answer, I start fixing a tomato sandwich. If there's one thing we still have aplenty on the farm, it's tomatoes. One of my few pleasures these days is to take a saltshaker into the garden, pick a fat, red specimen, and eat it right there in the sun. The girls watch me in silence. Finally, I answer, "Your father's mad at everyone, himself included. In his mind, life wasn't supposed to work out this way. He was certain that going back to the land would solve all the problems the Jews have had for centuries. So, he got his little square of earth, and it was going to support him and his family. Then he was going to pass it down to the three of you, never mind that none of you wanted it."

"But why couldn't he just accept that we had different paths?" Chaia says.

"Your father's a true believer. That's why he can't forgive you or Morris or Sala. If he did, he'd have to admit that you were right to leave the farm."

"Well," Chaia says with her usual bluntness, "that accounts for the three of us. Why is he mad at you?"

"He's hardest on Mama," Reyzel breaks in. "It's like all his bitterness comes out in whatever he says to her: 'The grapes are dead.' 'The chickens aren't laying.' 'The peaches are rotting on the tree.' As if this was all Mama's fault."

"Why do you put up with it?" Chaia demands. "He's always been a bully, and you just accept it."

"That's not fair," Sala jumps in. "She stood up for you many a time."

"Yes, she tried to protect me. But what about herself? She's been running that farm since we got here from Romania with never a kind word—let alone a thank you—from him."

"You just don't understand him," Reyzel protests. "He's not one for compliments, but he has other ways of showing he cares about us."

"About you," Chaia responds. "He cares about you. Maybe he cared about Sala, as long as she did what he wanted. He never cared about me. And he never cared about Mama."

This child does not pull her punches. Is she right? "Well," I say, "that's a little too simple. He was too hard on you, yes, but he cared about you. It's just that you never matched his idea of what a daughter should be like. To him, caring for you meant pushing you to be the kind of woman who would make a good match and be a *balabosta*, a housewife and mother."

"That's just another way of saying he didn't care about *me*—the real me."

I hear the sounds of Sala's brood squealing with pleasure as they dip their toes in the water of the lake, splashing each other in bright sprays. They're so free. How could they—or their mother and aunts, for that matter—ever imagine what life was like for Sender and me growing up. I try to explain. "You have to understand, in the world we came from, children followed in their parents' footsteps. They lived at home until they got married to the people their parents chose for them. Your father saw how bright you were, Chaia, but he couldn't fit that into the world he knew, where the men study Torah and the women keep house."

"I'm sorry, but that's not an excuse—although I guess it does explain how he treated me. Now, are you going to try to convince us he cares for you?"

Is this the girls' business? I always hoped I was keeping the hollowness of my relationship with Sender a secret from my daughters, but clearly, they figured it out a long time ago. I decide I might as well be honest. "Does he care for me?" I muse aloud. "Probably not in the way you mean. He never loved me. But I'm his wife. To his way of thinking, he carried out his responsibilities to me: he was faithful, he made sure I had food to eat (most of the time), he gave me children."

"Was that enough?" Chaia demands.

"It had to be. What choice did I have?"

Now it's Sala's turn to challenge me. "Well, now you do have choices. You could leave him today and come live with Morris and me. You know I love Papa in spite of everything, but it sounds like he's dumping all of his anger and disappointment in your lap."

Reyzel adds, "Maybe if you left, that would bring Papa to his senses, and he'd move into the city too."

"No, my sweet daughters, I can't do that to Sender. He's watered that farm with his own blood and sweat—and plenty of mine, too, to be honest. I don't think he'll abandon it, and I can't desert him. I just can't. If I leave him, what does that say about how I've spent the last twenty-six years of my life?"

"That you've had enough?" Chaia suggests.

I give her a rueful smile. "I guess I haven't."

Chapter 35

As AUGUST ROLLS IN, the lengthening days just give me more time to contemplate our losses. The grapes are dusted in white with slits like angry mouths. We have a good crop of peaches, and the garden is bursting with squash, melons, and tomatoes, but with only three people to do the harvesting, too much rots before we can get to it. Sender and I are locked in our separate desolations, him at the deterioration of the farm, me at the loss of Sala and Chaia. I could invent some pretext to go to Cleveland and see them, but by this point, we don't even have money for the train. Sender cannot let himself see that buying back the property is hopeless. Still the knowledge leaks into his mind and makes him surly.

Reyzel is the only one who brings the least bit of spirit to the place, buoyed by the knowledge she'll be going to music school soon. No matter how much work she has to do around the farm, she finds time every day to play the violin, at night by the light of a kerosene lamp and in the early mornings before Sender and I even get out of bed.

This morning, I spend a few extra minutes under the covers, enjoying her rendition of the Bach Chaconne and remembering all the compliments she received from Ernest Bloch. Sender has a different reaction: "I don't know why that girl has to be playing the violin at this hour," he grumbles. "She could be out milking Bubale."

"I'll milk the cow. Reyzel needs to keep in practice."

"Hmph," is all Sender says in answer. Throwing on his clothes, he winds the straps of his tefillin around his arm in preparation for his morning prayers. I hear him begin: "I give thanks to You living and everlasting King for You have restored my soul with mercy. Great is your—" The book snaps closed, an unheard-of interruption. "How am I supposed to concentrate with that caterwauling going on in the next room?"

"Sender, you've always loved hearing Reyzel play."

"It's too much of a good thing."

"But she's been doing this morning practice for months. It never bothered you before."

"Well, it's bothering me now! Reyzel!" he yells. "Reyzel, come here immediately." Reyzel's surprised face appears at the door. I'm sure she can't imagine what she's done to anger her father before the day has even begun. "Reyzel," he says sharply, "I want you to stop this violin practice. It's interfering with your chores, and it's interfering with my prayers."

"But Papa, you only have to put up with it for a few more weeks. Then I'll be leaving for the conservatory."

"I don't see how you can think about music school when your mother and I are struggling to hold on to the farm. You should be thinking of ways you can help, not gallivanting off to study something that won't even get you a job when you finish. How many women violinists have you ever heard of? Is there a female Heifetz?"

"You always said I would be the first," Reyzel says, flabbergasted.

"That was in another life. Your mother is always talking about what her mother used to say. Well, my mother, may she rest in peace, used to say, '*Vos toig dir der sheyner kholem, ven der frimorgn iz kalt?*' What good is a beautiful dream if the dawn is chilly?"

I have to step in. "Sender, what are you going on about? If Reyzel has a chance to make a new life for herself, you wouldn't stand in her way, would you?"

"Wouldn't I? The rest of us have done our part. Sala never got to finish school so she could help out on the farm. Chaia never got to go to college. Should Reyzel not do her share for the family?"

This is really too much. Sender has told himself enough stories about the family's noble mission to go back to the land. It's time he heard some hard truths. I blow up at him. "The girls didn't do it for the family. They did it for you. They did it for your mishugas: free farmers on our own soil? Hah! Is that what we are now?"

"It's what we will be again," he insists.

"But is it what the rest of us ever wanted—to muck the barn or tie back the grapes or milk the cow? Sala wanted to be a teacher. Chaia had a chance for a college scholarship. Now Reyzel *is going* to be a violinist. You can't keep sacrificing their dreams to yours."

I'm just getting up a head of steam when Reyzel interrupts me. "It's all right, Mama," she hushes me. "I'll do it. I'll stay." Although her lower lip is quivering, she manages to speak without bursting into sobs. "If it keeps you from being tossed out on the street, it's only fair that I should help out."

"You see," Sender says. "Reyzel understands. Besides, what would be so terrible if she didn't go to the conservatory? She doesn't need the violin. How can that compare to a piece of land?"

Reyzel is blinking away tears, but she stands up straight, taking the full weight of her decision on her shoulders. I don't intend to let her make this choice, but I've never been so proud of her. I'm about to intervene again when I notice Sender gazing at Reyzel's brave but miserable face. This is his pet, the child who always thought he was God's own cousin, the girl whose talent brought her to the notice of the great Jewish composer Ernest Bloch. He seems torn. I bite my tongue and wait to see what he does. There's a pregnant pause.

"On the other hand," Sender says, "I know the last few years have been hard on you." He shakes his head, as though clearing away some bleariness. "We could keep on, of course, make this place pay again. But I have to think about what's best for you." Another long pause. "You know," Sender says finally, "the Talmud tells us our duties to our children. There's a list in *Kidushin*—what you might expect: make sure the sons learn a trade, find them all spouses. But one thing on the list has always puzzled me. We're supposed to teach our child how to swim."

This is so far off the subject that I'm ready to break in until I catch the look of pain in my husband's eyes. Whatever he wants to say is costing him. I need to let him say it.

"What does this verse come to teach us?" Sender goes on. Reyzel would like to help him out, but she's as baffled as I am. She just shakes her head. "I never realized it until today, but I think it means we must teach our children how to survive. We have to make sure they can swim in whatever ocean they find themselves in. I always thought I was doing that. We never owned anything back in Europe, but in America, I had this farm—something I could pass down to you and your sisters, that you could live on when your mother and I are gone."

"I know, Papa. And I really appreciate it. I—" Reyzel begins.

Sender cuts her off. "But now I think maybe I was wrong, not because the land isn't good, not because you wouldn't work hard. But you— the Reyzel who's been a musician since she was singing little songs at the Shabbas table—*that* you wouldn't survive here."

I'm stunned. As my mother, may she rest in peace, would have said, "You should live to be a hundred and twenty . . . if only to see what happens." For once, maybe Sender's Talmudic reasoning has taken him somewhere useful. Of course, it would have been nice if he'd had this moment of insight with Chaia or Sala, but maybe losing them helped him see what would happen if he didn't change course.

I wish I had a minute to savor this victory, but Sender is going on. "I don't know how to swim in the ocean of music," Sender continues. "For that, you'll have to go to the conservatory."

Reyzel runs into her father's arms. "Thank you, Papa. Oh, thank you."

He turns to me. "Bluma, I know you won't want to hear it, but I just don't think this plan of buying back the farm is the right one. It's time we leave Geneva. We'll go to Cleveland, and Reyzel will go to San Francisco."

I'd shout hooray, but I know how important it is to Sender to save face. "Well," I allow, "you may be right."

"Of course I'm right. It's decided," Sender declares.

"All right, *mayn man,*" I pretend to concede, "as long as you think it's for the best."

#

This morning, we had our first letter from Reyzel. Maestro Bloch arranged for her to live in the maid's quarters of a San Francisco mansion owned by one of the Conservatory's Jewish donors. She tells us she can see the ocean while she practices.

Now every sign the girls ever lived in this house is gone. Today, I'm dismantling my loom. There won't be room for it when we move in with Sala and Morris. Yes, Sender has reconciled with his eldest and her husband. Who else would have us? Maybe someday, he and Chaia will make peace, but that seems further off.

I'll miss the loom, the fourth and most elaborate I've built since we came to Ohio. But I've been in this situation before. I put on my work boots and head off into the woods. I need to find a forked stick for making afghans, as I did back in Romania. If I'm not weaving something, who will I be?

The trees in the orchard are still heavy with peaches, although, since we're leaving soon, we've let many fall to the ground. The smell brings me back to the first day I set foot on the farm. I imagine I hear the racket of men disputing a point of Jewish law. When I reach the tree line, my mind flashes on Chaia holding on to Balagan's mane for dear life and how Sender rode to the rescue. As I near the path down to the Grand River, I can almost hear Sylvester crying out from the ledge.

By the river path grow several lilacs, the right tree for my purpose— short but sturdy. Their plump purple flowers are gone, revealing a mass of forking limbs. Now I do something I haven't tried since I was a young woman in Romania. I hike up my long skirt and reach one foot into the crotch of the tree. Grabbing the lower branches, I haul myself up. Hand over hand, branch after branch, I climb until I see the perfect Y for my hand loom. With a small saw we used to trim grapes, I detach my prize, grabbing it between my teeth as I make my careful way down.

Chapter 36

I KNOW IT'S COWARDLY, but I'm hiding on the porch as I watch everything we still own go under the gavel. The bank is auctioning off what remains of our belongings to cover at least part of what we owe. It's been going on for hours. I thought I'd be happy to finally be shed of this place, but with the sale of each item, I feel like a tiny piece of my heart is wrenched out. Yes, my oak table is full of dings and scratches, but I remember the little hands that made every one of them. The oven is old and cranky, but what meals Hodel and I wrung out of it. And our one piece of art—a needle-point I made of a rabbi leaning over a scroll—who in Geneva wants this? Perhaps Corbin Johnson would have bid on it if his farm hadn't gone bust just like the rest of ours.

Anyway, it's easy enough to hear the auctioneer from here: "All right, friends, what am I bid for this spike-toothed harrow? Can I start the bidding at twenty dollars?"

A man in faded overalls raises his hand. The bidding continues. I spot Sender chatting up Shloimie Ponsky. Sender's words float up to me where I sit in the shadow.

"Well, Ponsky, you're the only Jewish farmer who's managed to hang on. I envy you. If I hadn't invested in those grapes on the south hillside, I might have been able to pull us through."

"You can't blame yourself, Rappaport. I was reading in the *Ashtabula Star*: a third of American farmers have lost their land in the last five years."

"Misery loves company, I guess." The auctioneer has started a new item. "You should bid on that rotary cutter, Ponsky. I just got it a few years ago." Shloimie moves forward, waving his hand.

I'm surprised to learn Sender holds himself responsible for the catastrophe of the early frost. He's never said so to me. I guess that would have meant admitting I was right, which would, for Sender, have been the final indignity.

A parade of farmers is trooping through the barn, inspecting teeth and udders and eggs. Barney is so old now, I fear he's destined for the glue factory. Rozhinkes died just last month. I never thought I would miss his barking, but a few protest yowls would have been welcome today. Now they're leading Balagan out to the yard to take his turn under the gavel.

Mendel has come to help us move. He emerges from the parlor, where he's been packing up Sender's books to donate to a shul in Cleveland. This is a job I couldn't entrust to my husband unless I wanted to fill Sala's apartment with volumes of Rabbinic commentaries. It's enough to ask them to house *us* until we can find jobs. "How's the auction going?" Mendel asks.

"Not bad. So far, everything has sold, but I'm not sure about those final lots. They're full of odds and ends: screws without bolts, broken car parts, string too short for saving. I tried to get Sender to toss that stuff, but he claims it's valuable," I complain.

In the yard, the auctioneer is droning on. "That's fifteen dollars for the wine press to my friend in the green jacket. Now what am I bid on lot number fifty-seven: mixed metal hardware?" As I predicted, there are no bids. "Come now, people. Who doesn't need some extra nails and screws?"

"You mean, bent nails and stripped screws?" Old Man Custer calls out. Laughter ripples through the crowd.

Undeterred, the auctioneer says, "Let's start the bidding at a quarter."

Again, there are no bids. Finally, someone must have raised a hand because the auctioneer says, "All right, I have a quarter. Who will give me fifty cents? Forty cents? Thirty cents? Sold for a quarter to the gentleman in the white shirt. Now, we have a lot of spare parts. I see some hinges and metal plates. I see a tractor seat. Who'll give me a dollar? A dollar?"

Again, there are no bidders. A number of the farmers are starting to disperse when someone calls out, "A quarter!"

"I have a quarter, a quarter, a quarter. Going once, twice. Sold to the gentleman in the white shirt. And finally, we have this Franklin stove. Looks like it has a crack, but a little welding should fix that right up. What am I bid for the Franklin Stove? Can I get a dollar?"

I think of all the cold mornings we spent around that stove, in the good years drinking coffee or hot chocolate, in the bad ones, hickory nut tea. I remember all the homework that was done in its warmth, the dinner table arguments, the late-night talks. And now, no one even wants to bid on it.

I can see the auctioneer is about to bang his gavel, but he must have noticed a hand raised somewhere. "A dollar then," he says. "Sold to my friend in the white shirt."

"We owe that 'friend in the white shirt' a debt of thanks," I tell Mendel. "Someone must have taken pity on us."

Finally, the auctioneer is wrapping things up. "All right, folks, that concludes our auction. Please pay for your lots at the back table." The farmers file out, heading for their beat-up cars and wagons.

"Well," I say, "I'll just go get my valise. Sender must be in the barn with the last of the boxes. I got him down to two, though where we're going to put his stuff at Sala's, I do not know."

"I'll go help him," Mendel offers.

When I get back, Mendel and Sender are carrying his two boxes from the barn and lofting them into the truck.

"Hold on," Sender says. "I have a few more things."

"Sender, there are already two boxes here. That was our agreement. What are these few more things?"

"Just some bushels that turned up."

"Turned up? How does a bushel turn up?"

"Genug shoyn, Bluma. I have a few bushels."

While we're arguing, Mendel has lugged another two bushels out of the barn.

"Two bushels!" I say indignantly. "Let me see those. Let me see what was so important you had to add it to a house that's already so crowded, four children are sleeping in the living room."

"You don't have to see what's in them. You only have to know I need them."

Ignoring him, I march up to one bushel and peer in. "Aren't these the spare parts we put in the auction?"

"But no one was bidding on them."

"Maybe because they aren't worth anything?"

"They were at least worth the quarter I spent on them."

"You bought them from yourself?"

"You never know when these things will come in handy."

"And this other one is full of bent nails? Sender, please tell me there isn't any more."

"Only the Franklin Stove."

Mendel bursts out laughing.

"If the fool didn't belong to me, I would also laugh. What will Sala say when she sees this junk?"

"Don't worry, Bluma," Mendel tells me. "I'll find room for it at the grocery. Let's pack up and get going."

He and Sender go back for the stove and load everything into the truck. "That's it then," Mendel declares. "Hop in."

"Yes, yes. Just give me a minute," Sender says. I follow him to the side of the house, where we can see the whole vineyard. From a distance, you wouldn't know the plants were infected. We see only the carefully splayed vines, the neat rows marching up the hill. Looking out at it, Sender recites a passage from Isaiah: "What more could have been done for My vineyard that I failed to do in it? Why, when I hoped it would yield grapes, did it yield wild grapes?"

There are tears streaming down his cheeks. I pluck my handkerchief from my sleeve and wipe them away.

Glossary

Af mir di aveyre: Let the transgression be on me.

avade: Of course.

Avinu Malkeinu: High Holiday prayer, "Our Father, Our King."

azoy geshmak!: So delicious!

badekn: Literally, covering. A part of a Jewish wedding ceremony in which the groom veils the bride.

balabos: Man of the house.

balabosta: Literally, lady of the house. Also connotes someone who is a good homemaker.

balagan: Chaos.

bashert: Fated.

Borukh habo (with variations for gender and person): Literally, blessed is the one who comes. Welcome.

Borukh Hashem: Bless God!

bubbe: Grandmother.

cholent: A casserole with beans and potatoes. Similar to cassoulet. Often made on Friday and eaten over the Sabbath.

chuppah: A wedding canopy.

Daf Yomi: A daily regimen of Talmud study.

daven: To recite the Jewish liturgy.

Der mentsh trakht und Got lakht: A person plans and God laughs.

drek: Crap.

drey: Literally, turn around. Often used in the expression dreyn a kop, to turn someone's head around, to annoy or pester.

dudele: Little song.

edl: Refined

Es, khaverim: Eat, my friends.

farbisene: Bitter.

farkakte: Crappy.

farshlepte krenk: A long illness. Anything tedious and drawn out.

farshnikert: Drunk, inebriated.

frayndn: Friends.

freylekh: Happy. In reference to music, a joyful dance tune.

gehakte leyber: Chopped liver.

Gemara: Part of the Talmud.

genug: Enough! (Genug Shoyn, enough already)

gevalt: Literally, violence. Oh, no!

Gib zikh a shukl: Literally, give yourself a shake. Hurry up!

Got in himl!: God in Heaven!

Got tsu loybn!: Praise God!

Gotenu!: Dear God!

goy: A non-Jew.

goyishe meshugas: Non-Jewish craziness.

gut gezogt: Well said.

hametz: Grains prohibited on Passover: wheat, barley, oats, rye, and spelt.

hartsele: My heart. Term of endearment.

heymish: Homey.

Hok mir nisht keyn tshaynik: Literally, don't bang your teakettle at me. Stop rattling on at me. Don't bother me.

in a mazldike sho: Literally, in a lucky hour. Traditionally, Jews don't say "congratulations" before an event has actually happened.

ketsele: Little cat. A term of endearment.

Khas vekhalile!: God forbid!

khazn: Cantor.

kibbitz: To give unsolicited advice.

Kidushin: A section of the Talmud.

keyn en hora: Literally, not the evil eye. In Yiddish, when someone says something positive, this interjection is often used to ward off the evil eye.

kitl: A white linen or cotton robe worn for milestones and religious ceremonies.

kimpetbrivl: From the Yiddish cradle letter, a birthing amulet.

kleyn: Little.

knaker: A show-off. A big talker.

Koyl Nidre: "All My Vows," the prayer that begins the service on the eve of Yom Kippur.

kreplach: Soup dumplings.

kugel: A pudding.

kvell: Burst with pride.

Le khayim: To life! A toast.

Lomir Alle in Eynem: Literally, all together. A Yiddish song of celebration.

luftmensch: An impractical person. Someone who is more interested in intellectual matters than making a living.

macher: Literally, a maker. A bigshot. Often sarcastic.

mame loshn: Mother tongue.

mamele: Little mother—a term of endearment.

mamzer: A person born from a forbidden relationship.

mandlen: Almonds.

margeritkelekh: Daisies.

mayn man: My husband.

mekhaye: Something that brings delight.

mezinke: Youngest girl in the family.

Midrash Tanchuma: A collection of rabbinic homilies on the Five Books of Moses.

Misheberakh: A prayer for a blessing.

mishugener: A crazy person.

Naftule Spilt Far Dem Rebn: Klezmer tune, "Naftali Plays for the Rabbi."

nakhes: Great pride, especially in the accomplishments of another.

narishkayt: Foolishness.

Nisht do gedakht: Don't even think about it.

nu: So? Go on. Well?

nudzhe: Nag, pester, whine.

Ot azoy!: That's the way!

pareve: In the system of Jewish dietary laws, something that is not classified as either milk or meat. When used to describe a person, anemic.

paskudniak: A repulsive person.

patsh: A slap, a spank.

patshke: Tinker. Mess around to no great effect.

pekelakh: Little packages.

pisher: Literally, pisser. A young, inexperienced person.

rozhinkes: Raisins.

Shabbas: Sabbath.

shalakh mones: Literally, sending of portions. The packages of treats Jews send to each other on Purim.

shiker: Drunk.

shmegege: An idiot. A silly fool.

shmendrik: A jerk, a fool.

shmure: Watched.

shnor: To mooch. To take charitable gifts.

Sholem aleykhem: Peace be with You. A Yiddish greeting answered by Aleykhem sholem.

shtetl: A small town in Eastern Europe where most of the population was Jewish.

shtikl: A piece.

shvesterke: Dear sister.

Talmud: A collection of rabbinic discussions on matters of Jewish law, ethics and theology.

tararam: A big noise.

trombenik: Someone who isn't very accomplished but blows his own horn.

tsuris: Trouble.

tuchus: Rear end, tush.

tzimmes: A dish consisting of slow-cooked root vegetables. Also, anything that requires a big fuss.

ongepatshket: Tacky, ostentatious.

vayn: Wine.

Vey iz mir: Woe is me. Oh, no!

Yiddishkeit: Jewishness

yuts: Moron.

zeyde: Grandfather.

zisele: Sweetheart.